PRAISE FOR

Between You and Us

"Powerful, poignant, profound . . . *Between You and Us* takes the reader on a memorable, slow-motion roller-coaster ride they didn't know they needed. Broekhuis writes realistic, relatable characters with heart and emotion. This is a debut novel to savor."

—BETSY ST. AMANT,
author of *Tacos for Two* and *The Key to Love*

"Broekhuis has penned a beautiful story that will make you rethink all the moments you've wished for a different outcome. Moments of tears and moments of joy all come together in this story that culminates in one gut-wrenching decision. Readers will be left wondering, *What would I have done?*"

—JOHANNA ROJAS VANN,
author of *An American Immigrant*

"Broekhuis extracts love's essence in a story so creative and vivid, so tender and compelling, I scarcely came up for air. Smart, flawless dialogue and fluid plotting build to the unthinkable—and a woman's decision for her family that readers will ponder for a long, long time."

—CHERYL GREY BOSTROM,
award-winning author of *Sugar Birds*
and *Leaning on Air*

"*Between You and Us* is a masterpiece. With moments of humor and true tenderness, Kendra Broekhuis mines the complexity of longing for what might have been amid the wrenching reality of a life that did not go as planned. Readers will laugh and cry and ultimately consider the roads not traveled in their own beautiful and broken lives. Perfect for book clubs and anyone craving a heartfelt, moving, and ultimately transformative read."

—NICOLE BAART,
bestselling author of *Everything We Didn't Say*
and *Little Broken Things*

Between You and Us

Between You and Us

A NOVEL

Kendra Broekhuis

WATERBROOK

Between You and Us is a work of fiction. Names, characters, places, and incidents are the products of the author's imagination or are used fictitiously. Any resemblance to actual events, locales, or persons, living or dead, is entirely coincidental.

A WaterBrook Trade Paperback Original

Published in the United States by WaterBrook, an imprint of Random House, a division of Penguin Random House LLC.

WATERBROOK and colophon are registered trademarks of Penguin Random House LLC.

LIBRARY OF CONGRESS CATALOGING-IN-PUBLICATION DATA
Names: Broekhuis, Kendra, author.
Title: Between you and us : a novel / Kendra Broekhuis.
Description: [Colorado Springs] : WaterBrook, 2024.
Identifiers: LCCN 2023039947 | ISBN 9780593600757 (trade paperback ; acid-free paper) | ISBN 9780593600764 (ebook)
Subjects: LCSH: Self-realization in women—Fiction. | LCGFT: Domestic fiction. | Psychological fiction. | Novels.
Classification: LCC PS3602.R6364 B48 2024 | DDC 813/.6—dc23/eng/20231003
LC record available at https://lccn.loc.gov/2023039947

Printed in the United States of America on acid-free paper

waterbrookmultnomah.com

2 4 6 8 9 7 5 3 1

Book design by Jo Anne Metsch

For Collin, because I like you.

And for Aliza, because I miss you.

Between You and Us

CHAPTER 1

Present Day

"BARTOLOTTA'S, PLEASE," LEONA SAID AS SHE SETTLED into the back seat of the taxi. Though she was sure she botched the pronunciation.

The driver raised an eyebrow at her in the rearview mirror. "Fancy," he noted, then returned his face to neutral.

She finished rubbing her eyes and managed a smirk. "For one night, and one night only."

The French bistro was in the Historic Water Tower neighborhood of Milwaukee where residential properties were meticulously manicured and residents could—without having to stop and think—recommend their favorite interior designer or cleaning company.

The plan was to meet David at Bartolotta's. They both had to work late, but his commute was longer, so they decided he would drive the only car they owned and she would splurge for a taxi. She did her best to calculate the fees ahead of time and guessed it would cost her close to twenty-six precious dollars to get there and tip her driver. She may have reneged and taken the bus, but the summer school and aftercare programs she worked at went later than she anticipated, and the closest bus stop was still an eleven-minute walk from her destination.

This occasion was too important to be late for.

The taxi pulled away from the curb, and Leona took her journal—the one she kept with her at all times per Grandma Vera's advice—out of her purse. Besides taking naps, writing was Leona's favorite hobby. Her mouth exposed her as a bit of a bumbler, but her pen reminded her she had intelligent things to say. She fanned the pages of her journal, catching glimpses of the poems, short stories, and prayers she wrote in the cracks of her day between grading papers, planning lessons, and calling her students' parents.

The pages from the past year were mostly filled with pain.

She opened the journal to a fresh page and tried to write *Dear David,* but the taxi hit a pothole and her pen bounced across the paper. She turned to the next page to try again, but this time another car passed them on the right in the bike lane at a speed well over the limit. The taxi driver blared the horn, and Leona flinched. To help slow her heart rate, she took a deep breath, reminding herself that the travel would change the farther east they drove down Locust.

Dear David, she began again.

She was hoping to write something in honor of their tenth wedding anniversary. Although it wouldn't be difficult to inscribe pages of her deep affection for him, she settled for a succinct poem in honor of what their marriage had survived so far. David was more of a skim reader anyway, something she made a point to tell him was a crime against words.

She signed the note the way she always did: *Yours then, now, and forever.*

Leona tried tucking the journal back into her purse, but another pothole jolted the taxi and knocked it off the seat, spilling its contents onto the floor. Gritting her teeth, she tucked her wavy auburn hair behind her ear and leaned over. She held her glasses to the bridge of her nose as she gathered her keys and wallet, a crinkled pamphlet, and a confetti of gum wrappers. She spotted the other note she planned to share that evening too, a small greeting card with hand-painted flowers on the front. She picked it up, admired its delicate details, and carefully tucked it back into her purse. She'd been holding on to the note for far too long, and she was determined to show it to David at the restaurant. No matter how torn up she was about it.

For the rest of the fifteen-minute commute, Leona wrapped her palm around the back of her neck to knead away the tension sitting there, trying to focus on the entire decade they were celebrating tonight rather than just the past year they'd been through. This extravagant evening out was supposed to symbolize the start of learning how to live again.

The taxi pulled up to the end of a path that led to a majestic set of Corinthian columns. Leona moved her hand to the strap of her purse and began fidgeting. This was an establishment she wasn't bred for, she thought while inspecting the pristine architecture.

She paid the driver, got out of the taxi, and scanned the parking lot for her and David's taupe Toyota Corolla. All she saw was a wave of shiny black, save for one bright yellow Camaro in the middle of the convoy. She rolled her eyes and then chuckled. Whenever David saw one of these metal bumblebees on the road, he'd fawn over it and say, "Maybe in another life, huh, babe?"

She would shoot back, "Yes, another life when you marry an eastside heiress."

Leona was surprised she beat David to the restaurant. Then again, he might have parked farther away to avoid the embarrassment he would feel at pulling up next to vehicles with two hundred thousand fewer miles on them. She turned back toward the entrance and followed the path through the doors so she could check for him inside.

She crossed the threshold, taking in the walls filled with framed Parisian scenes that stretched out over warm refurbished floors as well as tables glowing with candlelight near windows overlooking Lake Michigan. The stunning ambience of wealth and romance—along with a heavenly aroma—made her stifle a gasp.

Was this restaurant plucked right out of a cheesy chick flick? she marveled, wishing she wasn't impressed. She was suddenly aware of the mulberry cotton thrift-store dress draping her pale body, advertising one who clips coupons and doesn't belong here.

She finished absorbing the grandeur of her surroundings and realized the hostess was watching each of her slow steps through the restaurant's corridor. The polished navy dress hugging her curves did not appear to be from a thrift store. Or made of cotton.

"Welcome to Bartolotta's Lake Park Bistro," she said. "Do you have a reservation?"

Leona cleared her throat and tried to cloak herself with poise. "Thank you. I am meeting my husband here. He might be seated already."

The hostess grabbed two menus. "Follow me," she said, then nodded toward Leona's arm. "By the way, that is a beautiful bag."

Leona looked down and realized the hostess was referring to the same purse she just spilled all over the taxi. It was expensive—her only possession that fit in a place like Bartolotta's. Her mother, having remarried one of Milwaukee's wealthiest silver bachelors, gave it to Leona for her birthday three years ago. Instead of giving it to her in person, Evelyn shipped it to her house without a card. Just a receipt with the price circled.

They crossed the dining room where more pleasing aromas hit Leona in the face. Her stomach growled, which earned her a quick glance from the hostess over her shoulder.

"There he is." Leona pointed at David.

The hostess stutter-stepped, which didn't surprise Leona. Most people seemed astonished when they learned her husband was David Warlon. She'd always been a bit amazed too and thought that he was out of her league in every way. A nerdy genius with the handsome charisma of a late-night television host who somehow managed to be humble about it.

Ugh. If it wasn't her David she was describing, she might throw up in her mouth at how corny she was about him—like he was some character written for the Hallmark Channel. But her David was all that, and they were happy.

At least they were, until the day everything changed.

"The waitstaff will be with you shortly." The hostess smiled at David, then offered a curt nod to Leona before leaving their table.

Leona turned to David.

It was the look in his eyes that first warned her something wasn't right. There was an unfamiliar glint in them—perhaps a distance or a steel barrier. His eyes were usually so full of light and playfulness and desire. When they'd land on her, for a split second she could almost hear them shouting "I love you."

But the words his eyes spoke now appeared bone dry, no longer drawn from that deep well of affection they'd shared.

His eyes said nothing.

She was caught off guard but not deterred. On the ride here she made a conscious decision that whatever happened, she would try to make their night special. It had been so long since they invested in their relationship like this. Literally, they had saved every extra penny they could for the past three months just so they could each afford a plate of Bartolotta's pan-seared tenderloin.

They'd gone back and forth on the practicality of spending all that money on one meal, especially when their home needed so many repairs, the ones their landlord claimed he couldn't address unless he drastically raised the rent. But every time Leona suggested they use the money to fix the plumbing in the bathroom, David pleaded with her about how much they needed this night out.

Against all her instincts to ask what was wrong, she leaned over, gently placed her hand on the side of his face, and kissed his cheek.

"Happy anniversary, David," she said.

He bristled at her touch.

CHAPTER 2

LEONA SAT IN HER LEATHER UPHOLSTERED DINING chair, noting David's cold reaction to her greeting. Their table was draped with a white tablecloth that felt like it cost more than their entire set of bedsheets.

Across from her, David's eyes bore into his menu, as if meeting her gaze would surely summon fire from heaven.

There was no "How are you?"

No "You look beautiful."

Not even a sarcastic "I could really go for a Big Mac right now."

She enjoyed silence in her everyday life, but this dead air between them was different, so unlike David. Even after everything they'd been through over the past year, he was never this guarded or detached. It wasn't just the stiff, silent way he sat in his chair, suggesting he'd rather be anywhere but across the table from her. His appearance was different too. He'd gotten a haircut, much cleaner than the longer style he'd stuck with for a while now. Every time she offered to cut his hair to save twenty-two dollars, he would gently pat her shoulder and turn down the "hack job from Leona's Butcher Shop."

"I'll have a glass of Bordeaux Supérieur," David told the waiter who'd appeared out of thin air.

His drink order startled her, but not because he flawlessly rattled off the name of a fancy wine in French. He was raised with menus typed in foreign languages, unlike Leona who—on the rare occasion she ate at a restaurant—grew up telling waiters she'd have the number seven.

But David never dropped French in the casual way he said *Bordeaux Supérieur,* as if he was still comfortable here. As if he belonged in this establishment. Because of their shared decade of leaky faucets and squeaky steps and the kind of financial stress that made their housing woes impossible to keep up with, he was often embarrassed by any extravagances reminding him of the world he grew up in and was revisiting tonight.

Where did he get that suit he was wearing? she wondered, noting the way it fit his shoulders perfectly. It looked like the kind of suit that didn't require saving pennies in order to eat pan-seared tenderloin and drink Bordeaux Supérieur.

She dug a few fingers into her shoulder, trying to mold away the returning tension. Her typical response to being out of place was to shut down until she felt safe. But her desire to do that conflicted with her heart's belief that David was a safe place to be. She didn't know how to reconcile the two.

"How was work? Did your presentation go well?" she asked, trying small talk to build a bridge toward him yet wanting an escape from this unfamiliar table of unease.

"Presentation?" He answered her question with a question.

"You said you had a presentation today about the updates on your research for FlourX?"

He paused. "We heard a presentation for a new drug last week, but I don't remember any by that name. Besides, I don't give presentations on new drugs, I listen to them and decide if Warlon Tech is going to buy them."

His confusion was now hers, and it came out of her mouth in rapid questions. "Warlon Tech? Since when? No, you've been working on this presentation for weeks. You've lost sleep over it. I would know because I'm not sleeping either, and—"

"What are you trying to do, Leona?" he cut in, his eyes now throwing shards of glass. "I have never even heard of the drug FlourX, so why would I talk about it, let alone lose sleep over it?" He ran a hand through his hair and adjusted his suit jacket. "Besides, you never ask me about work. The only reason I'm losing sleep these days is because . . . never mind." He stopped suddenly.

Leona didn't know what to do with that. She knew grief changed her, but the last time she checked she was still in touch with reality. Her husband worked for BioThrive, a clinical medical research start-up and certainly not for Warlon Tech, his father's beastly pharmaceutical company. And she didn't only ask about his work occasionally; she asked him about it every single night at dinner.

She looked down at her menu, but the words describing rustic French cuisine, imported wines, and delicate desserts were starting to swirl across the page. She was sure if she peeked at the cotton fabric under her armpits, she would find large rings of sweat.

When did the temperature rise from seventy-four degrees to Dante's Inferno in here? she wondered as a knot tightened in her chest and made it harder to breathe.

She picked up her goblet of ice water and choked half of it down. She should really ask David what was wrong with him and why he was wearing an expensive suit that made her feel like she was dressed as a peasant, but her thoughts were racing too fast to decide which question to ask first.

"Are you okay, Leona? You look ill." David startled her again, this time interrupting her spiraling thoughts.

She replied through quick, panicked breaths, "I'm . . . not sure. . . . What's—"

"Do you need to use the restroom or something?" he asked. His eyes had softened enough to be twinged with concern.

"I . . . don't know." She breathed in but couldn't push the air back out. Her hands were going numb, and her vision blurred.

David stood up, walked around the table, and placed his hand on her back.

The warmth of his touch calmed her enough so that she was able to say, "Ask me . . . three things . . ."

"What?" he asked. "What are you talking about?"

His blank-faced reaction to everything she said was getting old. She tried again. "Ask me . . . three things. . . . I . . ."

"I have no idea what you're talking about. Please, Leona, I don't want to fight tonight, and you really don't look well. Just let me take you home."

Leona couldn't compute. She and David had sat in that emergency room *together,* reading the pamphlet the doctor gave them about coping techniques for panic attacks—another frustrating symptom of her grief. The way he reacted now was as if none of that had ever happened.

David held her arm and guided her away from columned entries and fancy hostesses, across the parking lot to where Leona expected to find their taupe Toyota Corolla with 267,586 miles on it. Instead, he led her right up to the bright yellow Camaro.

If she wasn't already having an out-of-body panic attack reaching suffocating levels, she would have tried to stop David from herding her into his dream car. Then, when he took a wrong turn out of Bartolotta's, she would have asked why he wasn't driving toward the Sherman Park neighborhood where they'd rented a tired two-bedroom bungalow for the past ten years. And then, when he pulled into the driveway of 2638 Courtney Boulevard, she would have screamed at the top of her lungs, "Why did you bring me back here?"

Instead, shock froze her silent to the genuine leather passenger seat. She hadn't been to 2638 Courtney Boulevard since the day David proposed.

CHAPTER 3

Twelve Years Ago

LEONA WAS TERRIFIED OF THE CONCEPT OF A BLIND date, but the way Eden described David Warlon piqued her interest.

"On the very first day of the semester, Professor Draxler asked me if I was sure I was in the right classroom," her friend scoffed, curling her legs up onto their ratty dorm couch and opening a heavy textbook with *Genetics* printed on the spine. "But then David asked *him* if, quote, 'he was sure he could handle teaching our generation's prodigy because I outscored the other gentlemen in the classroom by a mile freshman year.' End quote."

"First of all, Professor Draxler is the worst," Leona replied from her spot across the couch. "Second, you've been bugging me about this David guy for months now, so he must be special. It's just that . . . I don't know. I have my doubts about going out with the son of Milwaukee royalty."

"He has some trust-fund-baby tendencies, but he's all right," Eden said, nodding. "I think the two of you would be amazing together. And I know what I'm talking about."

"Setting up one cousin with his future wife does not make you an expert matchmaker," Leona said. At her feet, she restacked all the required readings for Survey of English Literature, Beginnings to 1500. "And what about you? There's a long line of guys begging for a date with the smashing Eden Williams."

"You know I swore off men before the beginning of sophomore year so I can date my goals." Her friend clicked her tongue. "Besides, we aren't talking about me."

"Fine," she conceded as she stretched her back, which was tight after a long span of studying.

"Fine?" Eden asked as she perked up and leaned in.

"Fine, I said. I'll go on a date with him." She couldn't believe she was agreeing to this. "When is this date taking place, exactly?"

Eden looked down at her textbook. "Tonight. He'll be here in twenty minutes."

She gawked. "Twenty minutes? Are you kidding me?"

Eden waved a hand at her. "Twenty minutes is plenty of time to get ready. And I see you're done studying for the night, so why not? Now you don't have to waste an entire week of your life being all up in your head about it."

"But I will be extremely worried about it for the next ten minutes," she argued.

"Twenty. You have twenty minutes." Eden looked at the clock on the wall. "And now you have nineteen, so go get ready. You can thank me later."

Leona obeyed, not believing this was happening but also smiling about it. She pulled on her nicest pair of jeans and her only pair of boots, hoping her peacoat would wrap another layer of sophistication around her secondhand cowl-necked sweater.

Exactly eighteen minutes later there was a knock on their dorm room door. With sweaty palms, she opened it.

There was David Warlon, standing tall and confident in his dark jeans and black trench coat. He was holding a single long-stemmed rose in his hands. He looked like he belonged in a tabloid photo with the caption "Celebrity's kid spotted on university campus."

"It's a pleasure to meet you, Leona," he said with a smile, presenting her with the flower, which was full of velvety red petals.

She met his deep brown eyes for the first time. She wanted to say, "My goodness where did you get your gorgeous face?"

He had dark curly hair; it was styled but long enough to hint he enjoyed pushing boundaries. His glasses made him look smart, and the dimple on his right cheek—endearing.

Her stomach fluttered so much that what actually came out of her mouth was "I don't love roses."

She regretted it immediately, of course, and wondered if she'd just ended the date before it even began. She never made a good first impression, she knew this, but she thought she would do better than greeting a complete stranger with an honest opinion.

David tilted his head, pulling back the flower and letting it hang at his side.

Leona's eyes widened. "It's not because roses aren't beautiful," she said, trying to recover. "They're gorgeous, including the one you brought. And there's no reason you would have known this random fact about me. I even have a sister named Rose—another random fact." Heat rushed through her cheeks. She needed to rein in her rambling and nervous hand gestures. "I just think they're a little . . . cliché. Predictable."

He blinked twice.

"But I'm really sorry." She covered her face. "That was rude, and what I should have said was thank you because the gesture itself was thoughtful."

David grinned. "Honestly, I'm tired of polite first impressions."

He held up the rose again, but this time he looked past her into her dorm and yelled, "Eden? I brought you something."

Eden rushed to the door, her long box braids already tied up in a pink silk bonnet and her skin glowing under a layer of Jergens, ready to settle in for another long night of studying. Upon seeing the scorned flower, she took it out of David's hand and smelled it. "You should probably know Leona is weird about anything she thinks is too mainstream. And everything too pretentious. She isn't like other girls."

David's eyes locked with Leona's.

"Noted," he said.

Her insides tingled.

Eden shrugged. "Impressive that you got her to share her own opinion that quickly, though. It took me years."

With that, Eden patted Leona on the head and nudged her out of their dorm, closing the door and locking it for good measure.

Leona reached behind her back and jiggled the handle to see if there was still a chance she could escape. Maybe it would be a better use of her time to stay home and practice some self-loathing.

She looked up at David, sheepish.

"I'd like to take you out for dinner," he said. "I hear you don't like roses, but do you like food?"

She blushed again. She wasn't even done being embarrassed by the first words she'd ever spoken to him, and he was already joking about it. But there was something about him that emboldened her and made her feel safe. He not only brushed off her blunt remark, he was still willing to continue their date, and that made her want to get to know David Warlon a little more.

A smirk tugged at the corner of her mouth. "Do you have better taste in food than you do in flowers?"

David stared at her for a moment. Then he laughed.

THEY WENT TO Izzy Hops Swig & Nosh, a bar and grill that offered great meals at prices even college students could afford. Their unique menu kept the city's hipsters happy too. It was dark inside, but not in a seedy way that made you want to avoid touching the toilet handles in the bathroom. Everything was made of brick or reclaimed wood or wrought iron, and amber lightbulbs hung from the ceiling.

David and Leona sat themselves at a high table along the wall and placed their orders with their waiter shortly after.

"So, why did you choose Lake Michigan State University?" David asked, unfolding his napkin and laying it across his lap. "And to study English?"

"Location and in-state tuition costs," she said, not wanting to dwell on that answer any longer. "And, as far as choosing a major, my application just so happened to be due on one of the rare days my mother came around after the divorce. She hovered over my shoulder until I moved the computer mouse and clicked one; said I wasn't going to university to get a degree in indecision."

David grimaced. "Hmm. That's one way of deciding."

"I haven't always been great at choosing things. Sometimes I think it's because I have my dad's laidback nature. Most of the awards I got in grade school said something to the effect of, 'You were there.' "

David laughed.

"But sometimes," she continued, "I think it was because during my mother's few visits, she would criticize me no matter what I chose."

She thought back to tenth grade English when she honored this particular trait of Evelyn's during a unit on haiku:

Every step, disgust.
Is it not safer that I
take no steps at all?

"That would be pretty paralyzing," David affirmed. "Did that make it hard to choose your roommate? How did you and Eden meet anyway?"

"First day of grade school," she explained. "Eden walked up to my table and said she was going to sit with me."

"And the rest is history?"

"Pretty much. But the rest of the history is that it was 'my' table only because I was sitting there by myself, eating alone." She twirled a piece of her hair that she hadn't had time to curl earlier. "I wasn't popular or a misfit—I was flying under the radar as neither. But for some reason, Eden chose me."

"You two make an unlikely pair," David stated, a twinkle in his eye.

"It's true," she agreed. "She's confident, driven, and was offered rides to Friday night football games by upperclassmen when we were in high school. I, on the other hand, was not."

"And yet here you are, rooming together at LMSU."

"One of the nation's top research universities," she recited. "I'm just thankful Eden's path to becoming the next superhero of medical research was so close to home. I wouldn't hold her back, but I could also beg her to be my roommate. She's been there for me through a lot."

"Eden's pretty amazing. Girl Genius over in the science department too," David said.

"Yes, she is." She pushed her thick-rimmed glasses back up the bridge of her nose.

"I like your face furniture." He pointed at them. "How old were you when you got glasses?"

"Face furniture?" She wrinkled her nose as she pondered the phrase. "Hmm. I like that."

"Not too cliché of a term?" he joked.

She laughed. "Sixth grade. I couldn't see the whiteboard from the back of the room. I was so excited when I got my first pair."

"Excited over getting glasses?" David raised an eyebrow.

She crossed her arms and leaned into the small table. "I know I'll probably sound like a total dork for saying this. But, if eyes are truly windows to the soul, I like having a physical barrier between mine and other people. That way, my soul can keep a few secrets I'd rather not share."

"What you're saying is, your face furniture is actually a set of shutters." He folded his hands on the table inches from hers and narrowed his eyes. "Which philosophy courses are you enrolled in, exactly? Because I want to make sure I don't sign up for them and whatever flawed theories they're teaching."

She swatted his shoulder, surprised both by her physical outburst and by how much she enjoyed her body touching his. "Surely your science courses will back me up on this."

He laughed. "And when exactly did you start studying all the things people say with their eyes?"

Leona softened. "When my little sister, Rose, was a baby. Her first smile was at me. When she was two and I was seven, she would ask to play hide-and-seek, and I'd find her standing in the middle of the living room, her hands covering her eyes like she was saying—"

"'If I can't see you, you can't see me,'" David finished for her.

"Exactly." She nodded, stirring her glass of ice water with her straw. "And when I was older, I'd catch her staring at people at the grocery store. Our mother scolded Rose for being rude instead of taking the time to explain that people are made all different shapes and sizes and colors, and that's a good thing. But Rose was little; she was just processing stuff outside her own 'normal.'"

"That's actually quite fascinating," David agreed.

"Don't act so surprised. I already have science figured out. That's why I'm an English major."

"Aww," he drawled. "Saving the world one Oxford comma at a time?"

She wanted to swat him again, if for nothing else but to remove some of the space between them. Instead, she restrained herself by taking a sip of her cold water. "Yes. My Grandma Vera was the one who always encouraged me to write. She bought me notebooks, listened to every story and poem. She'd ask thoughtful questions, down to why I chose a particular word."

Suddenly aware of how much she'd talked, she took a deep breath. "But what about you? Saving the world one beaker or petri dish or whatever at a time?"

"Yes. And do you know what else? The other day I was doing some lab work, and when I put on my safety goggles, I thought, 'Wow, it's so nice that when I'm wearing these, people can't read what my eyes are sayi—' "

Leona swatted him for that. "It's science."

"It doesn't require X-ray vision to see through clear lenses, Leona." He rubbed his shoulder in mock injury. "Sheesh, what are you packing in that fist of yours anyway? A pair of brass knuckles?"

"They're an heirloom from my grandmother," she played along, holding up her bare hand.

"That's one classy matriarch you have there," he quipped.

"But seriously, what is it you hope to do with all that science-y, medical stuff you're learning?" She rested her chin in her palm.

"Seriously? I'm not sure I'm good at sharing my 'seriously.' " He took a sip from his glass, and she saw his blush before he could hide it.

David leaned in, so close she caught a hint of cologne. Then he opened his eyes wide and tapped on his glasses. "Maybe instead you can read what I'm thinking through these."

She laughed, wondering what it would be like to kiss him.

"Try me," she invited. "I promise I won't ridicule your childhood dreams too much."

David thought for a moment. Then he let it all tumble out in one long infomercial. "Right now, there's a lot of overlap between psychology and medical research. Kind of like studying the psychology of eye contact."

He glanced at her and then continued. "Let's say there's a kid who's had a traumatic childhood. Maybe he suffered abuse at the hands of a caregiver, and as researchers keep finding out, repeated trauma literally rewires his brain. His mind is always in overdrive; he's not able to suppress emotional impulses. He tends to strongly react to everyday situations. This affects his ability to have healthy relationships, or sadly, leads him to pass on that same abuse to others. But maybe, with therapy and new pharmaceuticals yet to be discovered by yours truly," David put a hand on his chest, "that kid could break a vicious cycle in one family tree."

David blushed again. "I know it sounds cliché, but I want to use my research to change lives."

Leona, however, soaked up the sacredness of him letting her in even though they'd only known each other for an hour.

To ease the intensity of the moment, she said, "I hate clichés too. You should really think about doing something less noble with your career."

David laughed, and she decided she liked the sound of it.

Their waiter arrived carrying two heaping plates of food.

"Chicken, mushroom, and spinach pizza?" he asked.

She raised her hand. "Me."

He set down her plate and turned to David. "Which means you, big guy, must have ordered the Wisconsin banh mi."

He glanced at Leona and then answered, "Yes, big . . . sir."

After the waiter turned away, the two of them dove in, making it clear how good their first bites were.

"I don't care if every student at LMSU likes Izzy Hops," David said from behind his napkin. "Some things are popular simply because they're that good."

"I can't argue with that," Leona agreed, trying to restrain herself from shoveling it all into her mouth at once.

When they had both emptied their plates, David pulled out his wallet to pay the bill.

"May I take you for a drive?" he asked.

She smiled wide and said, "Sure."

David looked at her mouth. He inhaled like he was going to say something but stopped. "Then let's go," he invited, holding out his hand for her.

She took it, following him out of the restaurant and down the sidewalk to his shiny black car. David made sure to walk her to the passenger door and open it for her. She climbed in, touched by the gesture but disappointed that it meant letting go of his hand.

He took a few turns, then followed the coastline north on Lake Drive, closer to where he grew up.

"Who are the two most influential people in your life?" Leona asked, looking out the window at the houses growing bigger, more lavish.

"What type of influence are we talking about?" he asked. "Good or bad?"

"Interesting question." She tapped her lips. "I suppose just because someone influences you, that doesn't mean they're your favorite. But let's stick with the most influential—good or bad."

"I would have to give that award to my parents, Charles and Delaney," David said. "It can be a lot of pressure to live up to their expectations. But on the other hand, they've given me everything I could ever ask for."

"That's a rather diplomatic answer."

"They're diplomatic people. My dad more so than my mom. My mom at least shows up to stuff, asks me about my day. She cares."

His words sounded more like a statement about his dad than appreciation for his mom, but she didn't pry any further.

"What is your happiest childhood memory?" he asked her, stretching his back as he shifted in the driver's seat. "Or is it too hard to pick one?"

"Honestly, it would take longer to tell you all my unhappy memories." She tucked her hair behind her ears and coughed back the sudden sting in her throat. "But Rose and I like to talk about our one good memory as a family. Whenever we need a happy boost of nostalgia."

David winced. "And what was that?"

Leona shifted in her seat and looked down at her hands. "It was on the Fourth of July. I was ten; Rose was five. My dad burst into the kitchen wearing a pair of jean shorts and no shirt and did his best Regis Philbin impression. 'Who wants to be . . . at the beach with their dad?'

"He said he'd pack a picnic but that we could stop at the gas station on the way to buy a can of Pepsi for each of us—a total splurge. Rose and I got some shorts and T-shirts we could swim in. My mother was never up for family activities, so the fact that she agreed to a day at the beach together tells you just how hot it was at the house with no air conditioning."

David glanced from the road to her.

"Rose and I spent forever building a sandcastle. We didn't have buckets and shovels, but we pushed the sand into rough piles and used the rocks, driftwood, and seagull feathers we collected to decorate the towers." She smiled.

"Then I remember Rose elbowed me and yelled, 'It's bigger than our house!' There was a big white boat out on the lake." Leona made a wide gesture with her hands. "It looked so majestic against the dark blue water, like a big white throne that must be sailing with a king and queen and princess on board."

She looked over at David, who was still listening intently as he drove.

"But the best part of that day was my mother. At first, she was busy reading her *Town & Country* and doing her sunscreen every ten minutes, but then all of the sudden, she was different. She took our hands and said, 'Let's have some fun, girls!'

"We played in the water, jumping over waves or pretending they were monsters we had to run away from. Evelyn—er, my mother—pulled us up whenever we got knocked over and celebrated with high fives each time we made it back to shore. She gave us hugs and marveled at our sandcastle. She watched the big white boat with us too, all the way until it sailed completely out of sight. She waved at it, then kissed me and Rose on our foreheads."

Leona felt burning tears gathering at the corners of her eyes.

"It doesn't feel fair to my dad to say my favorite memory was with Evelyn because he was the one who stuck around after their divorce. But that day was a taste of what our family could have been. Evelyn seemed happy, like there was no place she'd rather be than at the beach with her husband and two daughters."

She wiped away the one stray tear that managed to escape. "It was the only day I look back and think of her as 'Mom.'"

David paused for a moment like he was taking it all in. "That sounds like a complicated memory," he said, reaching over and squeezing her hand. "Family is complicated, isn't it?"

Leona didn't know what came over her, but when David started to pull his hand away, she held it tight, then interlaced her fingers into his.

David seemed to relax even more, smiling over at her.

She smiled back, grateful for the warmth of his hand that, in that moment at least, cushioned the pain she felt thinking about her family.

David continued on Lake Drive through the villages of Shorewood and Whitefish Bay, turning around before they reached as far north as Fox Point. The entire way, they asked each other questions, both serious and shallow: What were you like as a kid? What's your most irrational fear?

"What's your go-to study snack, and why is it not anything with raisins?" David had asked.

Leona didn't know how much time had passed, but she started paying attention to David's driving again when he took a right into a neighborhood and began driving around more square blocks of beautiful homes. The street he turned onto last was Courtney Boulevard, but that name didn't mean anything to her.

"Where are we exactly?" She watched as David pulled over to the curb and parked in front of the house labeled 2638. It seemed random to stop there, especially because he'd mentioned that his parents lived another mile or so north.

"My best friend used to live on this street," David said. "On the days both my parents were gone—my dad on business and my mom planning an event—I stayed with him. Based on your description, he was a lot like Eden."

She looked at the house they were parked by, taking in its features. The home at 2638 Courtney Boulevard was a Victorian, and it had to be at least a century old. The exterior was a timeless gray stone adorned with cream woodwork that contrasted against a stunning maroon door. An enclosed porch spanned the entire front of the house where Leona imagined soaking up the warmth of a sunny afternoon with a book and a cup of tea. It was utterly charming.

"I can't imagine growing up in a house like this," she said, feeling worlds away from the neighborhood she grew up in. She was used to sagging porches and chipped paint, not houses protected for their historical status.

She had a complicated relationship with her neighborhood. It was a tough area to grow up in, and the dynamics at home didn't make it any easier. But she appreciated that living there wasn't an anxious performance either. There were no restrictions about which flowers you were allowed to plant or rules about how long garbage cans should remain hidden from the curb before pickup. She hoped that after college she could find a job close to home, contribute to good change in parts of the city that often went overlooked. She already saw glimpses of progress with new small businesses moving into her area, home improvement grants, and groups organizing litter cleanups.

She kept these thoughts to herself, though, feeling like she'd already talked too much on their date. The surprise of the night was that she was the chatty one, thanks to David's warmth and charm melting away her defenses until she became an open book. Besides, her hopes and dreams for the future didn't make the Victorian home currently in her view any less exquisite.

So, she looked at David and said, "To be clear, I'm not interested in living in this neighborhood. But if I had to live here, I would want to live in this house."

AFTER THE DATE, Leona floated on a cloud of infatuation into her dorm. She found the door unlocked when she turned the handle this time. She couldn't wait to dish to Eden and immediately after call her other favorite human being.

Rose knew Eden had been trying to set them up for a while, but she would be just as surprised as Leona that the date was tonight. Leona would be giddy to answer all Rose's questions and also relieved to get the chance to check in on her little sister. She'd worried about her often in the four years since their parents' divorce.

"How did it go?" Eden called out in a tired voice from the couch where she was still studying. "Tell me everything."

Leona smiled at Eden, planning to praise her friend for her matchmaking skills, which were proving to be magical after all.

Before she could, Eden gasped. "Leona! What happened? There's some sort of green thing covering your teeth."

All Leona's good feelings vanished.

She sprinted on her unathletic legs to the bathroom, which was the most cardio she'd performed since high school PE. She took a deep breath and bared her teeth to the mirror. Sure enough, there was a giant piece of spinach stuck in them.

She lifted her face toward heaven and groaned, "Why?"

After she'd taken all those delicious bites of chicken, mushroom, and spinach pizza, she hadn't realized that a very big, very bright piece of spinach got stuck between her front teeth and remained there through the date.

She sighed. She'd accepted long ago she wasn't a stunning kind of beautiful. Her auburn hair—the combination of her dad's red and mother's ebony—had a limp personality. Her lips weren't full and pouty, begging to be kissed. She wasn't petite and cute like Rose or tall and gorgeous like Eden. Her skin was prone to breakouts, and when she didn't wear mascara, people asked if she was sick. Forgettable, like the aesthetics of a cardboard box. And she was fine with that.

The one thing Leona saw in a positive light besides her rare green eyes was her smile. In middle school, her parents scraped money together for heavy orthodontics to straighten it. She distinctly remembered standing in the kitchen, Evelyn's arm around her while she advocated on Leona's behalf, heavily enunciating the last word in every sentence like she always did.

"Look at her, *Frank.* She has the mouth of a *caveman.* We can't make her go through life like *this;* that would be *cruel.*"

At the time, Leona didn't understand why Evelyn seemed more concerned with her crooked smile than her weak eyes, but now she liked that her teeth were no longer distracting in a way that made one associate her with a Neanderthal. Until that cursed piece of spinach managed to negate her opinion in one single bite. It didn't matter how straight her teeth were if there was an entire vegetable blocking them from view.

In the background, Eden slapped her knees as she laughed.

Leona's embarrassment might have turned into humiliated rage if it weren't for the fact that Eden told her the spinach was there. Her friend would never let her walk around with something in her teeth for that long.

She did a round of violent flossing, then she picked up her phone and searched for her most recently added contact.

David Warlon answered after two rings. "Did you miss me that much already?"

She wasted no time with pleasantries. "Why didn't you say anything?" Her words were edged with interrogation and embarrassment.

"About what?"

She couldn't tell if he was playing dumb.

"I'll try to explain to your science brain the best that I can, but according to the *Oxford English Dictionary,* the definition of *friend* is someone who tells another person there's something stuck in their teeth," she explained.

Silence.

"Oh. That."

"Yes, that," she whined. "That piece of spinach was so big, David."

"I thought maybe you wanted to take it home and make a midnight salad with it or something," he teased.

"We hung out for five hours."

"I know. I really am sorry," he said, sounding sincere. "I saw it right away but didn't know how to tell you. I didn't want to embarrass you."

"Well, my bathroom mirror is making me feel pretty bad right now. You didn't even have to say anything. Hand gestures would have worked just fine."

"I would like to hear an example of the hand gestures you'd suggest."

"I don't know. Maybe pointing at a tree and then pointing at the giant leaf in my mouth?"

"I will definitely employ that the next time this happens."

She couldn't resist the smile pulling at her lips. "Either way, thank you for apologizing for Spinachgate."

David laughed. "If it makes you feel any better, I don't hold this against you, and I hope we can spend more time together to see if we are more than what the *Oxford English Dictionary* defines as friends."

"Wow, that's so dignifying of you to say you don't hold your silence in this scenario against me," she joked. "But how will we be able to move forward after this breach of trust?"

"We'll do fun activities together. Like playing board games."

"I do love board games," she admitted. "Though it feels a little random to mention them now. Like maybe you're deflecting, Mr. Warlon."

"My favorite game is Clue," he said, ignoring her. "And I think the answer is: Mr. Green. In the conservatory. With three bushels of spinach."

"I'm hanging up on you now," she said, even though she couldn't keep herself from laughing.

"It's a date then. I'll look forward to it, Leona."

CHAPTER 4

Present Day

AS DAVID'S YELLOW DREAM CAR PULLED INTO A GARAGE, Leona's survival instincts kicked in. Her brain, sluggish like the door closing behind them, agreed it was time to face the panic attack that started inside Bartolotta's.

"Once a panic attack begins, you can't magically make it disappear," the doctor had taught her. "You have to learn the skills to cope through it until it passes."

Leona closed her eyes, deeply inhaled four seconds of oxygen into her lungs, and then exhaled at the same speed, over and over. She made her fingertips feel the smooth cotton fabric of her dress, the sensation grounding her to the reality of the present instead of some unknown, foreboding future.

And then she told herself what she knew to be real. David probably borrowed this car from an old friend to be funny. They were just dropping it off and picking up their Corolla before the drive home to where they actually lived. On the drive home, they would talk through their confusing exchange at the restaurant, and she would hold David's hand, gently caressing it with her thumb. He'd react as if she made a sly innuendo and say something like, "Hubba, hubba." Then they'd go home and maybe even make love because they were celebrating ten years of marriage after all, and a lot of that time together could even be described as happy.

In the driver's seat next to her, David sighed. Since meeting him at the restaurant, he'd done a good job at making it seem like every interaction with her required a laborious effort.

"Are you okay?" David looked straight ahead. "Because we should probably go inside."

Leona knew what she should say. *Um . . . no?*

She had no idea why they were at the one place he had promised to never take her back to—the one place symbolizing everything they had worked so hard to leave behind. And she didn't understand why he was acting like such a tool.

The fact that she was no longer hyperventilating was, apparently, enough of an answer for him. He grabbed the key fob and climbed out of the car without so much as a backward glance.

"I just need a minute," she tried to say, but her throat was too dry.

It didn't matter. David had already closed the car door and walked toward what looked like some sort of large hallway from the garage to the house. Detached garages were the norm in Milwaukee, so the hall must have been an add-on.

Her eyes darted from the car window to the ceiling to the other window searching for answers, but the dim lighting turned every shape into an obscure blob, filling her mind with more intangible questions.

Am I dreaming? Or in a coma? Maybe I should try to wake myself up.

Being alone with her thoughts made everything worse. Until then, Leona had reason to address her anxiety—a restaurant full of patrons and a man who didn't act like her husband but certainly looked like him. Now her only audience was an empty car. She had free rein to freak out.

Wait. . . . Am I dead?

She pulled down the sun visor and opened the mirror. The sudden stream of light made her squint until her eyes could adjust. The reflection looked like her. Her glasses were still in place, though a bit sideways, so she adjusted them. Her eyes were still green, though smudged with mascara from her panic attack, which she tried wiping away. Her long hair was still auburn.

She gently slapped the sides of her face three times, like she was trying to keep herself from falling asleep during a long road trip. She slapped harder and then pinched until her cheeks stung.

I guess I'm not dead?

"Leona Warlon," she said to the mirror. The voice was hers, and the words were audible this time. She was still herself.

But then who drove her here? Her thoughts swirled down a drain of suspicion. As much as she wanted to believe everything she told herself, one detail threw a massive wrench into that: Warlon Tech.

She might be able to explain away this car she was sitting in, the garage they pulled into, and even the suit David was wearing—it all could have been borrowed. But she couldn't explain why he claimed to work for Warlon Tech. He turned down that opportunity years ago, right before they got married. It was the reason Charles and Delaney cut him off.

Have I been kidnapped by some look-alike? Was David secretly a twin all this time and I never knew it? Stranger things have happened!

Leona covered her face with her hands, fighting back the urge to scream. Maybe the weight of her life had finally gotten too heavy and her brain couldn't take it anymore.

Help! I need help! This was clearly an emergency. She needed to call someone. Someone who would speak sense into the nonsense.

Leona looked down and saw her purse, unsure how it got there. She didn't remember carrying it to the car, so David must have grabbed it in the restaurant. She picked it up and rifled through it for her phone, but it wasn't there. She remembered using it to call a taxi, putting it back in her purse, and then climbing into the back seat of the taxi.

Oh no. She'd spilled her purse in the taxi. She remembered putting back her journal and note and wrappers and keys. Speaking of keys, she didn't see those in her purse either.

She took out her wallet and opened it. Her credit card, insurance card, and library card were still tucked in their slots. She pulled them out to check them and noticed right away that her name was the same on the cards but that they looked different than the ones she remembered storing in her purse. Her driver's license was gone.

Leona's breathing shallowed. She had no way to identify who she was. She covered her face again, wishing she could pretend she was okay, but it was too much. It was all just too much.

She tried another round of mindful breathing techniques. She needed her heart rate to return to a regular rhythm so she could challenge her anxious thoughts into logic. Of course, that was easier said than done, especially when her surroundings and the events of the past hour all appeared to be completely illogical.

After a few more deep breaths, Leona still felt tense—especially in her neck and shoulders—but she was able to push her brain to name what she'd seen so far.

She met David at Bartolotta's for their anniversary. Everything about him seemed different. She had a panic attack. David drove her to 2638 Courtney Boulevard and pulled into the garage like he lived there. Then he walked into the house. He also claimed to work for Warlon Tech, and if that were actually true, it would explain the cashmere suit, the leather seats of this fancy car, and this house. Because if David worked for Warlon Tech, they'd be filthy rich.

She had no idea how that was possible, no idea what was real. Which meant she had no idea how to remedy the situation either. She felt like she was in one of those superhero sci-fi movies David made her watch three times too many. Some of them were about time travel or parallel universes or things like that.

She laughed at the absurdity of the thought, but the sound came out with an edge of hysteria.

Leona knew one thing. If she wanted to figure out what was going on, she'd have to do what she always did when facing problems in life, which was observe her surroundings and keep her mouth shut. The first task would help her gather information to figure out how she got here—how she and David got here. The second would help her stay under the radar as a complete stranger. She didn't want to stir up suspicion from David or anyone else that she didn't belong.

She pepped herself up with the thought that it would be just like all the true crime series she binged on the weekends. She would simply do whatever it took to solve the mystery of what was happening.

David hated true crime. "A little too much murder for my taste," he'd say in the perfect church lady voice with a self-righteous hand resting on his collarbone.

Leona reminded herself that to put her plan into action, she'd have to actually open the car door, get out, and walk inside the house.

Before she did, she practiced one more breathing exercise.

Inhale: *Irrational things are happening.*

Exhale: *But that does not mean I'm irrational.*

LEONA FOLLOWED THE trail of open doors and lights David left when he made his way in, which was a lot. The hallway ended up being an entire breezeway enclosed with thick glass and lined with potted plants, all the way from the once-detached garage to the back entry.

The first room inside the house was filled with coats and shoes. By the looks of it, an old pantry had been converted into a large closet too elegant to ever be called a mudroom. Dark wool coats hung in an impeccably neat line against the wall, and racks of professional shoes sat in orderly rows below. Wooden drawers that appeared original to the house separated the two. She ran her hands along the rack of stiff fabric. Everything was either black or navy, and she couldn't decide if it was timeless or boring.

There was one completely random pair of shoes sitting in front of the rack, a colorful pair of high-tops with iridescent stripes and mint soles, cluing her there may be a teenager nearby. She carefully slipped off the faux leather flats she remembered purchasing at a significant discount and gently set them next to the high-tops—every move she made more like a houseguest than someone who lived there. She noticed David's black lace-up shoes were kicked carelessly to the side instead of returned to their home on the shelves.

Some things about David hadn't changed, she thought.

Out of ten years of marital habit, she tidied them.

The door on the other side of the cloakroom—as she decided to call it—led to the kitchen. The cabinets were a deep forest green and were topped with dark marble counters. There was a large gas range and giant farmhouse sink, and the fridge was recessed into the wall and disguised as more cabinetry. Beyond the kitchen was a formal dining space, a blend of intricate oak woodwork and vintage wallpaper that was both regal and warm.

Every room followed this pattern: an old house stylishly modernized to be functional yet still so full of its original detail that it was brimming with character. She took it all in, her mind boomeranging between how frivolous it all seemed and how there was no need to wonder why people liked being rich. She could only daydream what it would be like to turn on the bathroom faucet without having to use a wrench.

Making her way past the kitchen, she found herself in a sitting room. There was a large oil portrait hanging on the wall that stopped her from roaming any farther. She stared at it, having a flashback to the first time she saw the giant portrait of her in-laws the day she met them. But this wasn't a painting of Charles and Delaney Warlon. It was of her and David.

It was her, and it wasn't her.

She firmly exhaled, wondering why she was in a picture that size on the wall of a house she didn't live in. She moved in closer to study the two subjects captured on canvas who resembled her and her husband. The David in the painting was identical to the David she met at the restaurant; he had the same short hair and a similarly crisp suit. The Leona in the painting, however, had her hair pulled back into a perfect French twist. There was a delicate diamond necklace around her neck, and she was wearing matching diamond earrings. Her face—empty of prescription glasses—looked thinner than Leona's own, but so did her smile.

In the portrait, David's arm was posed around her. They looked elegant and dignified, also stiff and unapproachable.

It didn't make any sense. She didn't know what was happening to her, why she and David were in this house. Why a portrait so out of character for them was hanging on the wall. None of it made sense.

Voices far off in the house interrupted her tour. She walked back to the kitchen, noticing for the first time the stacks of papers and dishes sitting out. This was the most lived-in space she'd seen so far, and it was where she guessed the voices—including David's—would reemerge to.

Unsettled as she was by their interactions earlier, she knew she needed to talk to him to learn more. David was mad at her, losing sleep for reasons she didn't know, driving her to houses they didn't live in. Perhaps some well-worded questions could reveal answers to the mystery of her presence here without setting off alarms in his head too. She stood, plotting her interrogation, until something across the kitchen gripped her attention and erased all her previous thoughts.

There, sitting out in the middle of the counter, was a sippy cup.

She stared at it, the bright pink and purple plastic starkly contrasting with the moody personality of the rest of the room. It was such a small item, and yet that one small sign of life was all it took to send a flood of emotion riding on a tidal wave of dark memories over her heart. She dragged her unwilling feet one step at a time toward the cup. As she got closer, she saw a small ring of milk at the bottom.

"No. It can't be," she whispered.

Seeing that sippy cup recalled something that caught her eye earlier but didn't register in her mind at the time. She raced back to the cloakroom and turned to the right. The only other spot of color in that entire utilitarian room besides the high-tops was sitting on its own shoe rack: a pair of tiny red Mary Janes. She picked up the shoes and held them in one of her hands, tracing the delicate strap and perfectly rounded toes with her finger. There were at least eight other pairs of shoes sized for a small toddler, but none were as bright—and more fit for childhood than a fundraising gala—as that pair.

She set the shoes back down. Now that she was on high alert to find more baby stuff hiding in plain sight, she noticed three miniature peacoats hanging above the rack of tiny shoes. She forgave herself for not noticing them before; they were black and navy too.

She fought the urge to sit down and weep, sucking in air as

tears stung the corners of her eyes. She leaned against the wall to brace herself while her empty arms ached. She would have given herself over to grief completely, but the voices she heard earlier were now arriving in the kitchen. One belonged to David, the other to a young woman.

She heard another sound too—a faint mixture of squirmy babbling and laughter.

David said, "I don't know where Mrs. Warlon went, but thank you so much for watching her."

"You're welcome, Mr. Warlon," the young woman said. Switching to a singsong voice, she cooed, "I just love watching this little bug. I'm going to miss her so much."

There was a fit of tiny giggles getting sharper and louder, as if whoever was laughing was being tickled.

"She is sure going to miss you too, Jaeda," David said. "Do you have orientation next week? Is that why you're leaving Bella's?"

"Freshman orientation isn't until the end of August. But I signed up for a session of summer studies to get a head start."

"Well, thank you for taking care of our girl for the past seven months. Marquette is lucky to have you, and congratulations again on that full ride."

"Thank you, Mr. Warlon. Let me give this precious baby one more squeeze before I go."

Leona listened in, a new feeling shoving her grief to the side and taking over her entire body. It was like a primeval instinct or profound urge: a need to nurture and protect and hold. Instead of thinking through what to do next, she stood up straight and walked with purpose into the kitchen.

There was a young woman who appeared to be in her late teens wearing a blue polo, her hair pulled back. She was holding a little girl who couldn't have been much older than one.

If Leona had to guess, she would say the little girl was fourteen months and twenty-eight days old. She wasn't a squishy baby, but she wasn't a verbal toddler either. She had David's curly brown hair and Leona's green eyes. She looked exactly how Leona imagined her baby would have looked like at this age.

Jaeda smiled at the little girl and said, "Look, Vera! There's your mama!"

Leona wasn't expecting this. She didn't know how this could be real or why this was happening. But even though she didn't know the how or the why, she allowed her brain to name the what, her new reality: She was not in her own life. Whatever that might mean.

Leona walked toward Jaeda and that precious little girl. Aggressively.

Exploring the house, talking to David, trying to figure out why she was here and how to get home—it could all wait.

Vera's here. She's alive.

CHAPTER 5

Eleven Years Ago

LEONA SLID EACH OF HER METAL HANGERS ACROSS the closet rod for the fifth time. "Eden!" she yelled across the apartment they'd moved into at the start of junior year. "Do you have a minute?"

Eden walked in and sat down on her bed. "I have twenty-six minutes before I have to meet up with Ryan."

Leona turned from the closet and wormed her eyebrows up and down. "Oh, Ryan. Is this the guy you met at the Bradley Symphony Center a month ago?"

Her friend tried to hold back the happiness all over her face. "Why, yes. Yes, it is. And he just so happens to be a gifted musician himself."

"Tell me more," Leona said. "Cello? Clarinet? French horn?"

"Piano, actually."

Leona lifted her hands in the air and pretended she was playing an invisible piano.

"Yes. The instrument played by skilled hands." Eden laughed. "Now, what is it?"

"Nothing in my closet says 'meeting my boyfriend's gazillionaire parents for the first time.'" Leona groaned.

"Are you sure this is actually about which outfit you're going to wear?" Eden cut straight to the chase.

"Yes, it's about my outfit," she lied.

Her friend rolled her eyes. "Look, your good heart is worth more than all their gold. And if David's gazillionaire parents can't see that, then they can go jump in a lake. Maybe that really big one they live right next to."

"I know," she huffed, "but there's so much more to it than meeting his parents."

"All right. Let it out," Eden invited.

"I'm going back to the world my mother was kicked out of and then remarried back into. After she divorced my dad, of course." Turning back to her tiny closet, she started sliding hangers again. "There's something simple about dating in college. Even though David and I are from different worlds, right now at least, we're revolving around the same campus."

"That makes sense. We're pretty insulated here," Eden agreed.

"Right? I'm nervous that once we leave, we're just asking for trouble." Leona's shoulders drooped. "I know what trouble can do to people who are supposed to love each other."

Eden sat up straighter. "Did you just say 'love'? As in, Leona Meyer is finally admitting, after over twelve months since their first date, that she's in love with David Warlon?"

Leona looked sheepishly over her shoulder at her friend.

She couldn't believe it had already been a year since her and David's first date, the date that made her pinch the bridge of her nose in embarrassment when she thought about it. And now, one year later, here she was, still paranoid after most meals that there might be food stuck in her teeth but thinking she might be falling in love.

She and David had spent as much time together as they could, and so far their most heated arguments were over whether a movie should be considered a work of art or a piece of trash. She was pretty sure the only thing holding him back from saying "I love you" was that she kept avoiding an introduction to his parents.

She'd tried to reason with him, saying, "There's no need to get too serious too quickly, to drag our family baggage into our relationship yet."

To which he countered, "Dating each other for a year isn't exactly casual."

She finally agreed, which was why she was standing in front of her closet agonizing over proper fashion for the occasion. She'd tried on six outfits so far and hated every one of them. Walking over to her bed, she plopped down next to Eden.

"It's not just about making them like me, Eden, it's also about David. He knows his parents can be intense, but he also really loves them, especially his mom. I'm used to family that breaks up and leaves each other behind. David is not."

She readjusted her glasses. "He's been off lately too. Like, a few days ago he started dropping hints about what I 'might want to wear.' And then yesterday, he said I might want to look for a little gift to bring along but then said never mind and wouldn't talk about it anymore."

Eden waited for a second and then held her arms out wide. "Come here. Let me hug you into serenity."

Leona let her, appreciating that her friend didn't pretend things weren't hard sometimes.

"Would you want to borrow one of my dresses?" Eden offered. "I'm sure I have something fabulous in my closet you can wear."

"Yes," Leona nodded. "Also, it's not fair that you're both a super smart scientist and a college fashion icon."

Eden ran to her room and came back with a dress that was bright purple, fitted, and glittering all over. "This dress is called

'Shake What Yo Mama Gave Ya.' You would look fine in this one, and when I say fine, I mean fine. I mean David won't be able to take his pretty eyes off your fine—"

"Eden!" Leona interrupted. "First of all"—she covered her glasses with her hands—"I think the sparkles might be blinding me. Second, I'm going to a dinner with someone's parents, not to dance with you at Mad Planet."

"That's fair." Eden agreed. "But we have to go back to Mad Planet sometime."

"How about a dance party in our own living room instead?"

"Silly introvert, that's not the same thing," her friend teased. "Okay, let me check my closet for a different option."

"Or," Leona offered, "how about I follow you to your room so you don't have to run back and forth and be late for your hot date."

"Even better."

The next time Eden looked through her closet, she pulled out a hanger and said, "What about my lucky interview dress? Every time I've interviewed in this dress, they end up begging me to work for them."

"It's not your clothes that're getting you your jobs, Miss Brain," Leona countered. She looked the dress over. It was beautiful and it was smart, but it was beige. "I love that dress on you, but even with what's left of my summer tan—if we can call it that—do you think it will make me look sickly?"

Eden looked the dress up and down. "I hate when you're right, but you're right."

She put it back and dug through her closet one more time.

When Eden turned around, Leona could tell by the look on her face that she found the one. The hanger held a chic yellow dress with a high neck and short sleeves that laid in loose waves. There was a belt around the middle, and the skirt had mini pleats. Eden was tall, so the dress came just below her knees when she wore it. On Leona it would be midi length.

"It's pretty. Business casual but cute. They won't even be able to sneak a peek at your collarbone." Eden pointed out.

It was a shade of yellow that popped beautifully on Eden, and when Leona held the dress up to herself, it complemented the red hues in her hair and her green eyes. The dress did both of them many favors. And, like Eden said, it was the perfect style for the occasion.

"Yes, that one is definitely the winner," Leona said with relief.

Eden fanned herself, pretending to tear up. "You're going to look so beautiful." Then she stopped and put on her go face. "Now, get changed so we can get ready together. We're amazing just the way we are, but that doesn't mean we can't get done up."

Leona did as she was told, eventually pulling up a chair to the vanity mirror in Eden's room, which they often shared because their bathroom was too cramped to do anything but shower and use the toilet. She had brought over her small makeup bag and a curling iron tucked under her arm, which she plugged in.

"So, how is college science these days?" she asked Eden, needing to think about something other than her own plans for the evening. "Is Professor Draxler getting any smarter?"

"You mean Introductory Survey of Organic Chemistry? Taught by that angry little man?" she huffed. "Today, I raised my hand and politely explained to him why the formula he wrote on the board was wrong, and he kicked me out of class. Again. Called me 'insubordinate.' "

"Were you able to meet with the department chair yet?" Leona gathered a section of her own hair to curl and picked up the iron. "I wish there was something I could do. Maybe I'll start sending anonymous emails."

"Not yet." Eden began the eyeshadow part of her glow up routine. "That meeting is next week. In her email she said they are working on finding hairnets that fit my hair, but she also said these are delicate matters because Professor Draxler has tenure."

"I'm sorry."

"Thanks, Leona," Eden exhaled. Her hair was pulled into a pineapple updo, and she tugged on one of the coils in her bangs. "It's good for me to talk about. Otherwise, I spend my whole day trying to pretend it doesn't bother me."

Leona nodded. Opening the iron, she let another curl fall warm against her cheek. "Speaking of obstacles," she added, "how are you feeling about this date with Ryan?"

This was her order of operations when she checked in with Eden. Science first. Boy stuff next.

"'Obstacle' is right." She twisted open her tube of mascara and leaned in toward the mirror. "I have all these gigantic projects going on, and he has the nerve to come into my life and make me want to think about stuff other than the microorganisms in my petri dishes."

"It must be hard choosing between your dream and your dreamboat," Leona teased.

"I know," Eden agonized, swiping her lashes. "Why can't I just forget about this guy? Oh, wait. I know. Because the man is a dreamboat."

"What do your parents have to say about it? I assume you told them."

"Of course. I tell my mama everything." Eden beamed, beginning to work on her other eye. "Mama jokes about me giving her grandbabies one day, but she also knows how passionate I am about my research."

"Well, I hope Ryan will be just as supportive of your passions. If not, he can go jump in a lake or something too."

Eden pulled away from the mirror, giggling. "You're going to make me smudge my mascara!"

Leona felt ready from head to ankle but got stuck on what shoes to pair with the dress. She didn't like any of her own, and unfortunately, Eden's feet were a whole two sizes larger. She settled with a pair of basic leather flip-flops, telling herself this unseasonably warm September afternoon might be her last chance to wear them for a while.

She and Eden left their apartment together, promising to catch up later about how their nights went.

David picked Leona up in his black BMW M6 convertible, top up—the car his parents gave him as a gift for graduating high school. She climbed in and found him with a large bouquet of cream, yellow, and marmalade dahlias covering his lap.

From behind the bouquet, he scanned her up and down. "You look good," he said, matter-of-fact.

Leona eyed him back. His curly hair was freshly trimmed. "I can't tell if that means I've stirred something romantic in you or I've met your approval."

He shook his head and said, more gently this time, "You look really nice."

"Sure," she returned, annoyed.

She buckled in, and he handed her the bouquet.

"David, these are really gorgeous," she said, "but what am I supposed to do with them during dinner?"

He avoided her gaze, shamefaced. "These . . . aren't for you. They're for you to give to my mom."

Leona didn't know whether to be embarrassed or angry. Right then, she was a hot mix of both, which was new when it came to her feelings toward David. She echoed slowly, "They're for *me* to give to *your mom.* Your plan is to pretend these are from *me.*"

"Yes?" David rubbed his palms together.

He was never this nervous around her.

"You want me to pretend I can randomly afford a bouquet that probably cost a hundred dollars?"

He looked down and mumbled, "Two hundred."

"Excuse me?" she raised her voice.

He closed his eyes. "The bouquet cost two hundred dollars."

"Whatever. This is outrageous." Her insides burned. Something told her she should run.

David turned to face her. "Leona, look, it's common practice for guests to bring a gift with them. My mom might not necessarily be expecting it from me, but it definitely wouldn't hurt." He raked a hand through his hair, messing up his styled curls. "This isn't about you. This is about the way my parents do things. I was taught to never show up to a new place empty-handed."

"Sure, David. Because we would never want your parents to know that I can't afford two-hundred-dollar flowers." She rolled her eyes. "This is how they do things? By what, living in denial?"

His jaw stiffened. "I'm just trying to make sure the night goes well. This is a really big deal for me, and—"

"Is it a big deal because this is a milestone in our relationship?" she interrupted. "Or because you're nervous about whether or not your parents will like me?"

He didn't answer.

"You know what?" She slammed the flowers back into his chest, petals raining down onto their laps. "I don't need this." She unbuckled and opened the car door.

"Leona! Come on, don't leave," he begged.

She got out of the car and started walking back to her apartment.

David pushed the flowers onto the back seat and rolled the passenger-side window down. Leaning over, he yelled through it, "So, you're just going to quit when our relationship hits its first bump in the road?"

She spun on her heels and walked back to the car window. "This is not a bump, David. It's more like a giant concrete wall. A wall meant to keep people like me out of your life."

She turned away again. She wanted a quiet place she could think. She wanted to wrap herself up in her soft tie-dye robe and cry.

David turned the car off and got out. "Leona, I'm so sorry. You're right. I shouldn't ask you to pretend about anything." He ran in front of her and held his hands up. "I'm just nervous. I wanted this moment of bringing you home and bringing these gifts to prove I'm growing up, that I'm not just their little trust-fund kid. I . . . I love my parents, and at the same time I care what they think about me. My mom . . . she can be a little critical at times."

She stopped walking and looked down. "I know what that's like."

He waited. Then—with caution—opened his arms.

She nodded, signaling permission to pull her into a firm hug, which he did.

After a moment of silence, he whispered into her hair, "I love you."

Leona looked up, a wave of emotion pushing her around. Was it happiness? Fear? It was strange to feel so safe and so vulnerable at the same time.

He said it again, louder this time. "I love you, Leona Meyer. I don't want our families' differences to come between us. I know it's a learning curve for me to not worry about what my parents think all the time. I love who you are, and you don't have to pretend to be someone you're not."

She appreciated his honesty but also couldn't help wondering about what was left unsaid. He did not say he loved her and he knew his parents would too.

The excitement of being told she was loved turned into unease. The world David grew up in had rules—a different set of rules—and he'd stayed in his parents' good graces all these years by following their rules. Sure, he chose to go to a school in state instead of the East Coast Ivy Leagues his parents would have loved to brag about. But he made up that deficit by reminding them Lake Michigan State University was one of the nation's top research universities. As long as it was "the best," it could pass as a loophole.

Leona, on the other hand, felt like she would be walking into that world with a scarlet letter. She was the daughter of a scandal—Frank and Evelyn's scandal, more precisely. Agreeing to go through with meeting Charles and Delaney Warlon felt like accepting an invitation to a lion's den, utter scrutiny.

But she loved David. And didn't loving him mean learning to play by some of the rules he grew up with?

Leona looked up at him, leaned in, and kissed him. She said it out loud too. "I love you, David Warlon."

They held each other a moment longer, then David put his hand on the small of her back and they returned to the car. He opened her door and gestured for her to climb in.

"I forgot to tell you. You look *really* beautiful." His smile was genuine. And genuinely handsome.

"I see you're making up for your flippant comment earlier," she joked. "Am I beautiful enough to be the arm candy you want to introduce to your parents?"

He tipped her chin up and placed a gentle kiss on her bottom lip. "Even beautifuller than that, my lady."

She laughed and sat down, buckling her seatbelt. "In that case, what's taking you so long? Let's get this over with."

David jogged around the front of the car and climbed into the driver's side. Picking up the flowers from the back seat, he handed them to Leona.

Her eyes widened. "You can't be serious. After all that—"

"Relax. They're from *us,*" he reassured her. "The flowers . . . and that fancy bottle of wine back there."

She shook her head. "Unbelievable. You realize you could have just said that in the first place, right? You realize you are your parents' son so they should just be happy to see you, right? And you realize the ridiculous irony of bringing them a gift they technically paid for, right?"

David restarted the car. "I never said the rules made sense."

A DOUBLE WROUGHT-IRON gate protected the entrance of Charles and Delaney Warlon's sprawling property, which David had to use a security fob to open when they arrived. The end of the driveway wrapped around a large stone fountain.

Leona knew Mr. and Mrs. Warlon were wealthy. David never pretended his nice clothes, car, and access to large amounts of spending money were the result of his own hard work. On their first date, he'd also driven her through some of Milwaukee's more affluent lakeshore neighborhoods and said they were near his childhood home. What he neglected to mention was that he grew up on the east half of Lake Drive, where renaissance mansions were nestled in the Wisconsin bluffs overlooking Lake Michigan.

David and Leona got out of the car. A house manager opened the front door. "Welcome home, sir," the manager said with a slight bow of his head.

"Mr. Benson, did you miss me?" David yelled, picking him up and twirling him around in a circle without dropping the bottle of wine in his hand.

"As much as I miss my gastroenterologist, sir." Mr. Benson smoothed his jacket.

Leona put her hand over her mouth to stifle her shock.

David wrapped his arm around Mr. Benson's neck like they were old fraternity buddies. "This guy. Forever the jokester."

Leona wondered how the man kept the energy to deal with someone who enjoyed pushing his buttons.

"Mr. Benson, this is my girlfriend, Leona Meyer."

Mr. Benson took a step away from David and held out a hand

to shake hers. "It's a pleasure to meet you. Now, miss, allow me to take your belongings so I can give myself a safe distance from Mr. Warlon's foolish antics."

She handed over her cardigan and purse but held on to the dahlias.

Suddenly, a woman arrived in the vestibule with her arms open. She was short and wiry and wearing an apron.

"There's my boy," the woman said, throwing her arms around David's waist.

"Mrs. Elliot, it's so good to see you." David hugged her back.

"I wanted to catch you before dinner. How is university? Are you acing all your classes? Are you getting into trouble? Is this your special friend?"

David didn't have time to answer any of the questions, as Mrs. Elliot had already turned to Leona and was pulling her into a hug.

Leona wasn't sure how to react to such a strong display of motherly affection.

"What a doll," Mrs. Elliot gushed.

Leona was uncomfortable but also a little sad when the hug ended.

"Yes, this is Leona," David said proudly. "Leona, this is Mrs. Elliot. She has been my mom's chef for decades. Her son and I practically grew up here together." He turned to Mrs. Elliot. "How is Hank, by the way?"

"Oh, he is fine. He had an accident at the factory a few weeks ago—split his finger right down to the bone. But the doctor said he's recovering well, thank goodness."

"That's awful," David said. "I'm sorry."

"Thank you. I always knew your kindness would outgrow your mischief." She pointed her thumb at David and said to Leona, "I have endless stories about this one. He used to sneak into my kitchen all the time to make trouble, doing things like filling the cupboard with hundreds of Ping-Pong balls so they'd pile onto me when I opened it. And that's just the beginning."

David tried interrupting, "Now, now, Mrs. Elliot. I don't think we need to bring up—"

"He almost got me fired once. Emptied the sugar canister and filled it with salt. I baked six Christmas pies with it. You should have seen the guests choking down each bite, still nodding politely to Mrs. Warlon as if it were the best dessert they'd ever tasted." She chuckled, brushing a loose piece of blond hair away from her face. "After Mrs. Warlon took a bite, she stormed into the kitchen, demanding to know who was responsible. I've never seen a nine-year-old cry as hard as when wee little David confessed to his mom what he did."

Leona shot a look of reproach at David.

He answered with a boyish grin.

"You're a lucky woman, Leona. You found a man with a heart of gold," Mrs. Elliot said, patting David. "He kept me on my toes, but he also filled this big house with joy."

Leona could have listened to Mrs. Elliot's stories all night. She wouldn't mind hovering close enough to get another hug from her either. But as quickly as she appeared, Mrs. Elliot started walking away.

"I'd better get back to work before your mother catches me out here," she whispered. "Enjoy the meal, and good luck, Leona."

Good luck? What did that even mean? she wondered.

David grabbed her hand and squeezed it, leading her through the hall toward the open foyer. There was a circular table in the middle of the room holding a fresh fall bouquet at least three times larger than the one in her hand. To her right, there was a fireplace with an armchair positioned on each side. The stiff chairs were far apart, like they were prepared for a news conference between diplomats of feuding countries.

Above the mantel, overlooking it all, was a large oil portrait of Charles and Delaney Warlon.

It was so quiet that Leona could hear the sound of her flip-flops slapping the bottoms of her feet. Moments later, her slappy steps were joined by the sound of high heels clicking against the marble floors. Feet flopping, heels clicking, closer and closer together. The audio was awkward, like pairing a harp with a kazoo. Before any more nervous butterflies could shove themselves into her stomach, the clicking arrived in the foyer.

Twenty feet away, a pretty—though that word didn't seem enough; elegant? regal?—woman held out her arms. She wore a blue tie-neck blouse and cream slacks with her short brown hair slicked back into a professional ponytail.

"Welcome home, David," she said. Her smile—worthy of a magazine cover—crinkled her forehead and the corners of her eyes.

He crossed the foyer and kissed her on the cheek. "Hello, Mom. Thank you for having us over for dinner tonight."

Mrs. Warlon brushed his cheek with affection. "Oh, David, stop it. You are welcome anytime. I wish you'd come home for dinner more often."

David held up the bottle of wine in his hand. Leona couldn't decide if it looked more like he was giving a gift or offering a sacrifice to appease an angry deity. She pictured that nine-year-old boy yearning both for what was right and for his mother's approval.

"For me?" Mrs. Warlon exclaimed, examining the bottle. "Oh, it's a 1998 Veuve Clicquot La Grande Dame. You know that's my favorite champagne! How kind of you." She kissed him on the cheek and then looked straight at Leona. "Now, David, I have been waiting for months to meet your significant other. Please introduce me to this sweet young lady standing in front of me."

Leona was confused. Mrs. Warlon seemed nothing like her

own mother or the witch Leona had made her out to be in her head. Mrs. Warlon seemed warm and genuinely happy to meet her. She raved for an entire minute over the dahlias Leona handed her before pulling her into a thankful embrace.

Even when Mrs. Warlon let go, she held on to one of Leona's hands and said, "It's just so wonderful to finally meet you, Leona. My David is special, so I know the girl he brings home for dinner must be special too. I mean, you are Evelyn Porter's daughter after all, who must have been the most beautiful young woman to ever be crowned homecoming queen."

In all Leona's anxious thoughts leading up to tonight, she forgot to brace herself for her mother being brought up in conversation.

Mrs. Warlon continued, "We were best friends in high school, you know. Though we lost touch for . . . a few years. . . . It's been nice to run into her again every once in a while."

Leona realized that it was possible Mrs. Warlon saw Evelyn more than she did.

"It's wonderful to meet you too, Mrs. Warlon," she replied.

"Oh, don't call me Mrs. Warlon. That was my wretched old mother-in-law, God rest her soul." She waved her hand in dismissal. "My closest friends call me Dely, and you may too."

All the hugging must have made Leona too comfortable, because instead of saying, "Okay, Dely," she asked out loud, "Like the meat?"

Mrs. Warlon laughed and laughed, but Leona saw something else flash across her face too. She wondered if "Dely" never considered that her nickname sounded like the precooked, ready-to-serve slices of meat sold at the grocery store.

"Oh, heavens, that is comical. David told me you were a clever girl." She shooed them away with a hand full of rings set with various gemstones. "Now, you two run along and get comfortable in the parlor. I'm going to have this wine chilled and these gorgeous dahlias put in a vase." She pronounced it *vahz.* "Can I send anything to drink? A glass of cucumber water, perhaps?"

"Yes, please," they said in unison, then glanced at each other.

When Mrs. Warlon was out of earshot, Leona whisper-yelled, "What is going on? Your mom is really nice."

David whisper-yelled back, "I never said she wasn't nice."

The next expectation to be shattered was the dinner menu. Leona didn't know why, but she was expecting that when they all sat down in the formal dining room, they would be served lamb. It seemed like that was what rich people ate in all the movies she watched. Mrs. Elliot, however, cooked grilled swordfish, eggplant, and pasta primavera.

"Charles and I are working really hard to eat healthier, so no more red meat for us," Mrs. Warlon explained. "It's practically immoral the garbage people put into their bodies these days."

It was the first elitist comment Leona heard her make, but it was mild compared to what she'd braced herself for. She let it roll off her back, too busy enjoying the meal to jump onto a soapbox about food deserts in other parts of the city. Her own mother had always fussed about dining etiquette, going as far as setting extra plastic utensils on the table so she and Rose could practice, so Leona didn't get nervous around multiple forks, and she was confident in her proper posture. But these were all new flavors to her, starting with the cucumber water garnished with mint leaves. The first time she took a sip, the bubbles bit her throat on the way down, sending her into a brief coughing fit.

Mrs. Warlon made sure there weren't any long silences, peppering Leona and David with questions about school and sharing the latest news regarding her volunteer work with the Medical Miracle Charity. When those topics ran dry, she threw in juicy tidbits about David's former classmates.

"If you think of it, please pray for Todd. He isn't faring well in his studies," Delaney said. "Poor Mrs. Wellington—that's Todd's mom, Leona—she had such high hopes for her 'Harvard-bound star.'"

Mr. Warlon didn't say much, not when he and Leona were introduced to each other mere seconds before the first course and not during dinner either. He zeroed in on his food and his glass of scotch, seemingly uninterested in anything being said around the table. She wondered where his mind was. Maybe tomorrow's meeting? His next sip? It didn't bother her that she didn't receive his attention. It bothered her that he was just as walled off from his son.

By the time dessert was served, she was so full of cucumber water she thought she might burst.

"Um . . . I need to use the bathroom?" she said, not knowing where it was located.

Mrs. Warlon said, "I'll call for Mr. Benson to—"

"That's okay, Mom," David interrupted. "I'll show her where it is."

The two exited the formal dining room, walked through the parlor, and crossed the foyer to where the restroom was located. On the way, David interlocked his fingers with Leona's.

"How are you hanging in there so far?" he asked.

"I'm good, just confused. What was all the hype about before coming here?"

"I'm glad you're good," he said, passing over her question. "I have to ask Mrs. Elliot something, so I'll meet you back in the dining room."

"Okay." She stood on her tiptoes and planted a kiss on his lips.

He fanned himself like he was all hot and bothered and then left her to do her business.

As Leona relieved herself, she thought about her night so far. Mr. Warlon was who she expected. The house, beyond ridiculous. A full housing staff—otherworldly. But the night was going well. Mrs. Warlon was nice—warmer than David made her out to be.

She didn't know why, but she came prepared to die a death of a thousand paper cuts.

She washed her hands and then dried them on the soft towel hanging next to the sink. She wondered if she would be able to find her way back from the bathroom but soon caught the frequency of Mrs. Warlon's voice. She followed the sound wave toward the formal dining room.

The tone of the conversation was different from when she left. Mrs. Warlon was spitting words at a volume just louder than a whisper. It caught Leona so off guard she stopped outside and waited to go through the door. She didn't want to stumble in on them arguing. As she listened in, however, she realized Mrs. Warlon wasn't arguing with Charles. She was talking about Leona.

"Seriously, who wears shoes that flop? The girl sounded impoverished before I even laid eyes on her." Mrs. Warlon changed her voice to a mimic. "'Dely? Like the meat?' And did you see her choking down her water? My goodness, it's like dining with a farm animal. What is David thinking? She's probably a gold digger just like her mother."

"It's just a college fling," Mr. Warlon muttered. "Let him have his fun. He'll graduate soon enough and then come to his senses."

The cloud of relief Leona sensed earlier turned into a fog of confusion and then a dark thundercloud of shame. She looked down at her sandals, scorched with embarrassment.

A maid came out of the formal dining room with a pitcher of water in her hands. She seemed surprised to see Leona standing there. Her light blue smock said *Bella's* in small navy letters. Leona recognized her as the woman who brought them their cucumber water earlier and who stood near the table as they ate, waiting to be beckoned to refill a glass, clear a plate, or perform any other task they asked. She looked older than Leona; she was maybe in her early thirties. Her bright red hair was pulled back into a tight bun. She was neatly put together in her uniform, but she carried a weariness about her too.

The woman nodded, then continued with her duties.

Leona understood now. Mrs. Warlon's charm was an act. It was all part of the game. Delaney Warlon was brought up to follow the rules too. To be polite, a warm hostess. But that didn't change how her real thoughts came out of her mouth behind closed doors—or doors that weren't actually closed.

In a twisted way, it made her miss her own mother. At least she knew where she stood with Evelyn, who'd say whatever she wanted, unfiltered, to her face. It never felt great but, listening to Delaney cut her down, she realized that being stabbed in the back didn't feel very good either.

What is safe? Leona wondered.

David came up behind her and wrapped his arms around her waist. "Is everything okay?" he whispered.

She startled, but she wouldn't look at him, her entire body fighting the urge to either run away or run into the dining room and rip the entire tablecloth out from under Mrs. Warlon's fine china. She couldn't tell him what she heard, not here. She bit back her humiliation, remembering her promise to play by his family's rules.

"I'm fine," she said.

They reentered the dining room.

Delaney greeted them with a million-dollar smile. "Ah, there's my two lovebirds. Are you ready for dessert?"

AFTER DINNER, DELANEY ordered David to give Leona a tour of the house. There was every kind of room imaginable. Nine bedrooms. Seven bathrooms. A theater room adjoined to a game room with Ping-Pong, air hockey, and a large gray sectional.

David dimmed the lights and walked over to the couch. Leona sat next to him, until he pulled her onto his lap. "Your parents might walk in!" she objected.

"They're at least two floors away."

Leona rolled her eyes. "Spoken like a kid who grew up in a mansion."

He put his hand into her hair and gave her a heavy kiss. She could feel her body reacting along with his, losing herself not only in a craving but also in love. She pushed herself back and caught her breath, forgetting for one sweet moment the words she heard Mrs. Warlon say about her.

"No, no . . ." She shook her finger at him, standing up.

David groaned but stood up too. Twenty rooms of touring later, they made their way back upstairs to say their goodbyes.

Mrs. Warlon took both of Leona's hands in hers like they were fast friends.

"Please come again, Leona. Come without David, if you must. We'll sip rosé out on the terrace."

In the foyer on their way out, Leona looked one more time at the large oil portrait of Charles and Delaney hanging above the fireplace. She studied their posture. Their tight smiles. Their coordinating power suit and dress. The pride in their eyes.

Is that what David wanted her to become?

LEONA GOT BACK to her apartment and was relieved to find Eden sleeping on the couch, a textbook lying open on her lap. She wasn't ready to tell her friend what happened, to articulate the shame broiling inside of her.

She tossed and turned all night, then woke up early the next morning. She had a couple of hours before she had to work a double shift on the campus cleaning crew, the job that would help her come within pennies of paying her bills that semester.

It was forecasted to be another unusually warm September day, so she grabbed a towel, her purse, and her journal and took the bus to Atwater Beach. She settled onto her towel in the sand, and it dawned on her she was only two miles directly south from the Warlon residence.

She didn't know how to navigate her and David's relationship colliding with the harsh realities of their divergent worlds. She remembered watching Evelyn nag her dad their entire marriage, and she didn't want to be the unhappy nag. She didn't know what the balancing act of give-and-take should look like in a healthy relationship.

She managed to open her journal. A previous entry caught her eye, one she'd penned right after her first date.

> *There once was a girl named Leona,*
> *could only take a man's breath with pneumonia,*
> *Because her mirror image,*
> *a smile covered in spinach,*
> *scared him away to Daytona.*

She laughed, caught off guard by the funny (though embarrassing) memory and the weird words she'd chosen to process it after.

She turned to a blank page, wanting to scribble something new to process what she was feeling now. Something even deeper than the embarrassment of Spinachgate. Her heart was heavy, which made her pen feel heavy too.

She started with:

> *Is love enough*
> *when it comes from*
> *two worlds*
> *on opposite sides*
> *of the galaxy?*

Then, because she wanted another moment of comic relief, she added:

> *Can lacrosse on a manicured lawn love the game of cans*
> *on an uneven sidewalk?*
> *Can Toaster Strudels love off-brand toaster pastries?*

CHAPTER 6

Present Day

LEONA WALKED ACROSS THE KITCHEN TO GET VERA from the babysitter, but Vera screamed and clung to Jaeda like a young koala to its mother. She didn't know how to respond. She was too uncomfortable to pull Vera out of Jaeda's arms even though that was exactly what she wanted to do.

She stood next to Jaeda and rubbed Vera's back.

"Hey, Vera. Want to come by me?" she tried.

Vera couldn't talk, but the panicked look in her eyes said it all: *You are not my mommy.*

The little girl leaned away.

David jumped in, holding out his arms and forcing a laugh. "She usually prefers Mommy," he said, catching Leona's gaze. It was the longest he'd looked at her all night. "I'll take her and put on her pajamas."

Vera's stiff posture relaxed as he gathered her. She stopped crying and snuggled her curly head into his neck while the two exited the room.

Leona fumbled around the kitchen, pretending to look for

something—anything—while Jaeda gathered her things. She wasn't sure if she was supposed to drive her home. Jaeda was old enough to have a license, but there wasn't a car in the driveway.

"Do you need . . . help . . . with anything?" she forced out.

Jaeda looked up. "No, Mrs. Warlon, thank you. A friend is picking me up. Besides, Bella's has strict rules about offering transportation to employees."

"Okay." Leona was relieved she didn't have to try to find car keys and a garage door opener. "Have a good night, Jaeda." Every word coming out of her mouth felt unnatural.

Jaeda left, and Leona released the air in her lungs she'd been holding on to. She still had no idea how she got here and why, but her fear was now laced with a happier adrenaline.

Vera is here.

I'm not living the version of my life that I know.

But Vera is here.

She started looking through the house for David and Vera, also hoping she could become more familiar with the layout, starting with the main floor. She didn't know how long she would be here, but she wasn't sure how long she could fake knowing where everything was either. She needed a system, too, to differentiate between the world she knew and the world she was currently in. Something concrete to orient her brain so she wouldn't feel lost.

She settled on this sophisticated arrangement: World #1 and World #2. Her house in World #1 was a rented bungalow on Thirty-Fourth Street. Her house in World #2 was—different.

She heard voices down the hall: more giggling, more tickling, and some bedtime songs too. She followed the noises, peeking inside different doors and discovering a large office, what appeared to be the master bedroom, and, furthest down the hall, Vera's nursery. In the master bedroom she assumed was hers and David's, she slid a pair of slippers onto her feet; they were a perfect fit and a welcomed comfort on the endless hardwood floors.

Every room had its own set of comforts to offer. The king-size bed with the fluffy comforter was so large she could curl up or sprawl out, toss and turn without kicking David in the back like she always did in their queen bed at home. The master bathroom—a monochromatic ordeal with white tiles, white sinks, and a white toilet—was luxuriously spacious. And the office, dimly lit save for one soft desk lamp, revealed walls lined with fully stocked bookshelves and attached rolling ladders. The kinds of things she'd only seen on the internet.

Each room also added more questions to her ever-mounting list.

The desk in the office was a mess of files and papers, which was typical of how David functioned. But there were other things out of place—a pair of dress pants and a button-down shirt lying crumpled on the floor, a sheet and blanket draped over the seat cushions of the leather couch, and a pillow next to the armrest. An end table held a phone charger, a journal and pen, and a pair of reading glasses too.

Was David #2 sleeping here? she wondered. It made her sad to consider their relationship crumbling that much, to co-parents but nothing more.

The sound of little feet toddling through the hallway startled her. She turned off the light in the office and followed David and Vera into the stately sitting room, keeping a safe distance from where they played. Vera was wearing a snug pair of pajamas with a pink unicorn that accentuated her diapered bottom and protruding belly.

She longed to hold her, to rub her nose in her soft baby skin.

The game they were playing was a mix between peekaboo and tag. There was hiding and chasing and tickling, and giggles filled the room.

Vera was walking, Leona marveled, wishing she could have witnessed her very first step.

She wanted to join in their play, whatever it was called and whatever the rules were. But she felt like an intruder on something intimate, even with her urgent need to belong there. The setting was off and she didn't know who her character was, but the scene was so right. Instead, she took a seat in a wing-backed chair at the other end of the room.

David seemed comfortable in his role, being the present dad he had always wanted to be. Leona's co-worker once joked that her attraction for her husband increased tenfold whenever he took care of the kids. Ever since she became a mom herself, she understood.

"What?" David asked. His terse question cut off her musings.

She flinched and stopped staring. It wasn't like she never fought with David, but this was next level, a complete mind trip. She had to remind herself this was not her marriage. Her David liked her. For the first time that night she decided to not overthink the moment and say exactly what was on her mind.

"It's sweet watching you with Vera. I always knew you'd be such a good dad."

He tilted his head but didn't say anything.

She traced his gaze from her face to somewhere else on her body. Shifting in her chair, she hugged her middle, hoping to hide any possible physical evidence that she was different.

David looked back at his daughter. "Will you feed Vera and put her to bed?" he said, more like a demand than a question. "I have to go into work early tomorrow."

Leona didn't love the way he dismissed her direct compliment, but she leaped at the second chance to spend time with Vera. "Yes, of course."

Her excitement fizzled into panic. What did feeding Vera entail, exactly?

She looked down at her chest. She was pretty certain she wouldn't magically start producing milk again. She didn't know what Vera needed or what she was used to. She hadn't gotten the chance to mother her baby to this age.

David stood up. "I'll warm up her milk."

Leona and her dry wells heaved a sigh of relief.

Two minutes later, David was back in the sitting room with Vera on his hip. He tried handing her to Leona, but the little girl protested again.

"Why does she keep doing this?" David asked.

"I don't know," Leona lied.

Instead of shrinking back, she took Vera, grabbed the sippy cup out of David's hand, and sped toward the nursery. One trick she remembered was that some kids handled being away from their parents better when their parents were out of sight.

"Hello, Vera," she said, once they were out of earshot. Being able to say that simple greeting filled her with profound joy and sadness—neither one canceling out the other. "I'm not sure if I should say it's nice to see you again or it's nice to meet you. Neither seems right."

Vera didn't fight to be put down, but she put her fingers in her mouth and whimpered. She kept looking at the open door, probably for her dad. Leona carried her away from the exit to the other side of the room where there was a shelf filled with plush animals of all sizes, fabrics, and colors.

"Look, Vera. I see a tiger with stripes," she said in a gentle voice. "Should we call him Mr. Stripes? Do you know what Mr. Stripes the tiger says?"

Leona put down the sippy cup of milk so she could pick up the tiger. "Mr. Stripes says, 'Roar.'"

Vera peeked at Mr. Stripes, then turned back to the shelf.

Setting down the small tiger, Leona picked up a much larger plush cat. "And what about Ms. Fluffy Cat? What does Ms. Fluffy Cat say?"

Vera glanced at Leona this time.

"Ms. Fluffy Cat says, 'Meow,'" Leona answered, nuzzling the plush toy into Vera's neck until it tickled her.

The toddler giggled, and her little shoulders relaxed. She even took her fingers out of her mouth.

"I like Ms. Fluffy Cat a lot, Vera, but do you know which one is my favorite?" She grabbed a small dog. "I love Spot the Puppy," she said.

She nuzzled Vera's neck again with Spot's soft nose. This time Vera's giggles were even louder, which warmed Leona's soul. She put the puppy back and looked around the nursery, ready to explore more of the room.

"Ruff."

Leona looked down. The whisper came from Vera.

"That's right, sweet girl!" She beamed. "The puppy says, 'Ruff.' Should we take Spot with us to look at the rest of your room?"

Vera nodded. She hugged the plush dog tightly to her body as Leona hugged Vera close to her own.

"Are all these pretty dresses yours?"

The closet next to the shelves had more clothes than any little girl could dream of wearing. On the wall near the doorway was a framed print that read, *Dream big, little girl*.

Though she hated to admit it, one good thing about accepting David's entire marriage proposal—which would have led to this very different version of her life on Courtney Boulevard—was that they could give Vera so much more. Instead of caved-in steps on the front porch, there were lush area rugs and glittery rocking horses. Instead of stressing about money all the time, there was enough to make at least some of their dreams for their little girl come true. Even if money couldn't buy lasting joy, it could buy moments of happiness every once in a while.

She turned back to the toddler she was holding. "Show me where you sleep, Vera."

The girl didn't point, but her eyes tracked to the crib in the corner. A padded rocking chair was next to it, as well as three baskets of toys and a tiered shelf full of board books.

Vera leaned as far down as she could toward one book that looked more worn than the others.

"Is this your favorite bedtime story?" Leona smiled.

Vera garbled a few excited words.

"Wow, that sounds like a wonderful book. Should we read it together?"

The toddler smiled and nodded.

The two of them eased into the rocking chair, Vera on Leona's lap. She still worried any sudden moves might send Vera screaming for her dad, but the toddler didn't fuss, cry, or even squirm. She laid back and drank from her sippy cup, her head warm against Leona's chest. Leona stroked her hair, examined her little fingers and toes, and pulled her pink pajama top back over her belly before opening the book. She had missed this more than anything over the past year—the room around her completely still except for the closeness of mother and baby. The smell of lavender shampoo and innocence.

She could have sat there forever, and she must have, because the next time she wondered how long they'd been snuggling in the rocker, she looked down and saw Vera was fast asleep. The sippy cup was still in her hands, and milk was dribbling out of her mouth.

Leona put her in the crib, grazing her hand against the heat of Vera's cheek one more time. She turned off the light and closed the door, remembering how important it was to make these moves without a peep.

The clock in the kitchen said it was already 9:47 P.M., a full seventeen minutes past Leona's own bedtime. She was tired, both body and brain, and she was starting to feel achy from the stress she'd been through over the past three hours. Even with the euphoria of being able to hold Vera again, tension was building in the muscles along her neck and shoulders, which always led to a raging headache she could only sleep off. As much as she wanted to explore the house and investigate further, this chronic reaction she had to stress would soon debilitate her if she didn't give her body the rest it was groaning for.

She went to the master bedroom. There was a large figure under the covers, which meant David wasn't sleeping in the office after all.

She rummaged through the large walk-in closet for clothes resembling pajamas, then searched the bathroom for an unopened toothbrush. Every item of clothing and toiletry bottle felt like a clue to help her solve who she was supposed to be in this house. She wondered if she was the one who bought the matching silk sets of pajamas neatly folded in the closet or if they were a gift from someone who shopped far differently than she did. Were the six different types of facial creams her own choices, or were they another small way she tried to live up to the expectations of those around her?

She finished in the bathroom, then walked over to the bed where David was sleeping.

This was so weird. It was all so weird.

She hovered nearby, but she wasn't ready to climb in. Instead, she looked around the room some more as her eyes adjusted to the dark. She noticed there were only two gold frames hanging against the cream walls, and there were no dusty knickknacks littering the nightstands or the cherry Larkin desk in the corner. It was exactly the way she would like her bedroom to look if she had to live here. Uncluttered but lovely.

She looked at the bed again. The man in it certainly resembled her David but not enough to be him.

She considered the couch bed in the office across the hall but knew that would be a nightmare for her aching back. She decided to use this bed only because it was so big she couldn't accidentally touch the man on the other side facing the wall. She pulled the covers back and climbed in, trying not to stir David #2 as he slept.

Who was she kidding? Dads slept way harder than babies, she joked, pulling the covers over herself less carefully.

On the other side of the bed, David rustled. "I'll take second shift with Vera," he mumbled over his shoulder, then turned back to the wall.

Second shift meant there would be a first shift. She smiled, excited at the thought of more parenting.

She knew she wouldn't feel that way under normal circumstances. When Vera was alive, she didn't exactly enjoy the many nights she had to stay awake or the mornings she had to bounce back from sleep deprivation. But whatever was happening right now was anything but normal. She would take what she could get.

SHE TOSSED AND turned and stared at the ceiling. Next to her, the covers over David's body heaved up and down in a consistent rhythm. He wasn't snoring; he was breathing heavily like he always did when he slept. The familiarity should have helped her relax and give in to her fatigue, but her adrenaline kept reminding her Vera might wake up at any moment and need her.

Just past midnight that finally happened. Vera started crying, and Leona jumped out of bed, awake and ready to mother.

Vera, on the other hand, was not ready to be mothered. She screamed when Leona tried to hold her, then cried even harder when she tried to lay her back down.

Leona did everything she could remember from past experience to soothe her. She bounced her, held her in a more natural sleeping position, rocked her. She walked her to the kitchen and offered her more milk. She turned on the exhaust fan above the oven to distract her from the sound of her own crying. She sang "Hush Little Baby."

Vera fought all of it, her cries reaching an even higher volume when Leona sang the line about papa giving her a billy goat.

As the minutes turned into a half hour, Leona's desire to comfort Vera turned into a frenzied effort to get her to stop crying. She would do anything to make the howling end.

David stumbled into the doorway of the nursery, his hair rumpled and his eyes only half open. "How long has she been awake? Do you want me to call the night nurse to come over?"

Leona was so frazzled and exhausted she forgot not to argue. "Night nurse! We pay people to parent our child during the night?"

David straightened against the doorframe. "You said you would pay anyone who's never been on *America's Most Wanted* one million dollars to take the night shift if it meant being able to sleep again."

That sounded like something Leona would say, but it was another extravagance she was shocked they could actually afford.

"Well, that was before I learned how to function as a parent," she huffed, knowing how silly that sounded against the backdrop of Vera's screaming.

"This is obviously a display of high functioning," David muttered.

"I'll take care of my own baby!" she yelled, sending Vera into an even louder fit.

David held his hands up in surrender but didn't retreat. He walked to the dresser and turned on a machine that filled the room with the sound of waves lapping onto shore, then leaned into the crib and grabbed a pacifier attached to a small plush unicorn and gave it to Vera.

Leona hadn't noticed those items before.

Vera clamped down on the pacifier and leaned her body toward the crib like she wanted to lay down. Leona put her in the crib, and the toddler's eyes rolled back until she was fast asleep.

Leona couldn't believe how fast that was. She turned to apologize to David, but he had already left the room.

She sunk down into the rocking chair, the ache in her neck and shoulders now pounding in her temples. She massaged them, listening to the waves coming from the sound machine.

She knew the noise was supposed to be calming—it obviously did the trick for Vera—but she spent enough time at the lakeshore to know waves could have more than one effect on a person. Sure, someone could be washed over by a wave of calm, but it was also possible to be knocked over by waves of fear or drown in a wave of grief.

Leona wanted to fall asleep right where she was, but she knew her anxious thoughts would probably turn into insomnia as they pulled her in opposite directions. She didn't know how she could fall asleep when she had no idea what was going on or how she'd gotten here.

And how could she sleep knowing that when she woke up, Vera might no longer be there?

CHAPTER 7

Ten Years Ago

DELANEY INSISTED ON PURCHASING A DRESS FOR Leona to wear to the Medical Miracle Charity gala, her treat. "I'll call my favorite designer—Maria Laurent. Do you know of her? She'll bring over some of her latest gowns for you to try on," Delaney said. "I'm telling you, this woman can alter a design to make anyone look fabulous" was her endorsement.

Leona never told David about the conversation she overheard between his parents the night she first met the Warlons. She even went through a brief phase of trying to make excuses for his mother's cutting remarks—maybe she was having a bad day or maybe she was worked up about her only son having a girlfriend. But those excuses didn't mesh with the way David described his mom at times.

For every nice word out of that woman's mouth in the five months since, Leona imagined what Delaney later said to Charles at the dinner table when she wasn't around to hear. She liked to think she had taught herself an entirely new language—to infer whatever Delaney wasn't saying out loud.

She knew exactly what Delaney was thinking about her gala attire. Delaney had a reputation to uphold, and she didn't need the guests distracted from writing big checks because her son's girlfriend was wearing something from Goodwill.

While Delaney and Maria Laurent played dress up on her in an upper room of the Warlons' estate, Leona tried to pick up on the rules of the gala's dress code. But as hard as she tried, she couldn't tell the difference between a dress and a gown, a timeless silhouette and one too trendy, decadent fabrics versus cheap. She thought all the dresses were pretty and that each one probably cost more than an entire month's rent.

The one thing she did know was that she really liked the eighth dress she tried on, and so did Maria. The designer went on and on about how the trumpet silhouette was perfect and how the long sleeves—fitted through the upper arm and puffed into a bishop cuff from elbow to wrist—added a unique embellishment. The open back was suggestive but not trashy.

In a French accent, Maria said, "You're sophisticated, stylish. And that emerald color on you, it makes your eyes practically pop out of your head. You look gorgeous—stunning, really."

Leona pushed her glasses up the bridge of her nose and smiled. What she liked about the dress was that she could walk in it, and it covered the parts she didn't want slipping out all evening. But she would be lying if she said she wasn't also happy to hear a fellow female go on about her like Maria Laurent just did.

The dress seemed to stun Delaney as well because her mouth gaped. She shook her head. "No, no. It's all wrong—much too fancy," she insisted. "This isn't a *white* tie event, Maria."

Leona had never even heard of a white tie event.

"It's perfection," Maria held. "She will steal the show."

And that was exactly what Delaney Warlon was afraid of, Leona translated.

Delaney studied Leona as they stood in front of a full-length mirror.

It reminded her of middle school when two girls looked her up and down with giggling whispers, sending waves of self-consciousness through her body and an anxious checklist through her mind. Back then she wondered if the problem was her clothes or her correct answer in math or the bubbly pimple she discovered in the mirror that morning.

In front of Delaney, she wondered if anything she said, did, or wore would ever be good enough.

Delaney smiled. The expression gleamed like ice. "You're right, Maria. It's a beautiful dress."

Leona understood. The dress was beautiful—not her.

THE GALA WAS scheduled for late February, the same season David and Leona's lives were scheduled to hit major forks in the road. They were less than a semester away from graduating from Lake Michigan State University, and David had to decide if he would commit to a life at Warlon Tech or if he and Eden would follow their mutual dream of starting BioThrive together.

David and Eden had made some huge breakthroughs in their research. Their formula had the potential to reregulate the part of the brain that processes emotions as well as renew a patient's ability to control impulses, basically reversing damage caused by early-life trauma. The drug would reduce anxiety, flashbacks, poor concentration, and trouble making decisions—all the stuff that can strain relationships and pull patients into substance abuse. Maybe for some, a lot of grit and resilience and intentionality could help a person overcome the past, but what David believed, and what Eden and Leona witnessed often, was that sometimes what didn't kill you left you too shattered to overcome your circumstances by sheer willpower.

David and Eden weren't close enough to the finish line to brainstorm names for their drug, but they had progressed enough to outline their pre-product, draft clinical trials, and fill out applications for grants. Until their product went to market—years, possibly an entire decade down the road—the work wouldn't pay well. Barely enough to cover living expenses.

At another dinner with Leona and his parents, David brought up his research to Mr. Warlon. He wanted to test the waters to see if Warlon Tech would be interested in funding the start-up.

"In my opinion, son, the drug sounds too good to be true," Mr. Warlon said as he set down his newspaper and folded his hands over his middle. "Also, medication related to brain research is highly regulated. It requires jumping through extra hoops for clinical trials and acquiring insurance."

"Yes, I know that, Dad, but—"

"Often, trials are done overseas where there is less regulation from the FDA," Mr. Warlon continued. "But those aren't the main reasons Warlon Tech could never fund your research. You seem to have forgotten that if people were healed from the chronic pain caused by past traumas, Warlon Tech would have a far smaller customer base to medicate for chronic pain." Mr. Warlon winked and picked his newspaper back up.

"Don't forget, David," Delaney jumped in, "having medical school paid for is contingent on you accepting a job at Warlon Tech postgraduation."

Leona knew this decision was ripping David apart. Pursuing BioThrive wasn't impossible, but it meant turning down a dynasty, free schooling, and what she saw as the conditional love of his parents. David had always wanted to please his parents, and he'd never had to think about money before except how to use it to its full advantage. BioThrive would be a hard road. Much different than the road he was raised on.

The other fork in the road was their relationship.

Leona loved David, but she didn't know what a future with him would entail. His parents were a link to luxury, but with so many strings attached to how they were supposed to work and dress and eat and present themselves, their safety net felt more like a safety ball and chain. She couldn't imagine an entire life as a doormat under Delaney's expectations.

For so long she'd ignored her objections to David's family in order to keep the peace, but it was starting to feel like she was living in denial of what marriage into the Warlon family would look like.

ON THE NIGHT of the gala, Leona pulled her hair into a simple updo. Rose had said she would come hang out while she got ready but called to cancel at the last minute.

"I'm worried about her, Eden," Leona admitted, opening a palette of eyeshadows. "And it's not her hair. We both know she gets unique haircuts just to piss off Evelyn. I think she looks adorable with them anyway."

"Have either of you seen Evelyn recently?" Eden asked from her bed where she was studying.

"Not since my last birthday." Leona started to paint, trying to mimic the tutorial she watched earlier. "And I think Rose stopped accepting her birthday brunch invitations when she turned sixteen. I guess that doesn't stop her from wanting to make Evelyn mad, even from far away."

Eden nodded, flipping the page. "Rose is tough."

Leona pointed at Eden's book. "By the way, I'm planning on studying together tomorrow. Do you still need me to quiz you?"

"Yes. Thank you. This class is killing me. Let's plan on it after church."

"And after lunch," Leona added. "But yeah, Rose is tough. Last time I went home for dinner with Rose and my dad, I found out she has a tattoo across her entire lower back."

Eden scrunched her face. "She isn't eighteen. That isn't even legal."

"Fake ID," she explained. "The tattoo says *fighter*."

Her friend frowned. "She may or may not regret that when she's eighty-three."

"Which is exactly what I told her—not too harshly because Rose is so sensitive these days." Leona held up two shades of lipstick to her face in the mirror, picked one, then slid the color along her lips and rubbed them together. "Whenever someone pushes back even just a little bit, it's like she's ready to explode. I don't know how to show her I care without lighting her short fuse."

"And she said . . ."

"She said I was probably right but that it's fun when she's seventeen." Leona set out a pair of lashes and glue on the table. "It's not even about the tattoo anyway. Not really. I'm worried about *her*. I think she's really hurting. She's only a junior in high school and already partying her senses away whenever she has free time. I don't want to be the badgering big sister, but it's hard watching a train go completely off the rails."

"That's a tough spot to be in," Eden agreed. "But, maybe next time, try being less passive and more aggressive with your interventions. So you can actually get your point across."

"You're probably right," Leona admitted. "Now, to attempt these lashes you so highly recommend."

It turned out to be a whole thing. When she tried to put the first lash on, her nose started itching so bad and she sneezed so hard the lash fell off her eyelid and stuck to her cheek.

Across the room, Eden giggled.

"I'm glad I'm providing you with some entertainment," Leona said, finally getting them to stick in the right spot.

"Oh, I forgot." Eden got up and walked to the kitchen. She came back with an envelope and handed it to Leona. "This came for you today. I think it's from Major Payne of the East."

Leona turned the envelope over in her hands. It was a different shape than a utility bill, and it weighed a lot more too. She recognized the handwriting because her name and address were written in the same calligraphy that was on her invitation to the gala. She ignored the flap that had been licked shut and hastily ripped the envelope open right through the middle. Inside was a heavy piece of cardstock pressed into an accordion fold. When she spread it out, she realized it was a Warlon family holiday card. A super belated holiday card arriving at the end of February.

"Is this what it means to be fashionably late?" she asked, angling the card toward Eden.

"Oh boy." Eden came in close. "What do we have here?"

There was a photo of Charles and Delaney posed in front of one of their many fireplaces, photos of David with each of his parents, and a centerfold of all three of them on the terrace with Lake Michigan in the background. They were attractive people, but that didn't make the poses appear any less forced.

Eden pointed to the last photo, which was of David posing by himself. "What a dweeb," she teased.

"Hey. He's my dweeb." Leona elbowed her. "I remember David saying he had a family photo shoot. I didn't realize it was for this."

Eden flipped the card over, and they both gasped. Typed across all three five-by-seven rectangles of the trifold was a newsletter about the Warlons.

"It's so long," Leona said.

"Leona? I would really love to read this correspondence together," Eden pleaded.

"I'm not sure I have time to get through this entire thing *and* be emotionally ready for the gala."

"It'll only be, oh, I don't know . . . a ten-hour endeavor?" her friend said.

"Okay," Leona relented. "But let's sit down. We're going to need all our energy to get through this."

The two made their way to the couch in the living room.

Holding the holiday card in her hand, Eden cleared her throat and harnessed her best impression of Delaney's voice. " 'We hope you and yours have successfully thrived through the first few months of the year.' "

Before she could read any more, Leona cut in with her own translation of Delaney's words. "We hope you are rich enough to pay someone else to lick your envelopes."

Eden looked at her, eyes wide.

"I'm sorry. I know I'm being petty," Leona explained, "but I just really need to vent right now. Get it all out before tonight."

Eden nodded, then turned back to the card. " 'We loved receiving your holiday cards, and we apologize for not sending ours in a timely manner.' "

"We are busier than you, and, therefore, we are better than you," Leona paraphrased, a little surprised by how angry she was feeling.

" 'Charles continues to ably lead as the chief executive officer of Warlon Tech, which broke through a major milestone of six hundred million dollars in revenue last year,' " Eden continued.

Leona rolled her eyes. "Ask us for pro tips on how to avoid paying taxes."

Eden started giggling. It took her a second to regain her composure. " 'After the unfortunate events of last winter, Charles spent the better part of January improving the security measures of the estate.' "

Leona leaned over to see for herself. "Wait, she seriously wrote that in there?"

"Yeah. What is she talking about?"

Leona shook her head. "A group of high schoolers egged their front gate."

Eden's face dropped. "Seriously? That's what they needed improved security for? You're going to really love the next line then."

"Oh no."

"Oh yes." Eden switched into an accent again: " 'We pray these measures will keep us safe on the streets of Milwaukee.' "

Leona balked. "Shut up! I wonder what kind of security measures would have been put in place if someone toilet papered the landscaping."

"I know. There's a lot to unpack there. But we must continue," Eden commanded. Switching back to her imitation of Delaney's voice, she said, " 'Delaney makes sure the operations of our residences are running smoothly when she can hire enough people to work.' "

Leona translated, "We still have not caught on to the fact that we are miserable people to work for. Also, what kind of lowlife owns only one residence?"

" 'Delaney also serves on the board of the Medical Miracle Charity,' " Eden read, " 'which is hosting its annual gala again this February. The event is on track to raise a record fifty million dollars in one evening.' "

Leona tried to keep a serious face. "Generosity is a competition."

"Yes!" Eden fanned her face with the card. "Our charity eats your charity for breakfast!"

They laughed together.

"Okay, okay," Eden said, wiping at her eyes, "now we get to read about your man. It says here, 'David continues to excel in his classes at Lake Michigan State University, the country's leader in medical research.' "

Leona didn't have anything sarcastic to say about that. "My man is amazing, and I know it."

"'We look forward to—'" Eden stopped and refolded the card. "Okay, I think that's it for today. You have to get into your dress or gown or whatever it's called."

"Hold on a second," Leona protested. "You can't just stop. What does it say?"

Eden pulled open the collar of her T-shirt and shoved the card down into her bra.

Leona crossed her arms. "You look ridiculous."

"But have I ever steered you wrong?" Eden challenged.

She rolled her eyes for the second time that evening. "No."

"Do you want to enjoy your fancy evening out with David?"

She uncrossed her arms. "Yes, but—"

"Then please trust me on this." Her friend patted the rectangular outline pushing through the front of her shirt. "You don't want to read the rest until after you're home."

Leona's curiosity raged. "But what if my night isn't as fun because all I'm thinking about are the millions of bad things that might be written on there?"

"Hey." Eden leaned over and put her hand on Leona's leg. "What's on here isn't the end of your life. I just think your night will be more enjoyable if you don't have to think about this."

Against all her natural instincts, she took Eden's advice. But not before she said, "I hate you."

"I know, I know. It's for your own good, friend."

MARIA SAID THE dress made Leona's green eyes pop, but it was David's eyes that popped when he saw her in it for the first time.

"You look ravishing, my lady." He bowed to her.

Leona never got sick of hearing ridiculous stuff like that come out of his mouth. She twirled so he could take in the whole picture.

David clapped and whistled. Then he held out the flaps of his jacket and did his own exaggerated twirl, ending with a curtsy.

"And? What about me?" he asked. "Do you like my tuxedo? It even has pockets." He stuck his hands into his jacket and then waved at her.

She took him in—his tux, sharp glasses, styled curls—and breathed in the faint scent of his cologne, which had drifted her way during his twirl.

"You look okay too." She bit her lip, still unsure how she ended up with someone like him.

The gala was being held at the art museum downtown. They would be in Windhover Hall, the illustrious reception hall located in the Quadracci Pavilion. The room had a ninety-foot-high vaulted glass ceiling as well as a clear view of Lake Michigan when the darkness of February didn't hide it. If all went according to Delaney's plan, the refined atmosphere would inspire all four hundred and fifty guests' historic generosity.

To Leona, what was even more impressive than the backdrop of the event was watching David be a complete natural in this environment. He remembered almost everyone's names and was able to ask gracefully when he didn't. He knew when to be businesslike and polite, and he knew when to turn up his lighthearted charm. And he never made her feel like she didn't belong. He introduced her to each guest that came up to him, saying to his parents' friends and business associates he was so glad he finally got to introduce them to his "one and only Leona."

On David's arm, people assumed the best of her. She was welcomed by association.

That changed slightly when Delaney began lingering near their party. At every introduction she had something to add.

"Did you know Leona didn't grow up on the east side?"

"She's practically our little Cinderella story."

"Young love. It's such a fleeting thing, isn't it?"

Leona interpreted that Delaney's fake nice was wearing off.

David seemed to notice too, and with a gentle hand on Leona's back, he led her away through the bustling cocktail hour and silent auction to find their assigned table.

They were seated with the three Warlon Tech bigwigs and their wives. Leona found her name next to Sandra Wellington, who was already sitting at the table with her husband, John. Sandra tried to make small talk with her—which she credited to her as kindness—but she had few applicable answers to offer in return. She didn't belong to a family who ran a business, invested in real estate, or had ever traveled to a destination across the globe. And no, she hadn't yet been able to afford to try the new Korean-Mexican fusion restaurant nearby.

Leona refused to bring up Evelyn—the one legitimate name apart from David's she could drop that people would know. And she didn't want to bring up Sandra's son Todd, as the one thing she knew about him was that, according to Delaney, he failed out of Harvard. Which meant the only topic the two women could equally relate to was the weather.

"Milwaukee sure got hit with a lot of snow last week," Sandra said.

"Yes," Leona agreed.

They both took long sips from their water glasses. Leona's sip was more like a gulp. She scolded herself for letting her manners slip.

Delaney appeared at the table, Cynthia Brand alongside her. Sandra greeted them excitedly, as if their arrival was her saving grace.

"What's wrong, Sandra?" Delaney probed. "Has the Warlons' little fledgling bored you already?"

Sandra blushed.

Leona wondered how Sandra would answer without disrespecting Delaney or lying about how uncomfortable she was sitting next to her.

"We were merely chatting about last week's snowstorm." Sandra straightened the cutlery next to her plate.

Leona tried taking another sip of water but was met with a glass of ice.

"I'm only kidding." Delaney waved her hand as she sat down. "Isn't Leona's dress fabulous, by the way? It's a Maria Laurent—almost too beautiful for anyone to be worthy of wearing."

Sandra blushed again.

Leona felt both belittled and relieved. She was so close to meeting the real Delaney.

All the guests were seated, and the presentation began. There was a lengthy video introducing the Medical Miracle Charity, including an overview of how last year's donations were utilized. The video then cut to three testimonials from people who received donations that paid their medical debt in full. Their stories were full of tears; the MMC literally changed their lives. Throughout the audience, cloth napkins dabbed at leaky eyes and quieted light sniffles. Leona wondered if any of the recipients were invited to feast with them at these gala tables.

The presentation paused for dinner, a meal with so many courses she lost count. They started with honeydew melon in a strawberry coulis, followed by egg mayonnaise on dressed salad leaves and cream of mushroom. Her only hurdle in this meal was the main course. It was roasted half duckling served with apple cider sauce surrounded by a pile of roasted vegetables. She had to tell herself she was actually taking bites of a Canada goose that once hissed at her grandma. Not an innocent, fuzzy duckling.

The conversation around the table fell into a predictable routine. One of the men gave an uninteresting, impassioned opinion about business politics, and then Cynthia butted in with the latest gossip about someone from a nearby table. Back and forth it went, between men convinced of their own importance and women convinced it was their job to tear everyone down.

David didn't say much unless he was spoken to.

Leona tried to play along, but she was nervous, thinking too much. She thought about how nicely David was welcoming her in and how blatantly Delaney was trying to push her out. She obsessed over what might be written on the Warlon family holiday card back at her apartment.

She needed something to busy herself, to quiet her brain. She noticed a glass of wine sitting next to her water glass and decided to take a few sips. Once she acquired the taste, she thought she'd make the conversation more interesting by playing a game. Every time Cynthia began a sentence with "I heard," she'd take a drink.

Thirty minutes in, the numbness felt so good.

She never drank—it was too expensive a hobby and not how she wanted to deal with the knot constantly growing in her chest. But she thanked the wine now for her newfound zen, the way the conversation around her became slightly more tolerable with each sip. Except for Cynthia, of course. She would really appreciate it if someone would put her in her place.

Isn't that what powerful men were supposed to be good at? Putting women in their place? She wondered for a second if she'd said her satire out loud, but nobody's mouths had fallen open and Delaney wasn't choking her with a cloth napkin.

The next time Cynthia started blurting "news," Leona had to focus hard in order to navigate her hand to the stem of her wine glass.

"Are you okay?" David leaned in.

"I'm fine, but someone should really tell Sister Cynthia over there to stop gossiping in the form of prayer requests," she said.

"Isn't that your second glass in twenty minutes?" he whispered.

His breath made her ear tingle. She giggled, which came out louder than she intended.

Mr. Wellington halted his speech about "our chokehold government" and glowered.

David whispered more urgently to her, "Are you sure you're okay?"

She nodded her head too hard and whispered back, "I'm amazing. Now, shhhhh." She tried to put her finger on his lips but it landed on his cheek instead. "Let me listen."

She wondered how she couldn't be amazing. She got to sit at a table where geniuses eating from silver spoons were solving all the world's problems. She glanced around again, hoping she'd only thought those words.

Mr. Brand changed the subject to Warlon Tech's cash flow, which reminded her of something she read recently about Warlon Tech's cash. She finally had something to contribute, so now was her time to speak. She didn't only feel numb inside; she felt bold, brave!

"*I* heard," she cut in over Mr. Brand, looking at Cynthia as she mimicked her gossipy tone, "that Warlon Tech made six hundred million dollars in cash last year." She raised her glass. "I'll toast to that."

The table went silent. Next to her, Sandra used her napkin to dab her forehead and cheeks.

Leona realized she had their table's attention, so she decided to take advantage of her newfound courage. "I have some thoughts on business too." She picked up a bite of duckling with her fork and waved it around in the air before popping it into her mouth.

"Leona?" David put his hand on her back.

She wasn't done chewing, but she continued, "You are all so rich, that what if—"

He whispered, "Maybe we should—"

"David." She pushed his arm away. "I read on the internet it's a 'fox pass' to interrupt someone at a dinner party."

"I think you mean faux pas." Cynthia glared from across the table.

Leona stood up from her chair, which made her brain feel like it was underwater. She wobbled but was proud of herself for not falling over. "Yes. Thank you, Thynthia," she slurred. She tried pointing at Cynthia, but her hand was unexpectedly heavy. "Now, please, do the entire table a favor and shut up."

Sandra and Cynthia gasped.

Delaney remained steely quiet.

"Leona." David was blushing bright red. "I think—"

"You all have so much money," she persisted, "and then you come here to be so generous. But what if—now hear me out—this is good." She leaned over to grab her glass of wine, which David moved out of reach. Her hand hit her water glass, which David also caught and steadied before it could fall over. "What if you made your happy drugs less addictive and more affordable, instead of making people cut off their arms and legs in order to be able to buy—"

Delaney bolted out of her seat. "That is enough." Turning to David, she bit through her teeth, "Take this girl to get some air."

Leona turned to David and offered her interpretation: "What your mother means is, she doesn't want you to marry me."

She was pretty sure everyone at their table and the surrounding five tables heard her say it.

DAVID USHERED HER to the ladies' room, gripping her arm a lot harder than the tender way he'd touched the small of her back earlier.

Once inside, she used the toilet, trying to navigate her dress without peeing on it. She finished the task with moderate success and then made her way to the long row of sinks, each movement more calculated than usual. The water coming out of the brass faucet mesmerized her, which added an extra three minutes to her handwashing.

She wasn't sober, but she was coherent enough to hear David and Delaney right outside the bathroom door.

"I'm sorry, Mom. I'm sure there's a reasonable explanation."

"David, if you are stupid enough to marry that girl, you'd better be smart enough to sign a prenup. Putting a green dress on a garbage can doesn't make it any less white trash."

Leona's insides raged. She wanted to rip her dress off and scream with the force of the Hulk.

The part she couldn't stomach wasn't the unforgivable faux pas she committed in front of Milwaukee's elite. Her display finally gave Delaney a reason—beyond the fact that she wasn't born into the correct social circle—to push her out. She wasn't worthy of the Warlons' son; anyone could see that. Everyone at the gala just saw that.

What made Leona fume beyond Delaney's cutting remarks was that when David's mother used words as sticks and stones to break her bones, he barely put up a fight.

Leona needed fresh air. Fresher fresh air than what was floating around the bathroom.

She noticed a second exit, a door David wasn't waiting outside of. She went through it, retrieved her jacket from the coat checker, and went outside to the terrace overlooking Lake Michigan. It was only eight o'clock, but the sun had set hours ago. She couldn't see the waves, couldn't hear their powerful churning. This was the short window when much of Wisconsin's coast was frozen still.

Leona leaned her forearms onto the railing. The bitter cold nipped the tips of her ears and started to clear her head.

A few minutes later, a door from the museum to the terrace opened. A silhouette in a black gown walked toward her. Leona remembered seeing the woman inside—and possibly on the cover of *BizTimes* magazine somewhere around campus. Her jet-black hair was tapered into a pixie cut, the crown of curls at the top grazing her forehead in a way that was soft and feminine. She was wrapped in a large fur shawl.

"I could hear you across the ballroom." The woman handed her a piece of bread. "Here you go. That's to soak up some of what's clouding your head."

Leona accepted the bread and took a bite, overcome by the compassion of a stranger. Now that she was starting to sober, the embarrassment of what she did at dinner was settling in. It wasn't like her, and she was beginning to feel the same turmoil that made her want to drink in the first place.

"I'm Patrice Perry," the woman introduced herself. She looked straight ahead into the darkness when she said it.

Leona turned to reciprocate. "I'm—"

"Leona. I know," Mrs. Perry finished for her. "You're here with the Warlon boy, which means everyone in that room now knows who you are."

Leona turned back toward the water, unsure how to respond.

Mrs. Perry grabbed the balcony railing, a small handbag hanging on her wrist. "So, you didn't grow up on this side of the city?"

"How did you know that?" Leona wondered out loud.

"I was nearby when Delaney sabotaged David's introduction of you to Mr. and Mrs. Kensington. Welcome to the ball, Cinderella." She nodded, then took a carton of cigarettes out of her handbag. "Do you mind if I smoke?"

Before Leona could shake her head, Mrs. Perry began rapping the carton against the palm of her hand. She removed the plastic and foil, then tapped the top of the carton, encouraging a few of the tightly packed cigarettes to pop up. Mrs. Perry pulled one out, placed it between her first two knuckles, and lit it.

There was something about the sight that made Leona feel a

little at home. Smoking a cigarette was one of the milder ways a lot of people she knew dealt with stress. Although a certain future medical professional named Eden always had a few words to say about it.

"Respect me as your elder when I say don't smoke," Mrs. Perry said before taking a long draw. "I started when I was fourteen, and I haven't been able to kick it, especially at these kinds of functions."

She held the cigarette at shoulder level, slowly releasing the smoke from her mouth. "My husband says it's the one thing I do he hates. I figure if he can only think of one thing, I must not be so bad of a wife." She took another drag. "Which neighborhood did you grow up in?"

"On the edge of Harambee, just west of Holton. It was my grandma's house," she said. Grandma Vera was one of the few who didn't flee the block when other white families were bolting to more restrictive neighborhoods. "Where did you grow up?"

"In North Division," she said. "Which, present day, is a little less gentrified of an area."

Leona felt uncomfortable, but at times, such was the truth.

"Did you live with your grandma then?" Mrs. Perry followed up.

"Only for a short time. By the eighties, my grandma was too old to keep up the house by herself. She gave it to my dad and let us move in with her until she passed."

"Ah, the eighties. Right when good-paying factory jobs moved out and drugs moved in."

A gust of wind blew off the lake and cut through Leona, making her eyes water.

Patrice took one last drag and then put the cigarette into the smoker's receptacle a few feet away. "The rules here are different, which I'm guessing you're catching on to. But hopefully tonight taught you that drinking isn't the answer to dealing with the pressure."

Leona wasn't ready to deal with her mistakes quite yet. "What about money? Is that the answer?"

Patrice opened her handbag again, moving through what was clearly a routine: antibacterial gel on her hands, spritzed eucalyptus on her neck, and a breath mint popped into her mouth.

"Now, that's a loaded question, isn't it?" She raised an eyebrow. "On the one hand, the answer is no. Money might have gotten me into that room, but new money is different than old money. Old money makes people feel safe. It represents generations of tradition. When there's new money in the room"—Mrs. Perry pointed to herself—"it comes across to some as a threat, like suddenly there aren't enough chairs for everyone."

Mrs. Perry reflected for a moment, then shared the other hand. "But in some ways, maybe the answer is yes. I don't think the original plan for this world included suffering in the kind of desolate poverty that plagues different parts of Milwaukee. I am an ode to the Garden of Eden, the fruition of my grandmother's wildest dreams."

Leona shifted her weight from one foot to the other.

Mrs. Perry continued, "But desolate places remind us that we're not truly flourishing if the people around us aren't flourishing too. Which is why I love the opportunity to support work that turns around and lifts others up." She petted her thick fur wrap. "And dare I say, I love a few frivolous things too."

The wine had almost worn off, and Leona was getting cold. She wasn't ready to go inside, but rubbing her own arms wasn't working anymore.

"You have to remember, the money in that room doesn't tell the whole story," Mrs. Perry said. "I'm sure you don't like it when people only talk about the bad parts of your neighborhood—

bullets flying into houses, low rates of graduation and employment. The assumption that all you're looking for is a handout. We know some of those numbers aren't always lying, but they certainly don't tell the whole story."

Leona thought about the time she tried to sell her TV in a garage sale group online. Three potential buyers immediately backed out when they found out where she lived. Two completely ghosted her. And one woman told her she would be more comfortable meeting up at the police station.

"I think of my old neighbor, Mrs. Lewis, who spent fifteen minutes every morning picking up trash she didn't litter along the curb." Mrs. Perry glowed. "And Coffee Makes You Black off Hadley that makes the best chicken and waffles."

Leona joined in. "I think of Mr. Harris, who shovels Ms. Kathy's sidewalk all winter long. And Casandra, who used her food stamps to buy my sister and me a carton of orange juice."

"We know the bad stuff about our neighborhoods, but we also know there's a lot of good. The same goes for that room behind you. The trick is having the courage to call the bad *bad*, and to sift out and celebrate the good."

Leona closed her eyes. She would need to ponder that for a while.

As if on cue, David burst through the balcony doors.

"Leona, I've been looking all over for you." He noticed her company. "Oh, Mrs. Perry, hello. I'm so sorry," he said, flustered, holding out his hand to shake hers. "It's nice to see you. You look lovely."

Patrice waited to answer, like she was willing David to take a deep breath, then shook his hand. "Hello, and thank you, David. I've been enjoying the chance to meet Ms. Leona." She pulled her shawl tighter around her shoulders and took a step back toward the gala. "You have a good one here. Partner with her."

Leona was struck. Mrs. Perry didn't say "take care of her" like she was some abandoned puppy at the animal shelter. She said it like Leona had something to offer too.

"Yes, ma'am," David said, but worry still furrowed his face.

The doors closed behind Patrice, and David turned to Leona. "Are you okay?" he asked.

Sometimes Leona really hated that question. Did he really want her to say no and then dive into all the layers of her childhood and their relationship that led her to get drunk at a fundraising dinner and make a fool out of herself?

"I'm fine," she lied.

THE CAR RIDE home was quiet; their goodnight kiss quicker, duller than usual. Leona unlocked the door to her apartment and went to the kitchen. She picked up, peeled, and demolished a spotted banana that was sitting out on the counter. Her body was screaming to get out of her dress, to shower off all the sweat and makeup and hairspray caked on it.

In the bathroom, the Warlon family holiday card was sitting next to the sink. It looked strategically placed, like Eden was rewarding her patience. She turned the card over to the newsletter, scanning the last five-by-seven rectangle to find where Eden left off.

Her heart sank.

Delaney had written, "We look forward to David's graduation, after which he will attend medical school and take his position at Warlon Tech. We couldn't be prouder of our son as he learns his role in the family business."

CHAPTER 8

Present Day

LEONA WIPED THE REMNANT OF DROOL AWAY FROM the corner of her mouth and reached back to massage the giant crick in her neck.

She never woke up ready to hustle. Her process was more like coming out of a season-long hibernation than a one-night rest. David liked to tease that she wasn't an early bird but a brown bat, the species that sleeps twenty hours of the day. She always told him to kindly keep his zoology to himself.

It took a moment to register where she was and what was going on. She had fallen asleep in the rocker in the nursery on Courtney Boulevard. She woke up in the same rocker. Vera was standing in her crib, gibbering at her to pick her up.

I'm in World #2.

Surprisingly, being here scared Leona less. Not because she didn't miss her David but because it was hard to think past the extra time she was being given with the baby she buried.

She turned to Vera. Her dark curls were a messy mop and her

green eyes still looked sleepy, but she wanted out. Like most toddlers she probably had two modes, asleep and high octane.

Leona stood up as fast as her aching lower back would let her and pulled Vera into her arms. "Good morning, precious baby." She drew her into a tight hug and rocked her side to side. She wasn't ready to let go, but Vera squirmed until Leona put her down, then toddled toward the kitchen.

"I appreciate a girl who likes to eat," Leona said, her stomach rumbling with morning hunger. She searched the cupboards and fridge for a suitable breakfast, settling on a pile of bright yellow bananas sitting out on the counter and a box of organic honey toasted oat cereal.

"Look, Vera, it's Cheerios' crunchy cousin." She poured each of them a bowl.

She opened more cupboards and discovered a collection of small kitchen appliances, including a coffee maker. Hallelujah, she thought. She may have gotten more sleep than she had anticipated, but she could still use some extra juice in her veins. On top of a busy day of snuggles and playtime, she had a mystery to solve—like how, when, and why she'd gotten here.

She slid Vera into her high chair and sat down at the kitchen counter next to her. As the coffee maker burbled in the background, they ate their bananas and cereal. Vera smiled, showing off the big gap between her front teeth now filled with yellow mush.

Leona couldn't resist. She rubbed the back of Vera's pudgy hand and said, "You are so sweet."

She took a bite of her banana and exhaled. It was nice to finally relax a little. Living a life that wasn't hers meant every move she made was trial and error, as she simultaneously hoped nobody noticed her blundering. But David had already left for work, so right now her only audience was wearing a tiny diaper.

She watched Vera as she picked up cereal pieces with two little fingers and put them into her mouth. Though Leona knew she should make a mental checklist of how to use her day, she would have preferred a slow morning where her only goals were to feed and clothe and play with the toddler sitting next to her.

There was a hard knock on the door. She looked at Vera and Vera looked at her, but that didn't give her any clue about who was waiting outside. She glanced at the clock.

"Seriously, Vera, who comes over at 7:20 in the morning? Before teeth are brushed and bras are put on?" She pushed back her chair and stood up. "This is why people raise guard dogs in my neighborhood. To keep the solicitors away."

Leona opened the door, hiding her pajama-clad body behind it as much as she could. A young woman was waiting outside, wearing the same blue polo shirt Jaeda wore last night. It had *Bella Luna Nanny* embroidered in navy.

"May I help you?" Leona tried to hide how annoyed she was by asking the question nicely, but her voice came out an octave too high. She hated how fake she sounded.

"Good morning, Mrs. Warlon," the young woman said, a professional smile on her face.

Leona guessed she was in her early twenties.

"My name is Kaili Man." The young woman didn't stop smiling, but her tone implied Leona should know who she was.

"It's a pleasure to meet you," Leona lied. "May I ask . . . why you are here? At this time of day?" She wished being flustered around new people didn't make her so awkward around them too.

Kaili straightened, adjusting the backpack strap across her body. "I'm Vera's new nanny."

Leona blinked. "Nanny. Interesting." She wondered if that meant she had a paying job she was supposed to be at in the next hour.

Kaili reached into her backpack and pulled out a blue folder.

"You scheduled orientation for today, Friday, so I can begin work on Monday." She held the folder out as proof.

Leona took it. It was stamped with gold lettering and had a clear protective cover. Underneath *Bella Luna Nannies* was a logo with a crib. She flipped it open and skimmed the first pages. There was a description of each service the company offered, which included a full-time live-in nanny, full-time live out, part-time, summer only, nanny share, night nurse, and occasional sitter. The boxes next to "part-time," "night nurse," and "occasional sitter" were marked. "M, W, F" was written in parentheses.

The next pages asked questions related to the family's schedule, the tasks their nanny was expected to perform, and their philosophies regarding childcare and discipline:

How will the nanny be paid for overtime?
Will they be given sick leave and paid vacation?
Describe your home and neighborhood.
Describe your overall experience with nannies.

The questions were answered in her own handwriting.

The last page listed fees for each service, revealing they'd paid five hundred dollars for a consult so they could "receive all the necessary tools to help you search for the perfect nanny."

Leona looked at Kaili, whose smile was fading with each minute her presence was being questioned. She didn't know what to do. She didn't want to leave Vera, and the fact that they could afford a personal nanny blew her mind. It also annoyed her for some reason. She felt stuck between who she was and who she was supposed to be acting as.

She closed the folder and held it out to Kaili. "Thank you so much, but I won't be needing your services today."

Kaili flinched. She didn't take the folder. "But . . . today is my first day."

"Yes. Something came up, so you'll have to come back another time. Besides, I think I can handle my kid on my own," she said, not thinking about what she was saying and how her flippant words might come across. She just wanted this to be over so she could get back to Vera. She stretched her arm to hold the folder out even farther, until it was almost touching Kaili's hands.

Kaili took it and shoved it into her backpack.

"Thank you!" Leona tried to close the front door. She felt anxious and weird and flustered, and she hated that she'd probably just made the young woman feel tossed aside and dispensable.

The door didn't shut all the way because it got caught on something. She looked down and realized Kaili's foot was between the door and the frame.

"Wait," the young woman said. She was no longer smiling, and her words were no longer sweet. "Are you going to pay me?"

Leona opened the door again. The forward question surprised her, probably because she was more prone to brood about people in her journal than confront them face-to-face.

"Of course I'll pay you," she said. Flustered again and not thinking it through, she lifted her hands in the air. "Look at how rich I am!" After hearing those words come out of her own mouth, she wanted to crawl into a deep, dark hole. Why was she acting like such a jerk?

Kaili was already halfway down their front walkway, so she closed the door and took two steps toward the kitchen. Then she remembered the blue folder.

The information in it might be useful, she thought.

She threw the door open again. "Hey! Is it okay if I hold on to that paperwork?"

Kaili stopped walking and turned around very slowly. Without breaking eye contact, she took the folder out of her backpack, held it out in front of her, and stood still.

The young woman had guts, Leona thought, deciding she liked her but was also slightly scared of her. She crossed her arms over her braless chest, jogged down the walkway, and took the folder out of Kaili's hands.

Kaili spun around and continued walking away, not saying anything to the effect of "Have a nice day."

Leona waved at her back and said, another octave higher, "Thank you!"

Back inside, Leona set the folder on the kitchen counter.

Vera was still in her high chair, but the banana was all over her face, hands, hairline, and tray, and on the floor beneath the high chair. Leona wiped her down and held out her hands as an invitation, which Vera quickly accepted. Apparently, Leona was easy to like when Vera's daddy wasn't available.

Leona gave the child in her arms a snuggle. "What do you think, Vera? Should we explore the rest of this big old house?"

Vera nodded yes, oblivious to what she was agreeing to.

"I think that's a great idea too," Leona said, smiling down at her. "Let's go upstairs first."

Morning sunshine streamed through a large second-story window onto the wooden staircase. Vera crawled up one step at a time while Leona followed closely, her arms open in a ready-to-catch position. Vera could likely climb up the stairs by herself at her age, but it was a lottery whether she knew how to climb down without serious injury.

They came across three more bedrooms, another sitting room with a TV, and two more full bathrooms. After getting glimpses into each space, it became clear most of the Warlon family's life was lived on the main floor. The rooms upstairs were neatly designed but not lived in.

"Not even you seem at home up here on this floor, Vera," she said.

They made their way down to the basement, Leona carrying Vera this time. There was a multipurpose room with cream linoleum flooring and dark wood paneling.

"We found an outdated part of the house. This is the aesthetic I'm used to," she joked with the toddler.

The room had a large sectional, an air hockey table, and a TV stand. If her memory was correct, these pieces of furniture used to be in the basement of the estate David grew up in. He had attempted more than one steamy kiss with her on that gray suede couch, and she had more than willingly kissed him back. She warmed at the memory of young, handsy love and also commended David #2 for not being too proud to accept hand-me-down furniture.

There wasn't much else to discover in the basement except a laundry room with double washers and dryers, a storage room with an iron sculpture of David's great-grandfather's head, and a state-of-the-art home gym. She didn't think she would be gracing the squat machine with her presence anytime soon.

"Let's just eat our doughnuts and be happy. Okay, Vera?" she said to the little girl hanging on her leg.

Vera clapped her hands together.

Back in the kitchen, Leona opened the blue folder from Bella Luna Nannies and noticed their tagline for the first time: "The Same Bella Quality Offering New Bella Services."

"Of course," she said out loud. "Bella Luna Nannies is a branch of Bella Maids."

She wasn't sure of the exact statistics, but she thought she heard once that the company was responsible for cleaning house, running errands, and making dinner for nearly 65 percent of residences in the area. And that there was always a waiting list to be added on as a client.

Two of Leona's classmates had family members who worked for Bella. Leona loved hearing stories about the luxuries they found in their employers' homes, like the perfume refrigerator that Crystal's mom found in the bathroom. Employees were expected to keep the family's business at home strictly confidential, but one time Anthony's sister spilled the juicy detail that there was a secret tunnel in Mr. Henkins's basement used to welcome his special friends. A discreet add-on to the blueprints when the house was being built. The rumor was that Mrs. Henkins still didn't know it existed.

From what Leona gathered, some of the families could be atrocious to work for and the commute was way too long, but the pay was hard to pass up. She continued reading the brief introduction near the top of the page.

> *We are not just the babysitter next door. We are highly trained professionals with the skills and experience to safely and effectively serve Milwaukee's parents and future generations. We pride ourselves on holding our nannies to the highest standards, ensuring each fulfills our rigorous list of requirements, including but not limited to: multiple background checks, comprehensive training courses such as CPR and First Aid, and a thorough interview process. Let us make your busy life easier by contacting one of our placement specialists today!*

She took a break from reading to address her younger counterpart. "I apologize, Vera. I told Kaili I could handle you on my own, but according to Bella Luna's requirements I'm not actually as qualified as one of their highly trained nannies."

Her interaction with the nanny was still bugging her.

"'I think I can handle my kid on my own'? Why did I say that?" she wondered out loud.

When Vera was alive, she had planned to work full-time to pay down David's medical school debt. She did the careful work of picking one of the many daycares in their neighborhood, one she double investigated to make sure it was the right place for Vera. She'd been a little skeptical when she saw that the sign on the building said Little Angles Daycare, but that turned out to be an honest spelling mistake. She liked the director, Ms. Brown, and she knew Vera would come to love being under her care for many hours of the day.

She didn't know what it was about a nanny showing up on her doorstep that bothered her so much. Maybe it was the absurd amount of money needed to pay for such a personal service or the stark contrast between having choices and just trying to survive. Maybe it was simply that her Vera died, and she couldn't imagine not spending every moment with her that she could.

She flipped through the paperwork, hoping to find out if she had a job she was accidentally ghosting that morning. A couple pages in, she learned that wasn't the case:

> *Hiring a nanny for Mondays, Wednesdays, and Fridays so I can volunteer for the board of the nonprofit Medical Miracle Charity, as well as engage in self-care.*

"Ugh, the Medical Miracle Charity?" she groaned. "Your father is in his family's pockets deeper than I expected, Vera. Remind me sometime to tell you about the gala I went to with Daddy ten years ago. Spoiler alert: It was my first and my last gala."

A large crash of plastic startled her. She'd gotten distracted and didn't realize Vera had gotten curious with the kitchen cupboards.

"Are you okay, Vera?" she asked.

Plastic bowls and lids had spilled from the cupboard onto the kitchen floor. The little girl was sitting in the middle of them all, smiling about it.

"An entire cupboard emptied in less than ten seconds? That has to be a record," Leona teased, relieved now that she knew Vera wasn't hurt.

Vera put a bowl on her head.

"Come on, silly. I bet your diaper is close to soaking through by now. Let's get you changed. We'll clean up this mess later."

Leona scooped her up and flew her like an airplane to the nursery. They looked through the closet for something practical to wear, but the task proved difficult.

"Is there anything in here that has less than three layers of tulle, kid?"

She flipped through a row of velvet-lined hangers, then stopped when she heard a familiar voice bellowing from the other side of the house.

"Leona?"

That voice still made her cringe after all these years.

"Leona, where are you?"

She was coming closer. Leona's blood pressure started to rise. Of course she'd been given a house key. Probably from David.

"Leona, we're already running la—Oh, there you are!"

She was in the hallway, close enough Leona could smell her. Her patronizing tone and plume of perfume always arrived in a room before she did, like the damaging winds and rains of an impending tornado. Leona wondered what egregious sin she had committed to deserve this harsh a punishment so early in the morning.

From top to bottom, Delaney Warlon was put together. Leona had never seen her not put together. Her mother-in-law once said the only way she'd get caught dead in loungewear—or the color orange—was if she went to jail.

"You're not dressed yet, Leona," Delaney pointed out then added, "One too many breakfast martinis?"

This was the way Delaney communicated once she got to know someone—with passive-aggressive barbs disguised as helpful advice and rhetorical questions. Every word was a power move.

Before Leona could answer, Delaney turned her attention to Vera.

In a maneuver she must have perfected with decades of practice, Delaney bent down gracefully in her heels without falling or flashing anyone. Then she gestured for Vera to come to her. "There's my future senator. Come give your grandma a hug."

Without hesitating, Vera ran into Delaney's open arms for a big squeeze.

Traitor, Leona wanted to say.

"Did you make that mess in the kitchen, young lady? Or was Mommy attempting to cook again? Also, where is your new nanny, and why isn't she doing her job?" Delaney looked at Leona for an answer this time.

She stammered, "I . . . uh . . . sent her home."

Using the power of her toned calves, Delaney pushed herself to a standing position, still holding Vera in her arms. "Firing someone on their first day? Leona, I approve. It sends a very clear message to the next nanny you hire."

Leona wished she had backup. "I didn't fire her. I sent her home for the day."

"Good heavens, child. People need to work for a living, otherwise you're just enabling them to become beggars," Delaney said. "And did you forget about our brunch for the MMC this morning? I'm going to have to hire you a nanny *and* a personal assistant to keep your head on straight. Come, dear. Go make yourself presentable so we can leave."

Delaney looked at Vera and brushed her nose against her granddaughter's nose affectionately. Then she grabbed a soft pink pantsuit from the little girl's closet. Their formal business outfits would coordinate. "I'll get this little politician dressed and teach her all about the family business."

Leona bit her tongue to keep from saying something honest like "corruption starts in the cradle." Instead, she tried, "I'm not feeling very well this morning, Delaney. I should probably stay home."

"Nonsense. I'll whip you up a quick hangover cure in the kitchen, and you'll be good as new," she insisted. "Besides, your mother will be there. I'm sure she'll be happy to see you and our precious grandbaby."

Being in the same room as her mother and mother-in-law was just asking to have her soul gutted.

"Ticktock, deary!" Delaney snapped her fingers loudly. "There's a big difference between being fashionably late and unacceptably late. Now, go do something with that hair. Goodness, it looks wretched."

Leona was not getting out of this.

CHAPTER 9

Ten Years Ago

"I'M JUST EXCITED TO BE WITHIN FOUR FEET OF YOU again," Leona joked into the phone to David.

"Four feet?" He pretended to be shocked. "Wouldn't that be an invasion of the personal space bubble you prefer to maintain from the general public?"

"Well, I've been thinking about it a lot, and I think I like you enough that you'd be an acceptable addition to my bubble."

David gasped. "Wow, I'm moving up in the world. Next thing you know, you'll be choosing to hang out with me on a Saturday night instead of reading books in your jammies."

"Who says we can't read books in our jammies together? That sounds like a lovely way to spend the weekend."

"You certainly are a wild one, Leona Meyer." David laughed.

She smiled into the phone.

"It really does seem like forever since we've been able to hang out," he said. "I'm excited to see you Saturday."

Three weeks had passed since the Medical Miracle Charity gala, and Leona hadn't seen much of David. They weren't distant on purpose. They still talked on the phone every day and made their paths cross for a few minutes between classes. They were just thick into their final semester at LMSU, so every spare minute was claimed by projects, exams, and papers. David was spending a lot of time off campus too, claiming he had meetings but never going into more detail. Leona noticed, but she was so entrenched in homework and getting in as many hours as possible on the campus cleaning crew that she didn't make it a point to question him.

"It's supposed to be close to seventy degrees on Saturday too," David said. "Pretty outrageous for March in Wisconsin."

"Don't fall for it," she warned. "Warm days in March are liars."

"Oh, really?"

"Yes, really. They make you believe spring has arrived when there's two more months of cold left."

"My, my, aren't we a little sun deprived?"

"I never said I wasn't going to enjoy the warmth," she explained. "I'll take a walk while I study, and I'll eat ramen on the patio while I study some more. I'm just saying I won't let myself fall for its empty promises."

"Here are a few promises that aren't empty," David offered. "I promise that my only plan for Saturday is to pick you up in my car. Then and only then will we decide what we want to do; no rigorous schedules allowed."

"I like it. And your other promise?"

"That the personal space between us will be a little less than four feet."

She laughed. "I'll look forward to it."

At first, she was grateful for the three weeks of distance. In her drunken state she'd humiliated herself at the gala. In every state, she was so humiliated by Delaney she was having recurring nightmares.

But now, she was ready to talk about everything—his parents' holiday card and what happened at the gala. She thought it might be a good idea for them to strategize how to navigate their drastically different backgrounds moving forward. She hoped the conversation would reassure her it was them against the world, not her boyfriend's world against her. She didn't say it over the phone, but that was her only plan for Saturday afternoon when they would finally get to hang out again—some genuine dialogue.

When Saturday finally arrived and David texted that he was parked outside her apartment, she ran to his car. But instead of buckling her seatbelt first, she leaned over, pulled his head in, and gave him a long, slow kiss.

"You can violate my personal space bubble anytime," David said when they finally came up for air.

Leona grinned as she buckled herself. "So, what are you hungry for?"

"Lupper," David answered.

Her face furrowed. "Is that an element on the periodic table?"

"It's lunch and supper put together," he explained. "Kind of like brunch but for people who get hungry in the afternoon. I can't believe you've never heard of this, Leona. All the cool kids are saying it."

"I've never been cool," she reminded him, "and I'm a little worried you've been playing with too many chemicals again. What you're saying is, you don't care what we eat?"

"The only thing I care about is that we eat right now. For lupper. See? Didn't that sound so cool?"

"So cool it's almost uncool," she obliged. "But I care what we eat, so let's get a burger from Crave."

Like many of Milwaukee's restaurants that Saturday, Crave was making the most of the unseasonably warm weather by dragging tables outside to the patio to seat their weekend crowd. Leona happily chose an outdoor table as well as a burger piled with portobello mushrooms and Swiss cheese. Her fries were thin cut and seasoned with Cajun, and she couldn't shovel them into her mouth fast enough.

They were almost done with their burgers when she asked, "Do you remember our very first date when I got spinach stuck in my teeth?"

David dipped one of his last fries into a little plastic cup of ketchup. "You mean that one time you adopted a pet leaf and invited it to live all over the front of your mouth?"

She balked. "I mean the time you saw something stuck in my teeth and didn't say anything for five whole hours."

He licked the salty residue off his fingers. "Vaguely. I remember the pet leaf better."

"Well, this is a test to see how far we've come in the last two years." She took his hand in hers. She thought about getting down on one knee for dramatic effect, but there were other people dining nearby. "David Charles Warlon, will you . . . look and tell me if there's anything in my teeth?"

She showed him her smile, knowing there was a minimum of two pieces of mushroom stuck there. David came in close, squinting his eyes to examine. He looked and looked, taking his sweet time instead of answering her.

She could tell he was delaying on purpose. "Hurry up, man," she grouched through her gritted teeth.

He sat up straight. "What, woman?" he barked, a spark of laughter in his eye. He lowered his voice to a gentle tone to explain, "These things take time, and I want to make sure I give you an accurate answer."

"Fine, but take less time," she said, trying not to laugh.

He leaned in again. Briefly. "Nope. I don't see anything."

Leona stood up from the table. "Liar," she said, taking their empty tray and walking toward the door.

David threw up his hands. "After all that, you still don't believe me?"

"I can smell the portobello in my teeth." She ducked inside the restaurant to return the tray, then started walking back to David's car.

"Where are you going?" He got up and followed her. "I thought we were going to spend this date together?"

"I'm going to ask the same question to my true friend, the mirror," she answered. "She always answers honestly."

"How about this? While you talk to your BFF about your mushroom teeth, I'll start driving to our next destination," David suggested.

"So there *are* mushrooms in my teeth," Leona accused.

He shrugged. She rolled her eyes.

Back in the car, Leona used the help of her reflection to floss out three pieces of beef and mushroom. Next to her, David drove aimlessly, making small talk. He seemed nervous, and the rate of his words per minute kept increasing until the pace was excessive, even for an external processor like him. She thought that, coming from someone like David who was usually so confident, it was adorable.

She reached over and took David's right hand off the steering wheel, intertwining her fingers into his. Sometimes she wondered what he saw in her to stick around for so long, but she was trying to unthink those thoughts. She liked that she could be a place for him to exist without unrealistic expectations.

David exhaled and slowed his sentences.

She thought it was the perfect time to start the conversation about their relationship, but right when she was going to open her mouth, she noticed David's driving had changed. Instead of driving aimlessly, it seemed like he was making turns on purpose, like he was aiming for somewhere specific. He drove a couple blocks off the lakeshore into a neighborhood she vaguely recognized.

She looked at the street sign and realized they were in the

neighborhood they drove through on their first date. On Courtney Boulevard.

David put on his blinker, then pulled into the driveway of the Victorian house labeled 2638.

She released his hand and scrunched her forehead. "We've been here before."

David nodded. He was biting his bottom lip.

"What are we doing here?" She searched his face for an answer.

"Get out of the car, and you'll see," he answered almost shyly.

"Do you know who lives here?" She unbuckled slowly.

Without replying, he opened his door and got out of the car. She tried her best to mimic his actions, but her limbs felt like they were on autopilot.

David held out his hand. She walked around the front of the car, then took his hand and allowed him to lead her across the grass to the walkway that connected the street to the home's front door.

Even the walkway was an ornate work of art. There were two sets of stairs bordered by iron handrails and small retaining walls, the perfect place to plant colorful varieties of annuals come May. The manicured shrubs weren't yet green, but they would certainly add to the property's already-lively curb appeal.

They reached the maroon front door.

David took both of her hands, which forced her to face him. He was pale, trembling.

He cleared his throat. "We've been reminiscing on our first date, and the other thing I remember about that night was when we drove around this neighborhood."

He squeezed her hands. His felt clammy.

"I blabbered on and on about my childhood and my hopes and dreams, and you listened. Patiently," he said.

Funny, she thought she was the one who blabbered that entire date away.

David looked down. "I knew then there was something special about you, that you were a person I could be myself around."

She treasured the sentiment, but her insides kept shouting that she wasn't ready for what was coming.

"That night, you also said that if you lived in this neighborhood, you would want to live here, in this house."

She did not remember the conversation that way, and the thought of where David was going with this terrified her.

"So . . ." He released one of her hands and fumbled around in his pocket. "I have a surprise for you."

He pulled out a single key.

"In the past two years since our first date, I made a point to drive past this house every time I visited my parents," David continued. "It reminded me of how lucky I am to have met you, to get to be with you. And then, one month ago, there was a For Sale sign in the front yard."

Oh no.

David smiled. "The reason I've been so busy the past few weeks is because I was making arrangements with my father, the financial advisor who manages my trust fund, and a realtor. I asked the realtor to take down the For Sale sign, but my surprise is that I bought this house for you, Leona. This house is ours."

She was speechless, but not like when someone was about to break down in gratitude. She was choking back shock and bewilderment and something else boiling up that felt like anger.

David kept going, putting the key back in his pocket and then fumbling around for something else. He pulled out a small velvet box.

She gasped. How much money's worth of stuff was this man gallivanting around town with in his pockets?

He got down on one knee and opened the box. "Leona, I love

you, and I want to spend the rest of my life with you. Will you marry me?"

The diamond was so big and so sharply chiseled, she could feel it cutting her apart from a foot away. She couldn't believe it. Any of it. She wasn't ready. They weren't ready. Not until they actually talked.

She stared until it got awkward.

From his position on bended knee, David chuckled nervously. "Remember when you asked me to look at your teeth and I took so long to answer, you felt uncomfortable?"

Leona knew she had to say something. She had to get her thoughts unstuck. She shook her head to jolt herself back into operating mode, to make her brain manufacture sentences and send them out of her mouth. "Yes, David, but I asked if there were any mushrooms in my teeth, not if you wanted to get married and live in this house together."

He squinted. "Is that your special way of saying yes?"

She ignored the sarcasm. She shook her head again, trying to make more words. "But what about what happened at the gala?"

David got up from the brick pavers and brushed off his left knee. He closed the ring box and put it back in his pocket. "What about the gala? It was a mistake. I'm sure you won't do it again."

His answer hit like a slap.

"*I* won't do it again?" Rage flamed in her temples. "I won't do what? Allow your mother to humiliate me? I won't drink my pain away?"

David's eyes widened. "Look, I know my parents are difficult, but I think you'll learn to grow thick skin and—"

"Thick skin? Made of what, heavy metal armor? Because that's what I'll need every time she stabs me in the back in front of her . . . posh friends. You know she hates me, right?"

Leona dug her hands into her hair. After a year of venting only a fraction of her frustration to Eden, she was finally letting all of it out. She was no longer shoving her feelings under her skin to keep the peace.

"*This* is the conversation we were supposed to have today, David, not . . . this house. I mean, I don't remember signing any mortgage papers; this house isn't *ours*. Who buys a house for someone without their approval anyway? We don't live in a Christmas car commercial!"

She started pacing the walkway. "You say you love me, but how can you love someone if you don't really know them? Because *this*"—she pointed at the maroon door—"is not me. This is not the life I want, and as far as I knew only one month ago, this is not the life you wanted either." She stopped and looked directly at him. "Were you ever going to tell me or your potential business partner, Eden, that you chose to work for Warlon Tech instead of starting BioThrive? Or do we need to find out about all your major life decisions from your mother's Christmas newsletters?"

He swallowed. "Leona, I—"

"You grew up learning how to sail," she cut in. She knew the statement sounded absurd, but it still annoyed her that David had the audacity to laugh when she said it.

"What are you talking about?" He squinted and shook his head.

"You have favorite restaurants in different countries. While, for me, an extraordinary day was when we could get a can of soda at the gas station."

David frowned. "Why does that matter?"

"It matters because I have bent over backwards to learn the rules of your world so I can fit in without embarrassing you or your family. But you still have no idea what that's been like for me or what it was like for me to grow up where I did."

"I've tried, but—"

"You have no idea what it's like to live in constant uncertainty, to never know if your dad's car will start or if you'll be able to get new glasses when your only pair breaks." She pushed her glasses up the bridge of her nose. "You have no idea what it's like to be playing with your sister at night, for the lights to suddenly shut off and your dad to come in with winter coats so you won't get too cold."

She kept going, the flame in her chest ablaze. "You grew up in a house with boxes of tissues and glass jars of cotton swabs in the bathroom. Fresh fruit on the counter bought by someone whose only job was to make your life more comfortable. You've never had to choose between something you genuinely need and food. I see what this neighborhood created in my mother, in your mother—"

"Stop it, Leona!" David yelled. "Just stop it. You say you hate clichés, but you're the worst cliché of them all." He glared at her. "You're like one of those people who claims to love the underdog until the underdog hits too high of an income threshold." He combed his hand through his curls. "I know you don't like either of our mothers, but are you really dismissing everyone in my life, in my circles, because of two people? Isn't that what you're always preaching? That we shouldn't assume things about someone just because of where they came from?" He held up his hands. "Are you willing to throw us away just because we grew up in different parts of the city? Because the big thing you're not saying is that this neighborhood made *me* too."

She'd never seen him this angry before. "I didn't say anything about throwing us away," she argued. "I'm just saying we still need to talk about all of this because it's a big obstacle between us."

"No, you're making this an obstacle between us." He shook his head. "I thought we loved each other and that was all that mattered, but I'm rich so now my thoughts and experiences don't mean anything. I'm the bad guy, and my life must be perfect." He clenched his fists. "Do I need to tell you about some of my classmates who feel like they have to earn their parents' love? A few of the girls I knew who threw up in the bathroom after meals so they could fit into the 'right size' dress their mom bought for them? The parents who were never home because they were off . . . accomplishing the next thing for their personal empire? The marriages based on social standing? Just because some people hide their hurt behind closed doors and perfect pictures online doesn't mean they don't hurt, Leona. And notice I said *some.* This might surprise you, but there's a few people in the upper class out there who know how to love their kids."

David stopped and shoved his hands into his pockets, pressing his foot firmly into the ground. "Yes, I took the job at Warlon Tech. *Some* kids on this side of the city don't get to follow their dreams; they have to follow in their fathers' footsteps. Even so, I took it because I want to be part of making changes there. I want to make a difference in a place I could have real influence over instead of scraping by to try something that might never work out."

Leona uncrossed her arms. "So, you're taking the job because you're afraid to fail? You're taking the easy way out?"

"You think all this is easy for me?" His eyes blazed. "Wow, you really don't get it, do you? I chose you. I've been sticking up for you. I'm trying to do exactly what my parents told me not to do, which is marry you. You know, when my dad realized he wasn't going to stop me from marrying you, he tried to convince me to buy a property along the lakeshore instead. But I told him; I said you'd love this house way more. It's far more down to earth."

It was clear they had different definitions of "down to earth," but Leona couldn't argue with the fact that David never hid his true feelings for her.

She sighed, ready for the yelling match to turn into a rational discussion.

"That's just it, David. You're fighting *for* me; you're not fighting *with* me. You never asked what I wanted; you just assumed. You're so disconnected from what I want, you can't even comprehend why I might not want to live here." She turned toward him. "The problem isn't your family's wealth; it's their complete disconnect from the rest of the world. It's the fact that their social circles welcome only their own or people who promise to give up everything else about who they are. I don't want that disconnect—from my neighborhood, from the friends I grew up with. From me."

David shook his head. "The only time we've even talked about this kind of stuff is when we got into that silly argument about whether or not the city bus was safe. I mean, we had that big fight right before you met my parents, but I thought we worked that out. How am I supposed to know when something's bothering you if you don't even tell me it's bothering you? I'm not a mind reader."

He wasn't wrong, Leona thought. While he'd made his feelings for her clear, she'd hidden her frustrations. She rubbed her temples, feeling jolted and frustrated.

It was then she realized that really liking David didn't mean their lives were headed in the same direction. Standing at an altar and exchanging vows wouldn't change that. She wanted only one part of what David was offering; she wanted him.

Leona closed her eyes. She knew whatever she chose to say next would greatly affect her future. She skimmed those choices in her mind, feeling a strange sensation running through her body as she did, like she was being pulled in at least five different directions.

She'd been standing away from David but came close, taking both of his hands in hers. Their eyes met, and she could tell he was wounded.

"I'm really sorry, David. I wanted to avoid conflict between us so badly that I shut my mouth and went along with everything asked of me the past two years. Even though it was killing me inside," she admitted. "I know now that isn't the kind of connection that can last in the long run. I can't pretend what exists between us is peace when it isn't honest."

Surprisingly, her voice didn't even shake. In fact, baring her heart to him made her feel more confident than she usually did about sharing her deepest hopes and fears. She wasn't sure of a lot in her life, but she was sure she wanted him.

"I know exactly what I want, David," she said, gently caressing his hand. "I want you. I love you."

He looked at her, a glimmer of hope on his face.

"But I don't want any of this," she said, looking at the large Victorian house.

He lowered his head and closed his eyes.

"You proposed to me, but now it's my turn to make you a proposition." She gripped his hands tighter. "I can't do Warlon Tech. I can't do Friday brunches with a bunch of high society busybodies. I'd rather struggle to build a life together on our own terms than inherit a life of luxury with so many strings attached."

A gust of wind whipped around them. The unseasonably warm weather on that Saturday in March was starting to turn, and Leona could feel tomorrow's chill in the air.

She shivered.

CHAPTER 10

Present Day

ONLY DELANEY COULD TAKE THE PERFECTION THAT was brunch and turn it into an occasion filled with anguish, Leona grumbled to herself. She couldn't believe that after ten years of avoiding this exact scenario with her mother-in-law, she was here.

Brunch was at Blu, a swanky cocktail lounge on the twenty-third floor of the Pfister Hotel downtown. The lounge, focused on premier beverages, appetizers, and desserts, was usually only open in the evenings. However, Delaney knew the owner and called in a favor to reserve the space and cater it to their needs.

The three of them got off the elevator, and Vera toddled straight toward the floor-to-ceiling windows.

Delaney smiled at her. "Enjoying the view of your future kingdom, little one?"

The toddler answered by putting her mouth and mitts all over the glass. When she turned around to look for Leona, there were two perfect handprints and a wet circle on the window.

Leona bent down and tried to wipe the smudges off with her sleeve. "You're one drooly princess, that's for sure," she whispered.

Vera put her face back on the glass, reminding Leona that cleaning up after a toddler was futile.

The panoramic view of downtown Milwaukee and Lake Michigan beyond was breathtaking. A paradox of man-made buildings—steel and brick—against an expansive body of blue water. She watched miniature whitecaps race toward the shoreline and realized she preferred the lake outside this wall of glass where she could smell seaweed and feel the sand prick her skin when the wind picked up. However, she also found it meaningful to be reminded of her smallness in the grand scheme of the landscape.

From behind her, someone said, "Leona. I haven't seen you in ages."

She stood up slowly, noticing a twitch in her eye that wasn't there a second ago. A muscle in her neck flared too. By the time she turned around, her mother was closing in to greet her cheek to cheek.

Leona did her best to fix her face into a polite expression. She wanted to say her mother was right; it was almost like they were long-lost acquaintances instead of mother and daughter. She settled for "Hello, Evelyn."

Evelyn looked down at Vera, who was now watching the tiny cars below travel from green light to red light. "My, my, isn't she getting big?" Without bending down to Vera's level, she opened her arms and said, "Come here. Give your glam-ma a hug."

Gross, Leona thought. Vera would not be calling her that.

She didn't ask, but Evelyn explained anyway, "*Glam-ma* is what celebrities are telling their grandchildren to call them so they don't feel so old. It's in perfectly good taste considering my youthful appearance," she said, framing her face with a hand that looked far more her age than her forehead filled with Botox.

Vera toddled into Evelyn's embrace more hesitantly than she

had to Grandma Delaney's earlier, which pleased Leona. For all her mother-in-law's faults, Delaney had more maternal instincts than Evelyn, including knowing the basics of how to hug a toddler.

Evelyn's arms were stiff around her granddaughter, like she wasn't sure how, or even if, she wanted to touch her. She ended the hug with two quick pats on Vera's back. It made Leona want to scoop Vera into her arms and give her the wholehearted affection she was worthy of.

Across the restaurant, a group of women arrived off the elevator, and Delaney invited them all to be seated. Leona thought she was being saved from more interaction with Evelyn until she saw her mother's name on the place setting right next to hers. Vera would have to sit on Leona's lap because she hadn't given Delaney enough of a heads-up that they'd need a high chair from the café near the entrance of the Pfister.

Leona scanned the faces around the room. The last she remembered, the Medical Miracle Charity was run by four wives of Warlon Tech executives. Delaney's husband was the founder and chief executive officer, Sandra Wellington was married to the chief financial officer, and Cynthia Brand was married to the chief operations officer. Helen Smith's husband was the regulatory affairs manager.

Leona could only assume by the way Delaney dragged her and Vera here that she was the newest board member of the MMC, although she still had no idea what David's position was at Warlon Tech. She would google it, but she still hadn't figured out the mystery of her phone's disappearance. She'd have to try using the laptop in the office later.

By Leona's interpretation, the work of the MMC board members consisted of meeting for brunch. Then, at brunch, they planned other elaborate meals for the upper class so they could ask them for money. Friday mornings were typically for board members only, but according to Delaney on the ride here, this meeting was meant to be a midyear check-in before the annual gala—MMC's biggest fundraising night of the year. Delaney had invited the wives of the men who owned the eight wealthiest companies in Milwaukee.

Which explained why Evelyn was at brunch too. She was representing her second husband, George Porter of Porter Law Offices LLC, the largest injury lawsuit firm in the city.

Leona would forever find that ironic since Evelyn had never acknowledged the extensive emotional injuries she'd caused in her lifetime.

She recognized a few other faces from the one gala she attended ten years ago, but the only other name she knew was Patrice Perry. She was surprised to see Mrs. Perry there because she was the only woman at the table more influential than Delaney. Someone Delaney might consider a threat. The Warlons might have been the wealthiest family in Milwaukee, but Mr. Perry was a prominent financial specialist, managing every last dime around that brunch table. He possessed something even more potent than money. He knew their secrets.

Leona could practically smell the power wafting off the group of women. The aroma was something like overly ripe roses and Benjamin Franklins. She guessed they would each lay a crisp one on the table as a tip for the waitstaff right before they left.

"Good morning, ladies," Delaney said to quiet the chatter, standing up from her chair. "On behalf of the Medical Miracle Charity, we are glad you could join us this morning. And may I just say, you're all looking fabulous—at least ten years younger than your actual age. Especially you, Vera."

Around Leona, everyone laughed.

"Speaking of charity"—Delaney looked straight at her—"Leona gave Vera's nanny the day off, so that is why we have this adorable addition in our midst."

The group of women smiled at them. Leona wished she could disappear into her seat.

"Today's menu," Delaney said, regaining everyone's attention, "is being specially prepared for you by Milwaukee's up-and-coming chef and James Beard Award finalist, Drake D'Gama. He is making for us a lentil kedgeree along with fresh grapefruit and rosemary mimosas—to loosen those checkbooks, of course."

There was another round of polite laughter.

Delaney continued. "Ladies, as you know, the executives of Warlon Tech have been very generous donors to each of your philanthropic efforts. We have donated to support our local art museum, fund childhood cancer research, begin quality education initiatives, and advance free markets." She nodded at each woman as she named their respective foundation's focus. "In five years, individuals on the board of Warlon Tech have given away a combined *240 million dollars*," she said.

The three other MMC board members clapped enthusiastically until the rest of the women around the table followed suit.

"So now, we are extending to each of you today, and at next winter's gala, the exciting opportunity to support the Medical Miracle Charity and its generous mission to fund chronic pain research and forgive medical debt," Delaney announced. "We are on track to set the record for the most money ever raised in a single evening: seventy-five million dollars."

When Leona was dating David, she learned that phrasing like this among the elite was not actually an invitation but an expectation. Favors and donations weren't given freely or of goodwill. They worked like friendly blackmail. *You scratch my back; I'll scratch yours.*

Out of nowhere, a server leaned near Leona's right side to place a plate topped with a stainless steel cover in front of her. The server removed the cover, releasing a burst of steam.

"Now, everyone," Delaney closed, "please enjoy this exquisite meal in front of you, and we'll continue to share more about the indispensable work of the MMC after brunch."

Vera did not need to be told twice. From Leona's lap, she lunged forward to grab a handful of peas, eggs, and haddock. She was probably the one person there who didn't care if she used the right utensil or if the bites she took were too big. Leona was grateful Vera had a palate for it and that she wouldn't need to ask the waiter for something more closely resembling chicken nuggets.

Around them, the presentation turned into conversation. On one side of her, two women talked about French wines. On the other side, Evelyn told Cynthia Brand about the latest art piece she'd curated for her great hall.

"You know, just your everyday business," she whispered into Vera's ear. Now that the toddler's stomach was full, she was ready to roam again. Leona didn't know how much longer she could keep Vera seen but not heard.

"I hear you're redecorating your house, Patrice," Delaney said across the table to Mrs. Perry, forcing everyone to quit their own conversations and join hers.

Mrs. Perry looked apologetically at Helen Smith seated next to her and said, "We'll continue our discussion later." Then she turned to Delaney. "Yes, we are reaching the end of a long renovation. I just hired an interior designer."

"Oh, delightful! Who did you hire?" Delaney asked. "Ember Finch is obviously Milwaukee's top choice. She did the Wellingtons' guesthouse last year, and it turned out stunning. Isn't that right, Sandra?" She only gave Sandra enough time to nod her head in agreement before continuing. "But I hear she is awfully hard to get ahold of—no website, no listed phone number, no office. Her only marketing is word-of-mouth. Not to mention, she can be incredibly picky about who she takes on as clientele."

"We hired Ember Finch," Mrs. Perry answered evenly, not breaking eye contact.

Delaney looked away first.

"Really?" Evelyn jumped in. "I got her number from Sandra. Our manager tried to hire Ember, but she wouldn't return any of his calls. So, I fired him and tried calling her myself to schedule a consult, and even *I* couldn't get through. How ever did you manage to get her to schedule you?"

Mrs. Perry didn't flinch. "I also received Ms. Finch's number from Sandra after the Wellingtons had us over for dinner one fine Tuesday evening and gave us a tour of her work. I decided I wanted to hire Ms. Finch, so my house manager left a message with my name. A mere two hours later, Ember herself called back to inform me personally she would be honored to direct the project. Our first meeting is tomorrow." Patrice turned back to Helen Smith. "Now, Helen, where were we?"

Even if Patrice was finished talking about Ember Finch, the other women were not. Evelyn couldn't seem to grasp that she was unable to get one measly phone call with Ms. Finch.

She lowered her voice and leaned over to Leona. "I guess I'm going to have to drop by the Perrys' for an unexpected visit tomorrow. Did you hear Patrice say what time Ember is coming by?"

Sandra spoke up to the whole table. "Such an interesting person, that Ember Finch. She has a rather . . . alternative look."

Leona wondered what Sandra's definition of "alternative" was when that word could mean so many different things. In this circle, it probably meant the woman's ears were double pierced, she thought, annoyed at how quickly stuff was assumed about someone based only on their appearance.

"I hear she has a daughter," Cynthia added pointedly, "out of wedlock."

One woman, who Leona didn't know, inhaled loud shock and disgust. "Shouldn't we be hiring the talent of individuals who better align with our family values?"

Leona looked at Evelyn, wondering how she would react to

the woman's statement. They were sitting right there, a mother and her child conceived out of wedlock. For a split second, she actually felt sorry for her mom. These were some of the people Evelyn grew up with; some had seen the exile she went through as a pregnant teenager. But there Evelyn sat, shaking her head against some designer's assumed immorality and nodding at "family values." Was she so far removed from her past that it was all forgotten, or was this simply how she survived?

Cynthia broke the silence. "I'm not defending Ms. Finch's choices by any means, but I think fornicating is just what the artists are doing these days."

"Yes," Sandra agreed, sounding grateful for her friend coming to her aid. "And her talent is truly unmatched."

Those who had seen the Wellingtons' finished guesthouse concurred.

"Yes."

"Oh, absolutely."

"Unmatched."

"I think it's true, though, that Ms. Finch has an illegitimate child," Sandra said, returning to the gossip. "I overheard her on the phone once, talking about having to pick someone up from school. But whenever I asked her questions to try and find out more, she either ended the conversation or was vague with her answers. She wouldn't even tell me what part of the city she lives in. She's a private person. Very mysterious."

"Maybe that's why she's in such high demand," Delaney reasoned. "The mystery adds to the allure of hiring her."

Vera started to squirm and whine. The smiles she received earlier were turning into sideways glances.

Leona pushed back her velvety blue chair and maneuvered Vera to her hip. She heaved the diaper bag over her shoulder and said to the table, "Excuse me, I need to take care of her."

She swore she heard "that is why" and "nanny" being muttered nearby.

They started toward the bathroom, but behind her Evelyn said, "I'll come with you."

Leona pretended she didn't hear her and picked up her pace, but Evelyn closed the gap between them, catching up right before they reached the bathroom.

"There's something we need to talk about," Evelyn said.

"I have to pee," Leona lied, enjoying the opportunity to annoy her mother with what she considered coarse vocabulary.

Leona pushed the heavy bathroom door open with her free hip and ducked inside. The door closed heavily against Evelyn, who caught it with an "uff" before using her scrawny upper body to push it open the rest of the way. For eighteen years, Leona had wished for her mom's attentive company and almost never received it. Now Evelyn couldn't seem to take the hint that her presence was no longer desired.

Leona set Vera next to the sink and tried to make herself appear busy, then grabbed a folded paper towel from the basket and got it wet so she could clean Vera's face and hands.

"When is the last time you talked to your sister?" Evelyn asked while staring at her own reflection in the mirror.

"I can't say I remember." Leona acted disinterested, pulling a few peas out of Vera's hair. She could feel her anxiety rising. This was the kind of question she did not know the answer to, one that could easily reveal her as someone who didn't belong.

"I think there's something going on with Rose," Evelyn said. Her words swarmed with suspicion.

"I wouldn't know anything about that," Leona answered truthfully.

"But has she called you, contacted you in any way?" Evelyn pushed.

"I don't really want to talk about Rose," Leona asserted. She could pretend it was because she might say something that would contradict this version of her life. But deep down, she knew it was actually because Rose was a reminder of her own past mistakes.

"But why? Why hasn't she talked to you?" her mother asked again, this time more like she was thinking out loud instead of torturing her daughter for answers.

Either way, Leona was frustrated. She put a hand on Vera's knee so she couldn't make any sudden moves off the counter, and turned so her shoulders were square with Evelyn, who was still looking at herself and primping.

Leona tensed up. "You have now asked me the same question three different ways. Is there something going on, Evelyn?"

Her mother rotated slowly, cocking her head to the side. "Goodness, Leona. There is no need to be so aggressive. And I am not just 'Evelyn.' I am your mother. Show me a little respect."

Leona learned a long time ago that arguing with Evelyn was a losing battle. There was no use trying to make peace with someone who only wanted to make war. But Evelyn had crossed a line; she always crossed the line.

Leona's hands started to shake. She tried setting a boundary. "Please don't go there."

Evelyn didn't back down. "Go where, Leona? The fact that you call me by my first name even though I gave you life?"

"Dad was the one who—"

"Oh, you want to go there?" Evelyn interrupted. "To your drunk father?" The words spewed out of her mouth.

Leona didn't know what she was talking about. It didn't register with any of the memories she had of her dad. Sure, some of his behaviors were a little strange at times. He could get too emotional for what circumstances called for. When Leona was eight, she'd brought him a picture she drew of the two of them standing in front of their house. There was a tree, some pink flowers, and a yellow sun, all in crayon. She'd written "I love my dad," and he thanked her, but his words seemed thick. She remembered he smelled like stale cigarettes too. He'd burst into tears, and she was so upset, she didn't draw him another picture for a long time.

But drunk? No.

Evelyn went on. "Let me tell you something, Leona. You might think your father is the hero and I'm the big, bad spoiled diva. You might believe you were abandoned. But it wasn't always roses for me. Your father made plenty of mistakes."

Leona knew her parents' marriage—built on the foundation of teenage pregnancy and nothing else—had always been fragile. But it didn't help that for sixteen years, Evelyn tried to build a life in the opposite direction of the rest of them, tried to get back to the comforts she grew up with. With that relationship model, the walls were sure to cave in eventually.

"Whatever mistakes Dad made, he was there for me and Rose while you were . . . you were . . ."

"I was what, Leona? You have no idea what I was. My mother was an obnoxious worrier. She tried to control everything I did. 'You'll either be killed, or you'll ruin your reputation,'" Evelyn mimicked her mother's mantra. "That fueled every decision she made—other people's opinions and murder. And so, when I met your father that night, he was supposed to be an . . . escape. A rebellion with someone my parents would never approve of."

Evelyn sighed. "It was homecoming night my senior year, for heaven's sake. It was supposed to be one night out, not . . . not . . ." she trailed off.

Tears stung the corners of Leona's eyes. "Just say it. It wasn't supposed to end with me being here."

"It's not about you." Evelyn rolled her eyes and crossed her arms. "*I* lost everything. In a matter of a month, I went from being homecoming queen to the knocked-up outcast who couldn't afford to fill her car up with gas."

Leona turned away. This was the most Evelyn had ever talked about her past, about their family. And it hurt. "But at least Dad tried. He tried to make the most of it. He worshipped the ground you walked on."

"Oh, his constant positivity was exhausting," Evelyn scoffed. "He was always trying to focus on the bright side of life. I went from being smothered by my mother to being smothered by my husband." She turned to her reflection and put on another layer of lipstick. "I wish you'd appreciate me a little more. Maybe the bright side of me leaving was that because I finally took control of my own life, you didn't have to be smothered by all the things you so obviously loath about me."

It was too much to process in the bathroom of Blu. "It's always other people's fault, isn't it?" Leona said. "But the truth is, you pushed him away, and then you left us."

Evelyn laughed. "A child should never claim to know the truth of their parents' marriage. Remember, when I was a kid about to give birth to a baby, I wasn't given the option to stay with my parents. My mother had a panic attack, and my father wouldn't look at me. He told me I was a disappointment and asked when I was getting married. I went to your dad because I had no other choice. My mother didn't want to send me away, but she had the standards of the PTA to live up to and the 'duty to submit to her husband' or however she put it."

Leona muttered, "Every villain has a sad origin story."

"What did you say?" Evelyn asked.

Leona pursed her lips. Strangely, her happiest childhood memory came to mind.

"Why couldn't we be like we were at the beach that day?" She didn't know where she was going with her question. She just knew it was the one thing about the memory that haunted her. Why couldn't they have made more memories like that?

"What are you talking about?" Evelyn seemed clueless.

"That day at the beach. When you played with me and Rose in the water and we saw that big white boat. You seemed so happy to be with us."

"That white boat?" Her mother's eyes widened. "Let me tell you a little story about that big white boat. It was my father's; I recognized his favorite line of flags hanging across it. That was the last day I ever saw them. A remnant of them, I guess."

Leona couldn't believe it. "But that doesn't explain why you acted so different. Like such a . . . mom." The word came out almost a whisper.

"I wanted to make my parents pay."

Leona flinched. Evelyn's version of payback was pretending to be happy with her kids. "So, it was all a lie?"

"It was revenge. Honestly, Leona. Do you think everything is about you?" She put her hand on her hip. "My father never hugged me. Never told me he loved me. But he named his precious yacht after me: the *Evelyn*."

Leona wanted to lean in to hear better and run away all at the same time.

"The name *Evelyn* is derived from the French name *Aveline*. Did you know that? My father explained that to me once. The name eventually traveled to England where it evolved into a surname, a masculine name, and finally, a girl name in the early 1900s."

The strength behind Evelyn's words seemed to waver. "Some say the name *Evelyn* means 'wished for, desired.' But every once in a while, I've wondered—by the time my name crossed the channel to England where my father's family was from—if *Evelyn* became a better way to describe a boat than a child."

Sitting on the counter, Vera leaned over to splash water around the sink.

Leona felt bad for Evelyn; she did. But it didn't change how her mother lived out her pain. "You left us for the money."

"No, I put my life back together. And don't get all judgy with me. Judging by the size of your husband's wallet, you don't have yourself that bad of a life either. So, this whole victim act you play whenever you're around me is getting old."

Leona thought her lungs might explode from the unease growing inside them. There was so much to think about, but she couldn't keep doing that. Not here. And not now, when Vera needed her morning nap.

Leona removed all emotion from her face. "May I borrow your phone?" she asked.

Evelyn seemed surprised by the change of subject. "What?"

"May I borrow your phone?" Leona asked again. "I don't have mine."

Evelyn dug into her blue crocodile Hermès Birkin handbag and then pushed her phone into Leona's palm. This was the kind of dependency that irritated her mother.

She searched for the contact she wanted to call, but before dialing, she looked at Evelyn. "I would like some privacy."

Her mother huffed one more time and then turned to the door. She had to wrestle it open before she could leave.

Leona looked down. Rose's name and number were on the screen.

Her argument with Evelyn, as well as something about the conversation at brunch, reminded her of her little sister. She wondered if—in her strange life travels—she would get to see Rose. She missed her. Eden was her closest friend, but Rose was the only other person on the planet who knew exactly what it was like growing up under Frank and Evelyn's roof.

She pressed the call button. The phone rang until it went to voicemail. The recording said, "It's me. Why are you calling instead of texting?"

She hung up before the beep. Hearing Rose's voice summoned a deep sadness she'd been feeling for a long time.

It was possible Rose didn't pick up because she thought it was Evelyn calling. She tolerated their mother even less than Leona did. But even if Rose knew it was her on the line, it was possible she wouldn't pick up. Maybe Rose didn't speak to her in this version of her life.

Leona took Vera into her arms. The toddler kicked and screamed as Leona left the bathroom and crossed the lounge to Evelyn.

"Here's your phone. Thank you."

Everyone was looking at Vera's overly tired tantrum. The time to exit was now.

Leona turned to Delaney. "Vera needs a nap, so we'll take the bus home."

There was a loud gasp. It came from the same woman who reeled over Ember Finch's rumored illegitimate child.

Leona forgot. These women would never, unless there was a zombie apocalypse and it was their only means of escape, use public transportation.

CHAPTER 11

Ten Years Ago

THE DRIVE FROM COURTNEY BOULEVARD TO LEONA'S apartment after David's proposal was uncomfortable. To top it all off, they didn't know how to say goodnight to each other. She leaned in for a hug, but he leaned in for a kiss. After two failed attempts, she waved and got out of the car.

Her apartment was empty. Eden had a group project and was going to pull an all-nighter to get it done. She wouldn't be back until Sunday morning when they planned to go to the small Presbyterian church a few blocks from their apartment.

Which meant Leona could go straight to her room, put on her favorite fleece robe, and begin to cry.

Just as David put himself out there, so did she, and they completely missed each other. She was worried. They weren't broken up, but even the thought of that possibility made her heart feel like it was crumbling. It was out of her control now. All she could do was wait.

The fleece robe she craved wasn't the most stylish piece of

clothing she owned. The tie-dye was fading, and the seams were coming apart. It was a gift from her dad on her sixteenth birthday, right after her parents divorced. She and Rose rarely got gifts on holidays, especially stuff that wasn't from the dollar store, but even in his wrecked state he'd saved up for it. That robe was what she imagined love to be like—a comforting presence. Someone who asks as much of themselves as they ask of others.

She pulled the robe tight around herself, turned off the lights, and climbed into bed. An hour ago, she was so confident she made the right decision. Now she wondered if she ruined every chance she had at being with David.

She cried some more, worried some more. She was pretty sure she slept some too. A while later, she heard someone calling her name.

"Leona?" the voice whispered.

It wasn't Eden, but she didn't feel like getting up to see who it was. "Please leave me alone. I just need a little more sleep."

"You've been doing that for a whole day now." The person was now standing next to her bed.

She propped herself onto her elbow. "Rose?"

"No," she said. "It's your other sister, Tulip."

Leona wiped a salty mixture of snot and tears from her face with her sleeve.

Rose sat down next to her on the bed and presented her with a few squares of toilet paper. "For the next round," she said.

"How did you get into the apartment? And how did you even know to come here?" She took the toilet paper and blew her nose.

"Eden called me," Rose explained.

"I thought she wasn't going to be back until Sunday morning?"

"It's Sunday night, Leona."

"What?" She sat up straight. Her head started to pound.

"According to Eden, you've been sleep-crying in the dark for almost a day now." Rose stood up and turned on the lamp. "She said you refused to get out of bed, so she called me and asked me to come."

Leona covered her face. "The light is too bright. And I'm too sad."

Rose sat next to her again. She was wearing a shirt that said *Ew, People.*

"What happened? Is David okay?" The concern on her sister's face was genuine.

"Yes, David's fine. It's nothing like that." She shook her head. "It's just that he . . ."

"He what? Did he hurt you?" Rose demanded. "Because if he hurt you, you know I will hunt him down and—"

"No, he didn't hurt me," she interrupted. "You can put your hunting gear away."

"What, then?" Her little sister sounded like an exasperated teenager, which was exactly what she was. "You crying in bed for an entire day means something must have happened."

Leona sniffled. She didn't know how to explain everything that happened last night, or over the past year with Delaney, so she tried to say it as succinctly as possible. "David proposed."

Rose's mouth fell open and her eyes sparkled. She looked like she wanted to scream. "David proposed? Leona, that's—" She stopped when she saw Leona's face. "Wait. That's . . . bad? Why is that bad? I thought he was the best thing to happen to you since . . . well, me and Eden and sliced bread or whatever?"

"Yes, it's bad. It's terrible!" She flung herself back into her pillows. "And that's not the only thing he did."

"What did he do?" Again, Rose asked like she was gearing up for a fight.

"He bought me a house too."

"He bought you . . . a house," Rose repeated, monotone.

She nodded. "He bought me a house," she said, emphasizing each word.

"He bought you a house. Wow, you're right, Leona," Rose responded, her words dripping with sarcasm. "This is terrible. This is the worst news I've heard in years. David is a total jerk for . . . buying you a house and wanting to commit the rest of his life to you."

"You're mocking me," Leona said. "My little sister comes to me in my time of trouble only to mock me."

Rose took Leona's hand. "Maybe it will help if you tell me more of the story."

"More of the story? I'm not sure what else there is to say. I said no. To . . . some of his proposal. Kind of. I don't know; it's complicated."

Rose shook her head. "No, I'm sorry, that doesn't help. Maybe it's because I'm just a dumb high school teenager and you're a cool, grown-up college student, but I still don't see the problem here."

Leona massaged her temples. "How can you not see the problem? I've told you all about his mother."

"The Wicked Witch of the East?"

"Exactly. If David takes a job at Warlon Tech, and if I say yes to his proposal, and if we live in this house bought with his trust fund, that would mean being a doormat to Delaney for the rest of our lives."

"Oh. That doesn't sound great," Rose agreed.

Leona wiped her eyes. "But am I overthinking this? Did I make a mistake?"

Rose shrugged. "You might be. And you might not be. His mom sounds pretty awful, and we both know how we feel about our own mother. Which means you've only seen the worst of what David's social circle has to offer."

"And the worst is pretty bad," she said. "It's just that . . . I love David so much that I'm also questioning saying no."

"Out of all the guys you've dated, David is definitely my favorite," Rose stated.

"All the guys?" Leona asked. "I dated one other guy, and that was back in high school."

"I remember him. Derek, wasn't it? He was a total sleaze." Her sister scrunched her nose. "But back to David. Maybe it would help if you took an extended cruise through the Mediterranean with his family first. Or figured out which restaurant in Vienna is your favorite. Spend some time experiencing the good of his luxurious lifestyle."

"Super helpful, Rose," she replied.

"Well, I aim to please." Her sister flipped her hair with a dramatic flair. "And to approach your life's problems like Evelyn would."

Leona laughed. "I appreciate you."

They sat in silence for a moment. It was too dark outside to see much through the window, but they could hear the rain pouring down heavily.

"After I told David what I wanted, he said he needed time to think. Said he was going to visit his parents today to talk about a few things. But I don't know what that means or how long he'll need. Delaney's probably thrilled to have dinner with just the three of them. She'll raise her glass of pinot noir and toast with fervor to 'the original Warlons.'"

Rose's eyes flashed with an idea. "Let's go egg her front gate."

Leona thought about the Warlons' increased security measures. "Wait, was that you? Please tell me that wasn't you who egged their front gate last year."

"I plead the fifth." Rose brushed aside the claim.

Leona guessed she was joking, but she would probably never know for sure. She also didn't feel like laughing. "What if I scared

David away forever? He saw a different side of me tonight. I mean, last night. I stood up for stuff that mattered to me, but maybe that threw him off too much. Maybe he doesn't want that side of me."

Rose rolled her eyes. "Leona, I love you, but your whole peace-monger thing isn't sustainable. Don't you think it's a good thing he saw that side of you? Doesn't he need to see every side of you for the rest of your life if you're going to last?"

Leona looked out her window. The rain was pouring even harder now. "You've always hated my desire for world peace."

Rose laughed. "No, I hate that you think world peace is possible without ruffling a few feathers. I'm just not wired that way."

"Were you wired to give me a hug?" she asked.

Rose opened her arms. "Of course. I love you, big sister. And I'm sorry. Really, I am."

Leona pulled her sister close. "I love you too, little sister. Thank you so much for coming."

"You love me? Even though you hate my tattoo?" Mid-hug, Rose traced a line across Leona's lower back.

"I really do hate it," Leona admitted, resting her head on Rose's shoulder. "But everyone gets to be a dumb teenager once in their life. Besides, I'm worried about your heart, not about what you look like."

Rose pulled away and repositioned herself. "You know what might make me feel better?"

Leona could tell Rose was avoiding the subject, which was easier to handle than an angry explosion. "What's that? Name it. I'll do anything to help you feel better."

"How about you choose option C where you don't accept David's marriage proposal, but you and I still get to live together in the house he bought."

Leona laughed. "Option C is definitely worth considering. Let me call David up a second and ask what he thinks about that."

Eden popped her head into the room. "Leona? I'm glad you're up. Your man is here."

Leona and Rose looked at each other.

"He answered that call fast," Rose muttered to Leona.

"Bring towels," Eden suggested. "He's dripping all over the floor like he just went on a walk with Aquaman."

Rose gave Leona one last big hug. "No matter what happens, you always have me."

"And me," Eden added.

Leona's shoulders slumped. "Thank you. Both of you."

She ran to the bathroom and splashed water on her face, wishing her eyes weren't so puffy and her nose wasn't so red. Then she grabbed three towels. She had no idea how the next half hour would go, but it felt like a span of time that would change the course of her life forever, for better or for worse.

She rounded the corner of her apartment to where David was waiting in the hall. He was peeling off his coat and hanging it on their small coatrack. All the rainwater absorbed by his thick curls was now running down his head.

The sight of him here in her apartment made her catch her breath.

"I brought you towels," she said.

David took one and began drying his hair. "Remember how all the romantic comedies we've watched include rain? Boy and girl date. Boy and girl break up. Melancholy music. Rain."

"I hate those movies so much," she joked. "They're so predictable."

"And yet, when boy and girl finally kiss, I look over and catch you wiping away tears."

"It was probably allergies," she lied.

"Either way, I'm beginning to doubt the whole 'making up in the rain' trope." He took another towel and draped it around his shoulders. "Because what the movies seem to forget is that in real life, inclement weather is a miserable setting." He took the third towel and set it to the side. "Because here I am, fighting wind and rain to come back to you, and I look like a drenched poodle."

Leona tried to keep her face under lock and key, but she couldn't keep her heart from starting to pound.

"A handsome poodle," she corrected.

"I'll take it," he said, then took a deep breath. "Can we sit down somewhere and talk for a while?"

Leona nodded. "I think Rose went to Eden's room to give us some space. How does the couch sound?"

"Perfect. Anywhere but outside in the pouring rain."

She led him through the entry to the small living room. She wanted to take him by the hand and pull him close, run her fingers through his curls, but she held back.

"I visited my parents today," he said as they sat down.

Leona felt like she was holding her breath. She wished they were on the other side of this conversation. She wanted to peek at the last page of their story to know how it ended.

"I decided the most mature way to handle your counteroffer to my proposal was to make something that worked almost like a pros-and-cons list." David was smirking. "I'd go to dinner at my parents' and then award both them and you points based on how dinner went."

Leona blinked. His humor came out at the strangest times. "I hate this already, but go on," she said.

"I love my mom," he said. "She gave me so much stability growing up, and she wins a million points for that. But when you weren't at dinner with me, she spent most of the time trying to tell me that I should consider getting back together with a girl I dated in high school."

"I hate her already, but go on," she repeated.

"Elise Mason." He shook his head. "She broke up with me at a steak house because she thought her food was too cold and I didn't complain enough to the waiter. Said I should have 'defended her right as an American to quality service.'"

"Is that how the preamble starts?" Leona joked. "What did your mom say?"

"At first, my mom said customer service isn't what it used to be. And then she went on a tangent about how I would 'never ridicule a man for being confident in knowing what he wants,' so I'd better make sure I wasn't ridiculing a woman for having the same traits."

"How feminist of her."

"That's what she called herself, actually. She was very proud of how open-minded she was being toward her own gender." David arched an eyebrow. "I told her that standing up for women didn't mean acting like an idiot at a steak house."

"I'm sure she loved that," she commented.

"Then I asked her if knowing what you want and fighting for it is an important trait to find in a spouse."

"Which I assume . . . that she assumed . . . you were talking about Elise."

"Oh yes. I'm pretty sure she thought she'd successfully planted an influential seed in the soil of her family's future," he declared.

"So, what did she say?" Her stomach was full of butterflies—the nervous kind.

"She said yes. But, of course, Elise wasn't who I was thinking about." David smiled at her, but his eyes were sad.

Leona tried to make herself exhale.

"I also asked her if *she* had everything she wanted in life. It was one of the first times I've seen her stumble over her words."

Leona imagined a thousand stories of sacrifice and submission flashing through Delaney's eyes. Stories of the person she was before she became Mrs. Charles Warlon.

"When she finally regained control of her face, she said of

course she got what she wanted. She talked about the pleasure of watching my dad build an extremely successful company and serving at the Medical Miracle Charity. And she talked about being blessed with a wonderful son who she's so proud is going to take his place at Warlon Tech."

David looked down at his hands. "So, I told my parents that I had something to say and it would be hard to hear. My mother immediately blurted out that I must have broken up with you."

Leona's heart hurt. "That was her first guess?"

"I couldn't believe it," David confessed. "And yet I could believe it, because it was exactly the kind of detachment you've been talking about. My mom can read when I need space and when I need management, but she can't read when I'm in love."

"Wow, David, I—"

"I corrected her," he continued. "I told her that we hadn't broken up but that I changed my mind about working at Warlon Tech after I graduate grad school. I said that I still want to pursue a degree in medical research, but I'm going to start a biotech company with Eden. And I told my dad I needed help putting the house back on the market."

Leona couldn't believe it. She felt shock and excitement, as well as an ache for what David was going through with his parents. "Wow. How did they react?"

"Oh, my mother protested as if I'd literally stabbed her in the back. She cursed you and all the ways you've tainted me. And then she told me that if I was rejecting everything my parents worked so hard to give me, *I* must be an ungrateful child too."

She couldn't take it anymore. She needed to touch him, show him she cared, even in a gentle way. She reached out and squeezed his hand. "What did your dad say?"

"He set his newspaper down and said, 'It's your grave, son.' And then he said he had to go to bed because he had a red-eye flight in the morning." David paused. "He did pat me on the shoulder before he left the room though. Closest thing to a hug I remember from the patriarch in nearly twenty years."

Listening to how Delaney and Charles tossed him to the side, Leona felt her inner peacemonger vanishing. She looked at David but didn't know what to say.

He pulled his hand away and ran it through his wet hair. "It's not like I told my parents they couldn't be part of my life anymore. I just told them I wanted a different job and that I needed to sell a house. Their reaction said everything. I'm not Delaney's son. I'm her prop. I'm not Charles's son. Warlon Tech is. Their security is financial; it's not love," he said.

"David, I'm so sorry." She didn't hold herself back. She pulled him as close to her as she could, relieved to feel him put his arms around her too.

David continued, "But I know exactly what I want now. I want to be with the woman who knows what she wants. Whose desires are far more meaningful than how she's served at a steak house." He pulled away far enough to look into her eyes. "I'm sorry I tried to start our life together without you, Leona. That wasn't fair."

She smiled, tears filling her eyes again. How many different kinds of tears could one cry in a day?

David added, "I do need to tell you one interesting fact about my family though."

She tilted her head. "And that is?"

"Last night you brought up those Christmas car commercials. And, well, my cousin Kimberly was in one of those once."

Leona's eyes widened, and her mouth dropped. "You've got to be kidding me."

David shook his head. "I'm not. I had a vague memory about it, so I asked my mom today. It turns out my Uncle Jim's friend—who happens to be a prominent advertising director—owed him a big favor, so he gave Kimberly the part. According to my mother, she was 'a dreadful actress on her best day.' Her unfortunate career began and ended with that commercial."

"It's so shocking," Leona said, laughing. "And yet, with all your family's connections to wealthy and powerful people, it's not shocking at all."

David looked down. "But let's talk about more interesting things now."

"Like what? How your hair doesn't look like a drenched poodle anymore?" She scrunched a few of his curls.

He got off the couch and down on one knee, glancing at the floor. "The rug on laminate is a vast improvement from the concrete for today's proposal."

"What a weird thing to be able to say." She laughed.

He took her hands in his and looked up, straight into her. "I have nothing to offer you, Leona, not even a house like the one I tried giving you yesterday. I mean, what a dump, am I right?"

"David . . ." She blushed.

"I'm pretty sure it's the same for you," he continued. "You have nothing to offer me. I was hoping for a cow or at least a spring chicken, but here we are and no dowry." His thumbs grazed her hands. "I want a life with you that isn't cliché, Leona. And what is less cliché than being partners in the crime of turning down vast family fortunes?"

"Literally nothing is less cliché," she said.

"Instead of fighting for you, I want to struggle with you—through rent, medical school bills, and car repairs."

This feels so right, she thought. *It all feels so right.*

He continued, "I want to be a safe place for you, just like this ugly robe you love to wear."

She looked down at the soft, swirly garment, and a tear rolled down her cheek.

"Eventually, I want to make babies with you."

"Don't you mean you want to *have* babies with me?" she cut in.

He shook his head. "No, definitely make babies. Hush. This is *my* proposal."

She stifled a giggle.

"I want to be with you until we're old and decrepit and I have to buy you highly absorbent, disposable undergarments."

"This is getting oddly specific," she said.

"But most of all—" The words caught in his throat. He cleared it and started again. "Most of all, I want to spend the rest of my days loving you, because I genuinely like you."

They were both crying now.

"That is, if you will accept my second proposal." He smiled. "Leona Meyer, will you, for the love of everything, please marry me?"

He let go of one of her hands and started searching his pockets.

Then he groaned. "The ring is in my coat pocket."

"The coat that's hanging on the rack back in the hallway?" She laughed.

"Exactly." He looked at her, blushing. "I can't get anything right with this whole proposal thing. And yet I've never felt so comfortable being a complete failure."

Leona pulled him up, her heart so full it could burst. "I don't need a ring. I just need you, David Warlon."

"Is that your special way of saying yes?" he asked, his eyes filled with hope.

"Yes, David." She wrapped her arms around his waist. "I will marry you. I was yours then. I'm yours now. And I'll be yours forever."

She kissed her fiancé.

CHAPTER 12

Present Day

DELANEY HAD HER DRIVER TAKE LEONA AND VERA home from brunch at Blu. Leona was about to insist they were fine but then realized that instead of it taking them thirty minutes to get to Courtney Boulevard—and that was only if the city bus was on time—she could get home in ten minutes and not have to walk the last five blocks from the bus stop.

She figured she might as well enjoy the conveniences of wealth while she had them.

At home, she laid Vera down for a nap and then started looking for her phone. Her best guess was that it fell out of her purse in the taxi last night, but she wanted to scour the house just in case. It could have also fallen out of her purse at the restaurant or David might have picked it up for her and brought it home.

Like many homes owned by people in her generation, the house had no landline she could use to call David, the restaurant, or the taxi company. It drove her nuts that she couldn't find her cellphone. She was a neat freak, not only because she preferred her living environment to be calm but also because she hated misplacing things.

"Every item in our house has a home," she'd preached at her husband when they first got married.

This was a big adjustment for him. He was used to everyone picking up his stuff, whether it was his pampering mother or Mrs. Elliot or the yoke of maids who cleaned for them. He was never trained to hang up his wet towel, put his dirty clothes in the hamper, or put his keys in the basket so he wouldn't have to search yesterday's pockets when they were trying to get out the door. He just threw stuff on the floor and a few hours later it magically appeared in its proper place. Even when he went to college, Delaney would regularly send an employee to launder his clothes and give his apartment a once-over. His roommate might have mocked him about it more if he wasn't throwing in his dirty clothes to get washed too.

In their early years of marriage, David turned Leona's tidiness into a game. He would take something from the cupboard—a book or deck of cards—and misplace it on the coffee table to see how long it would take her to notice and put it back. He typically bet himself under ten minutes, and he almost always won.

But her David wasn't here moving her stuff around, so she had to think harder about where her phone might be.

The other possibility she had to consider was that her phone didn't come here with her at all. She couldn't know that for sure. She didn't make the rules about jumping from one outcome of her life to another.

Even without a phone, it was possible she wasn't completely off the grid. She went to the office and flicked on the dim light to find out. The desk was still covered with a mess of files and papers, so she hovered over it and carefully gathered them into a neat pile. Hiding underneath was a laptop.

"See, David? This is 'the life-changing magic of tidying up,'" she quoted Marie Kondo out loud to her husband a world away.

She missed him—his banter, his presence. She was acutely aware her heart was trying to exist in two places at once. Her David didn't leave without saying goodbye in the morning like David #2 did today. Her David didn't sleep on the couch when he got mad at her. He didn't dismiss her anxiety.

"I miss you," she whispered.

She also missed herself, who she used to be when she first married him—before her grief.

"I miss you too, Vera." She knew that didn't make sense when the toddler was asleep down the hall, but she still felt the ache to say it.

Her temples throbbed and the tension in her neck reminded her she wasn't dreaming, but she still wondered if she would suddenly wake up and find this reality gone. Vera was the reason Leona was willing to accept the unknowns of this other reality. Of David #2 and House #2. Of not knowing how she got here and why. But without Vera in the room, she was thrown off. Her acceptance faded just a little, forcing her to look for answers.

She opened the laptop and sat down in the firm leather chair. She felt like she was in one of those movie scenes trying to log in to a computer and download something before getting caught. The password would end up being related to an estranged son's birthday, and the camera would cut between the percentage of files downloaded onto the USB and the door where someone could walk in at any moment.

She hated how nervous those scenes made her, even though she had yet to see a movie where the person got caught. Besides, she had no reason to be nervous now. The laptop didn't even have a password-blocked entry. That surprised her a little until she remembered this computer was probably used for everyday emails, online shopping, and checking the score of last night's game. Warlon Tech would never allow work files to be accessed from a personal computer.

Leona started her investigation on Instagram, searching first for Eden's page. Her friend was easy to find, and her zest for life was glowing from every square. Her bio read: "Research scientist @BioThrive. The Next Patricia Bath."

While their high school classmates put up posters on their bedroom walls of the many Hollywood boys they swooned over, Eden fed her drive by printing pictures of scientists like Patricia Bath and Alice Ball. She taped them next to her one music poster of Black Violin. She was going to use her genius to change the world like the accomplished women looking over her.

"They were used to bring sight to the blind and cures for leprosy. And I'm next," she explained when Leona asked who they were.

Leona scrolled through her latest pictures, which didn't have much for captions. Under one selfie of Eden in all lab gear she'd written, "Science Queen." There were quite a few pictures of her with the same guy though. Scrolling further, Leona came across a photo of him kissing Eden on the cheek. Eden was holding up her left hand, and there was an ornate band on her ring finger.

He must be her fiancé, she thought. The guy in the pictures wasn't Ryan, Eden's on-and-off-again boyfriend since college, which filled Leona with all sorts of questions.

Out of pure curiosity, Leona typed in her own name. There was an Instagram profile for Leona Warlon with a few photos of their family of three and many more related to her work at the Medical Miracle Charity, including snapshots from last year's gala. Leona was well-dressed and well-groomed, right down to her flawlessly shaped eyebrows. Every photo looked like it was taken by a professional photographer, and every caption was impersonal.

There weren't any social media profiles for David or Delaney, which Leona had anticipated. When your family name was directly connected to an international company, you were allowed either a carefully curated page or nothing at all. Social media usage was strategic, not instant. You had to protect yourself—and the company—from liability.

David never saw the point of keeping social profiles anyway. "People on there are either bragging or lying or making themselves lonelier," he always said.

Leona clicked back to Eden's profile and followed the tag to BioThrive's page. She wanted to reach out to Eden for help, but she wasn't sure how to do that except by chasing her down at work. The address on BioThrive's profile confirmed it was in the same location, but she was still glad she double-checked.

Finally, Leona looked up the unfinished business in her real life. In the search bar she typed "Rose Meyer."

There were only a few results, all links to art shows her sister contributed to in college more than three years ago.

Leona sighed. *I'm so sorry, Rose.*

If she ever got back, she was finally going to tell her she was sorry.

THANKFULLY, GETTING TO BioThrive wasn't an issue. Leona was able to find the keys to what she assumed was her car in the garage, and there was a car seat for Vera already installed.

Unthankfully, Vera did not like her car seat. It was like wrestling an alligator just to get the straps buckled around her. Every time they braked for a stop sign or red light she started screaming. They were still fifteen minutes away from their destination.

Leona tried making a shushing sound, and then she tried distracting Vera by calling her name. She even dug out a bag of fruit snacks from the diaper bag, opened the wrapper, and cautiously handed it back to her—all while trying to avoid running a red light or hitting the car in front of her.

"You know what, Vera?" she said to the screams. "Operating a vehicle while soothing an angry toddler is even more dangerous than texting while driving."

She gripped the steering wheel, while her head pounded from the sound of a howling child. It was like being in a maddening echo chamber on wheels. She wanted the crying to stop, but she had to get Vera there safely. In one last ditch effort, she turned on the radio. If she couldn't make the noise stop, maybe she could drown it out. She pressed the power button to turn on the car's audio. A high-pitched, nasally version of "The Wheels on the Bus" blasted through the speakers.

Vera stopped crying.

Leona found the little girl's reflection in the rearview mirror. "You have poor taste in music, kid. This is making my ears crawl."

Vera smiled a toothy grin.

"I'm so glad the princess is satisfied with the state of her carriage." She glanced in the rearview mirror one more time.

Even with a newfound calm inside the car, Leona felt a jittery exhaustion come over her as they got closer to BioThrive. She was tired of walking into situations not knowing where she stood with people. When she ran into someone who knew her in this life—in World #2—they would assume there was a relationship built on time together and past conversations. But she had no memories with them in return, good or broken. She didn't know if they were close or if they were feuding, if they shared the same values or if different experiences had driven them apart. She was having a hard time not projecting her own assumptions and memories from World #1 onto everyone here too. Nothing felt certain.

She pulled up to BioThrive and parked, wondering how Eden would react to her showing up here unannounced. Their friendship might be on the fritz like her relationship with Rose #1 or David #2, but she wouldn't know until she went inside and found out. She got out of the car and unbuckled Vera, putting the diaper bag over her shoulder and holding Vera's hand as she walked beside her.

The biotech start-up occupied the first floor of an old warehouse. The floors above it remained abandoned, a mangled mess of broken windows and graffiti, and the sidewalks leading up to it were littered with old pieces of cement block and fresh trash. BioThrive's logo—a green leaf—hung from the door, standing out against a landscape otherwise overwhelmed by demise. Like a seed of hope.

The inside of BioThrive looked like what one might expect of a biotechnology laboratory. There were lots of things made out of glass. Glass walls separated individual labs filled with glass beakers connected with tubing, and computers monitored what was happening inside each of the glass beakers. Whiteboards filled the back walls with chicken scratch Leona assumed was part of the research process.

She couldn't help but feel a sense of pride—this was Eden and David's dream come true. It looked different than she remembered, but that was probably because David's half of the dream wasn't included in this version of BioThrive.

Leona herded Vera's wobbly steps toward the reception area where she picked up the toddler and placed her on her hip. A young woman was at the desk, standing but not still. Her movements were like a hummingbird's, darting back and forth and up and down. She alternated between typing notes into a computer and wiping down beakers, then scribbling words onto sticky notes and putting them on her computer screen. The computer screen was so full of sticky notes that this one had to be placed on top of another.

The young woman's name tag said *Raven.* She looked familiar, but Leona couldn't place her.

Raven didn't notice Leona and Vera. She moved from task to task, whispering urgent reminders to herself.

"Hello?" Leona said, trying to get her attention.

Raven jumped. "Hi. Oh my goodness, I'm so sorry. I didn't see you there. I was trying to finish cleaning these beakers and then trying to get this data filed on the computer. I've just been . . . It's just so . . . I just can't keep everything straight."

"It's okay." Leona smiled at her oversharing. "I'm hoping for a chance to talk to Dr. Williams. Is she here today? And available for any sort of meeting?"

"Yes, she's here. I'm actually supposed to finish opening these packages for her and also call someone to try to set up a meeting. Oh boy. Oh no." Raven pinched the bridge of her nose and shook her head. "This is not good. I forgot to get that set of files over to UPS . . ."

She waited for Raven to say something else, to move toward the phone or an office door to call Eden, but she didn't.

The young woman was staring into the air and mumbling words to herself about what she needed to add to her to-do list. She scribbled another sticky note. The poor girl was clearly overwhelmed by her job.

She leaned onto the desk and kept her voice gentle. "Um, so, do you think you could call for Dr. Williams?"

Raven looked at Leona. "Of course! I'm so sorry." She grabbed an unopened package and slid a box cutter through it. "It's just that when you mentioned Dr. Williams, it reminded me of this package she wanted me to open to see if it was the cell proliferation kits she's been waiting for, so that's why I needed to open this box."

Leona watched as Raven opened the box and squealed in excitement. "It's them! I ordered the wrong kits last time, which delayed Dr. Williams's work for a couple weeks, and let me just say she was—"

"Hey, Raven?" Leona interrupted.

She stopped rambling and looked at Leona. "Yes?"

"Do you think you could call for Dr. Williams right now?"

Raven dropped the box of cell proliferation kits.

Leona thought she heard the sound of glass shattering. She tried to stifle her shock.

Raven stood frozen in place. "The beakers. I dropped the box of cell proliferation kits on the beakers I just cleaned."

She wondered how Raven came to work for Dr. Eden Williams.

Raven stooped down to the mess.

"Um, before you start that," Leona began, "do you think—"

"Oh yes!" Raven swung around and yelled toward the hallway of labs. "DOCTOR EDEN WILLIAMS? YOU HAVE A VISITOR! PAGING DOCTOR EDEN WILLIAMS?"

Three seconds later, Eden appeared from around the corner, her head buried in a file.

"Raven. Girl," she whispered gently. "Please either use the phone I paid to have installed or get up out of that chair and—"

Eden looked up from her file and stopped talking. Leona locked eyes with her but couldn't read what she was thinking. Her friend narrowed her eyes, closed her file, and looked Leona up and down.

"Follow me," Eden said, then turned and walked away.

Leona hurried after her, remembering all the times she'd struggled to keep up with Eden's long legs. Lugging a toddler didn't exactly help the speed of her steps either. They went through the hallway into a lab that had a makeshift office set up in the corner. She braced herself for the anger about to come her way. She was grateful to have Vera with her, even though it wasn't right to use a child as a shield in relational combat.

Eden tossed the file onto her desk and turned to look Leona dead in the face. Her insides cowered.

"How dare you . . ." Eden said slowly.

Leona was pretty sure she visibly winced.

". . . keep this baby away from me for so long!" Eden gushed. "Look at you, Vera! You're so big! Come to your favorite Titi Eden!"

Leona exhaled. She hadn't known what to expect, but it certainly wasn't that.

Eden closed in on them, but Vera buried her face into Leona's shoulder.

"No? Okay, okay." Eden put her hands up and backed away. "Girl got boundaries. I can respect that."

Vera pulled out from hiding just enough to take a small peek at Eden, who leaned in closely one more time to whisper. "Don't let anyone disrespect you, sweet princess." She rubbed the back of Vera's hand and walked back to her desk.

Leona couldn't be more relieved. She thought for sure she was about to get ripped into and was pleasantly surprised by her friend's warm greeting.

"So, tell me about your receptionist," she began.

"That's my godmother's niece, Raven," Eden explained. "I've been trying to give her some real-world experience to put on her college applications. She's really sweet. And she's . . . learning."

"That's probably why she looked familiar. I must have run into her at your parents' house sometime." She looked around the office. "You've done an amazing job with the place, Eden."

She set Vera down so she could roam. Vera started by pulling at a locked filing cabinet drawer, looking far more relaxed than when they first arrived. Leona felt that way too.

Eden, on the other hand, crossed her arms. "Did you come here to chitchat, Leona?"

Leona blushed. She thought everything with Eden was fine, but maybe she thought wrong.

"Um, no." Leona fiddled with the hem of her shirt. "Actually, I . . . uh . . . came here because I wanted to ask for your help with something. I'm not sure you're going to believe me, but I—"

Eden held up her hand. "I'm going to stop you right there. It was really nice to see you again, but—"

But. Leona knew what that word meant. It meant that she thought her friendship with Eden might have survived this trajectory of her life, but it hadn't. This life was starting to give her whiplash. It felt like she'd plucked each petal of their friendship, ricocheting between "she loves me" and "she loves me not," only to find out the last petal was "clearly not." Leona wasn't sad or angry about it; she was scared.

"You can't walk in here after all this time asking me to help you," Eden finished.

"Is it because . . . we don't see each other as much as you'd like?" she tried. She needed to know what happened.

Eden raised an eyebrow. "Leona, I'm not mad at you. It's not like we broke up." Her friend massaged her temples. "Our lives just don't overlap anymore. You have important board meetings and bougie galas, and I'm drowning trying to get this start-up to perform an actual medical miracle." She turned and started tidying a few of the files on her desk. "Every time we have a breakthrough around here, there's more hoops I have to jump through with the FDA. I wanted you here for this. I still need David here for this. But you and David chose a life that doesn't include me anymore."

Leona knew that technically she wasn't responsible for walking away. The life she'd built and grieved through was light-years away. But she felt a deep sorrow for what her likeness did to her friend in World #2.

"Eden, I—"

"I know, I know, David has offered to bring me to Warlon Tech, but that place isn't going to be welcoming to someone like me." She graced a hand across the bottom of her coils, which spread as wide as her shoulders. "And I think you know that."

"Eden, you're—"

"My parents took you and Rose under their wing. I tried to be a good friend through everything you went through in high school. We've been friends since kindergarten." Eden was on a roll. "But even though you're only five miles away, it's like we're living in different dimensions."

Leona pictured a weight being lifted off her friend and slowly placed on herself.

"I'm not asking for a thank you, Leona. I'm just saying you can't cut me out of your life and then complain I'm not in it to help you anymore. I'm not holding a grudge; I just need to set a healthy boundary."

Leona hung her head. What Eden said was true. When Frank and Evelyn got divorced, Jackie and Winston checked in on her all the time, inviting her and Rose for dinner and letting them sleep over whenever they wanted. The air of their home radiated warmth and gave off a lasting strength. When anyone tried to give her the credit, Jackie took the opportunity to deflect: "Just grace, baby. And lots of laughter."

Their hospitality together with Eden's friendship carried her through adolescence into new adulthood.

"Eden, I'm so sorry—"

"Stop," her friend cut in again. "If you're seriously trying to apologize, then call me and ask me out for coffee instead of interrupting my workday. Whatever is going on, you have to take care of it yourself this time."

Leona had to say something. She had to get Eden's attention. She knew that if Eden heard what was really happening to her, she would at least consider helping her out.

Gathering all her courage, she said, "Eden. I'm not who you think I am."

Eden scrunched her face. "What do you mean?"

Leona took a deep breath. She was finally going to tell someone the truth. As if she actually knew the truth of what was happening. She wasn't good at processing her thoughts out loud, but she decided to open her mouth and see what would come out.

"I'm not sure how to explain this, but I'm not the Leona you know."

DAVID MUST HAVE left work early. He beat them home, and it wasn't even five o'clock yet. He met them at the door but looked right past Leona to his daughter.

"There's my baby girl," he said, pulling her into his arms.

Vera seemed happy to see him too, until two seconds later when she wriggled herself down and ran off.

"I missed you too!" he called after her.

"We've been out most of the day," Leona explained. "She's probably excited to see her own toys for a few minutes."

In the distance they heard toys being pulled out of their baskets and thrown onto the hard floor.

David looked down and crossed his arms. "I guess you're right."

An uncomfortable silence filled the space between them. Leona had always been the quieter one in their marriage. She couldn't leave a room without David asking how she was doing. But David #2 didn't even ask about her day, let alone how brunch was this morning. The only pleasant surprise was that he didn't immediately exit the room with Vera.

"I saw Eden today," she tried.

His eyes widened. "Seriously? You haven't seen her in forever. How long has it been?"

She told the truth. "I don't even know."

David nodded but didn't ask any follow-up questions. Uncrossing his arms, he took a step toward Vera's room.

"David?" She tried to call him back, wondering where the David was that she knew.

He stopped but didn't turn around. "What?"

"Did you happen to see my phone? Either at the restaurant or in your car? I think I might have left it there by accident last night."

"No." He didn't seem eager to start a search party for it. "Emily said supper is in the oven," he said, then disappeared around the corner.

Leona didn't know who Emily was, but she was too struck by her distance from David and too drained from her day to ask more questions. She wanted to put on her very old but favorite tie-dye robe and curl up on the couch under a fluffy blanket for an hour. She went to her room instead, settling for five minutes sprawled out on the fluffy king-size bed. After she recharged, she would dish out Emily's supper.

One minute into her adult time-out, she heard a phone ding twice across the hall. It wasn't the ring of a phone call but the kind you'd hear while receiving a series of text messages.

Her curiosity—along with the fact that she still hadn't found her own phone—gave her the drive to get out of bed. One more ding led her back into the office, over by the couch made into a makeshift bed, and up to the end table pulled next to it. Next to the charger and reading glasses, underneath the journal, was a phone.

She hadn't noticed it there yesterday, but she picked it up now, wondering whose it was and if she'd be able to get into it. She opened the welcome screen to find a baby picture of Vera as the background wallpaper. It was the Vera she remembered, when she was less than four months old.

The phone needed a pin to unlock it, but the privacy settings still allowed her to see who the message was from as well as a preview of what it said.

The text was from "Krissy."

Leona could feel all her jealous insecurities rising to the surface, flaring into anger. *Who is Krissy?*

Her breathing got shallower as she tried to make sense of this. Was Krissy the reason there was a bed made up in the office? Was Krissy responsible for David's chill toward her? Was David having an affair with Krissy?

Leona stopped her spiraling thoughts and told herself she was overreacting. Krissy was probably just one of David's co-workers.

She dragged her thumb down against the screen to read the preview:

Missed sweating with your bod today. Its been too long.😘

CHAPTER 13

Five Years Ago

DAVID AND LEONA WENT TO BRADFORD BEACH ON Lake Michigan to celebrate their fifth wedding anniversary. It was hard for them to get away, even for just a few hours. David and Eden were in the middle of looking for a building where they could start BioThrive, and on top of Leona's main job teaching English at Berrien High School, she took on summer school and did the aftercare program to help pay the bills.

But they tried to set aside this one day to celebrate, and what they could afford was sitting on towels in the hot sand and, later, getting two small custards from MooSa's Custard Stand. David was reading his loaned copy of *Neuroscience and Behavioral Reviews* while Leona took notes on the book she would be teaching next school year.

Her brain needed a break though, so she pulled her phone out and sent a quick text to Rose: *I miss you already.*

David noticed and closed his journal. "Is she settling in yet?"

"It's only been a week since she left, but I'm guessing so. She never does anything half-heartedly." She thought about her sister's tendency to be vocal about who she liked and who she didn't. "Knowing her, she has ten new friends already. And maybe one or two enemies."

It had been almost four years since Rose graduated high school, and she'd finally gotten bored of what she described in her own words as "sticking it to the man by getting fired from every big-box retailer in the greater Milwaukee area." A few months back, she told Leona she was now ready to stick it to the man by proving she could hold down a job. And signing up for art school far, far away.

David put his hand on her leg. "This seems like a really good fit for Rose. Far better than the paint department at Home Depot, at least."

"I know." She laced her fingers into his. "The part about art school thrills me. Rose has been drawing on every surface she could ever since she was a kid. Scrap paper, napkins, our bedroom wall. Her stuff was miles ahead of my stick figures."

"That's because you were busy being nerdy about words," her husband teased.

"True," she agreed. "Rose was obsessed with design too. She'd weave dandelions into original décor for the house, and as a teenager, she bossed Dad about how to move our furniture around to liven up the place."

"How's Frank handling her moving away?" he asked.

"Oh, you know Dad," she said with a shrug. "He struggles to understand the practicality of an art degree just like he did with my English degree. But he's the type to say his piece once and then let it go. Besides, he always called Rose his little 'artsy fartsy one.' He knows she loves it."

She tightened her ponytail and repositioned her sunglasses. "I have no doubt she can do it. She's stubborn, so it's just a relief to see her put effort into something other than self-medicating her misery."

"It's the long distance, though, isn't it?" David squeezed her hand.

"Exactly. She's four whole states away now. I didn't want Rose to feel guilty for leaving, but I'm sad. I couldn't keep it together at the bus station when I dropped her off." She dug her feet into the sand.

Rose may have been five years younger than her, but they raised each other in different ways. She was Rose's quiet protector, and Rose's feistiness kept things light when the weight of their world threatened to crush them.

David got his water bottle out of their small cooler and took a drink. "How did it go at the bus station? I'm sorry I forgot to ask earlier this week."

"It's okay. I know you and Eden have been swamped," she said. "It was good though. Rose told me I did such a good job facing our childhood ghosts but that she needed to run as far away from hers as possible for a little bit. I told her I'm cheering her on, but that I need her to answer her phone every once in a while."

"Do you think she will?" David asked.

"Not a chance." She laughed, grabbing her water bottle and taking a drink. "But now that we have a day to ourselves and not to our jobs, I want to hear more about your job and this building you and Eden are looking at."

"It's in the Metcalfe Park neighborhood just like Eden wanted. Which is in line with her goal of someday being able to employ people in the area who don't have transportation outside our shoddy bus system." David grabbed his phone and pulled up his email. "But I came across an article about a school seven blocks away that was going through some long-overdue updates, and vandals stole ten thousand dollars' worth of copper wiring and pipes off the jobsite. I sent the article to Eden and signed it, 'Hesitantly, David.' "

"What did Eden have to say?"

"I wanted to read it to you word for word so I don't mess it up. She wrote, 'About the assumed correlation between poverty and crime: Let's address the poverty factor by creating new jobs and see how that affects the maths.'"

Leona loved her friend.

"And then she added, 'PS: Every investment of love involves risk.'" David tucked his phone away.

"That sounds pretty on brand for Eden."

"I agree." His brow was twinged with worry. "I just need to convince our tiny group of investors and our contractor that it's a good idea."

"Not easy," Leona said.

"Nope," he agreed.

Leona looked up and saw a couple with their baby crossing the sandy beach to the shore. They were carrying what she considered to be an absurd number of bags on their shoulders. She wondered if they were here to visit for the day or to move in.

The child sat in a canvas wagon pulled by his dad's free hand, like this was his chariot and the parents were his steeds—their sole purpose to cater to his every fancy. The couple sat everything down in the sand with a crash, then they proceeded to set it all up, telling their son they would get him out of the wagon in "just a second."

Leona didn't think going to the beach was supposed to be this much of a workout. The dad floundered with their giant umbrella while the mom spread globs of thick sunscreen on the baby's cheeks and hands and feet. The rest of him was covered by a full-body swimsuit so tight that his neck rolls were spilling out of the top of his collar. His mom also tied a floppy hat on him, which he immediately pulled down over his face.

The parents plopped down onto the blanket, but their son crawled toward the edge where he proceeded to stick his pudgy hands in the sand and put them up to his mouth. The parents did their best to distract him, but he was not deterred. The child had a craving he planned to satisfy.

Leona looked at David and saw he was watching their juggling act too, the slightest smile grazing his lips.

Before they got married, they had agreed they wanted to have kids someday. David told her the one thing he desired more than becoming a medical research scientist was becoming a dad. "The kind of dad who shows up to baseball games *and* looks happy to be there," he joked, but she knew the words came from deep wounds within.

It was Leona's loudest desire lately too—to become a mom.

Parenthood always seemed far off in the face of David's schooling and residency. So, after she graduated from Lake Michigan State University with a less-than-honorable GPA and a degree in English, she succumbed to the stereotype that all English majors become teachers by becoming one. And after spending five years with her students in all their oily, anxious, malodorous glory, something shifted inside her. A whisper that grew one decibel at a time.

She'd wonder what her students were like when they were young and outwardly vulnerable—if Aaron used to hold his mom's hand crossing the street or if Ciara scribbled pictures of her mom for Mother's Day. Even when she saw a mom struggling to vacate the store with a cartful of groceries and a screaming toddler, Leona felt the desire to be a child's safe place.

David broke their focused silence by leaning over and saying, "You know, I really like being just the two of us. It feels . . . simple."

She studied him for a second and noticed a hint of mischief in his eyes, so she decided to play along. "Yeah, it's nice going to the beach and only having to take a cooler and a couple of towels."

"We can just sit and relax—even read a bit of intelligent literature."

"And I don't have to keep you from eating sand all day," she added.

He picked up a handful of sand and brought it an inch from his mouth.

She swatted it away.

"Not to mention," he continued, "all the expensive costs of a baby like diapers and a shiny yellow Camaro to take him to preschool in."

"True, except the car thing. Also, I don't know if you know this about me yet, but I really like to sleep, and I hear kids can mess with that a little."

David acted shocked. "You? Like sleep? I've only known that since the morning you informed me you prefer not to speak to humans before 8:30 A.M."

Leona raised her nose to the sky. "I'm not afraid to have standards."

"About the hours of sleep you need or the humans you talk to before 8:30 A.M.?"

She turned away from him. "Yes."

"Humph."

"Oh, don't act like you're all sunshine in the morning, Mr Crotchety-Before-Coffee," she countered.

"I think we're getting a little off topic here," he sidestepped the accusation. "The point of this conversation is that we shouldn't have a baby."

She nodded. "Because they're too much work. I mean, you just finished medical school and are finally starting BioThrive with Eden."

"Babies are too expensive."

"And don't forget smelly. Very, very smelly." She pinched her nose.

"Actually, I once read an interesting article that claimed parents enjoy the smell of their own baby's poopy diapers." He said it like he was enlightening her. "At least, they find their own baby's diapers less revolting than the poopies of a stranger's baby."

"Oh, so now you're reading articles about parenting?" she teased. "And using the word *poopies*? If I didn't know any better, Mr. Warlon, I'd say you were actually interested in having a baby."

"Having a baby?" David pulled down his sunglasses, smiling wickedly as he pulled at the strings on the side of her swimsuit. "Or making a baby?"

This was his recurring joke. She swatted his hand away but gave him a sultry grin. "Yes. I want to have a baby with you by first making a baby with you."

His whole face lit up like a sparkler. "Really? Because I'm not kidding anymore, Leona."

She grabbed his hand and locked it with hers. "Me either, David."

It was settled then.

CHAPTER 14

Present Day

LEONA ONCE AGAIN MADE HER BED IN THE NURSERY next to Vera's crib and once again woke up in the rocker feeling like she needed a neck and spine transplant. She knew her sleeping arrangements were not sustainable, but last night when she mulled over where to lay her head, she couldn't stomach being next to David or far from Vera.

Getting out of the rocker quietly proved difficult. All her aching body wanted to do was groan. But she managed and made her way over to Vera's crib to hover over the sight of the still-sleeping toddler. Vera's hands were resting above her head, vulnerable but safe, and her curls were a glorious mess.

Leona had to fight the urge to touch her rosy cheek, knowing how easily she could wake.

Her heart felt so full staring down at her—and so deeply sad too. The thought was always looming in the back of her mind, the lesson she learned a year ago in the worst way possible: A tomorrow with Vera was not guaranteed.

She crept across the nursery and snuck out of the room, grateful for floors that didn't creak and door hinges that didn't squeak. As she walked to the kitchen, she could smell that coffee had already been brewed. She did the math and realized it was Saturday morning, which meant that David would be home from work.

She needed coffee but she also needed restraints—a leash or maybe a pair of handcuffs—to hold her back from committing a felony against David #2. Her whole body felt like it was on fire, and she wanted to scorch every bit of earth in front of her.

"Missed sweating with your bod today. Its been too long." What else could that text mean besides David having an affair? She didn't know the full dynamics and history of her marriage in this world. Maybe she was overreacting. But what responsible adult texted sexy words that could one day be leaked onto the internet and get them canceled? These thoughts lit her blood on fire. And the English teacher in her couldn't help but side-eye the use of *its* instead of *it's.*

David was sitting at the kitchen counter scrolling on his tablet. Without looking up, he said, "I made a pot for us."

She didn't reply, which seemed to get his attention more than any of the words she'd spoken to him the past two days.

"I made it just the way you like it. Practically on steroids." His comment sounded more like an accusation than a joke.

"Thanks." The word came out flat as she rummaged through the cupboards for a mug.

"To the left," he directed.

She opened the correct cupboard and grabbed a mug, keeping her back toward David #2 to hide any more behavior that might come across as suspicious. She held her breath and braced herself for an interrogation on why she'd been acting so weird recently. She could feel his gaze boring into her neck.

At the same time, she couldn't believe his audacity to watch her every move. She'd spent the last thirty-six hours walking on eggshells around him as she tried to figure out what was going on and not be discovered as an impostor. But now that she had seen Krissy's text, it was her turn to be the one stomping around in disgust, ignoring his questions, and avoiding real conversation. She knew that wasn't how a healthy relationship built on ten years of loving trust was supposed to act. But she reasoned with herself that she hadn't been married to this David for ten years.

"You seem stiff," David said.

She didn't know if he meant her demeanor or her body. "I'm fine. I slept in the rocker again."

He stood up and walked around the kitchen counter until he was only a foot away. They made eye contact, and it was so intense Leona thought her retinas might go ablaze.

With her David, close proximity like this usually led to him wrapping her up in his large frame and squeezing the worry out of her. It led to a tender kiss and each of them apologizing for their morning breath. She had no idea what David #2 was about to do.

He turned to the cupboard, grabbing a canister and setting it on the counter before opening it. When he faced her again, she realized he was breathing heavily, like he was trying to hold something back. Like he wanted to say something, do something.

He shook his head, then walked back around the kitchen counter to finish his coffee and morning headlines.

She let out the breath she didn't realize she'd been holding and looked at the canister sitting on the counter. It was full of sugar.

David didn't take his coffee with sugar. She did.

She put two scoops in her mug and stirred, her thoughts as muddled as the grains being absorbed by the scalding coffee. David just did what parents do to sustain shreds of intimacy between each other—thoughtful acts in a season when tender moments must be stolen.

But why?

She wanted to process their confusing interaction more, but

she heard babbling over the baby monitor. Vera was awake and oblivious to the pain looming outside her crib between the two adults in the kitchen.

The noise gave Leona the will to move. David shifted too, but she sped ahead of him across the kitchen. "I'll get her," she said, leaving no room for argument.

She walked into the nursery, and when Vera saw her, she held on to the side of her crib and jumped up and down. Then she pointed at the open door. "Dadda," she stated once, then again as a question. "Dadda?" Vera was excited to get out of her crib, but apparently she still had an opinion about who was there to get her.

Leona knew she shouldn't take it hard. She couldn't expect to walk in after two days of making Vera's acquaintance and have her trust her, like a mindless sponge content to soak up just anyone's love. Trust was hard-earned and easily lost. A single text message reminded her of that.

She took the little girl out of her crib and pulled her close, still in disbelief she was here, mothering Vera. They enjoyed a morning cuddle, and the warmth of Vera's head cooled some of the anger in her chest. The only thing that ruined the moment was the smell. The toddler reeked of wet diaper.

"Whew, Vera. You're a sweet girl but a stinky one too. I need to give you a bath, don't I?"

She changed her soaking diaper and then brought her to the kitchen. She didn't want to talk to David, but she knew the next half hour would go more smoothly with his help. "Will you get her breakfast while I get her bath ready?"

"Yes, of course." He took Vera and spoke to her in a much gentler voice. "Does my little girl want some breakfast? We can't start the day with you stinky *and* hungry."

Leona excused herself to the bathroom where she filled the tub with water. She looked through cupboards for baby shampoo and a washcloth and came across much more than that. There was a giant bucket of bath toys and a rubber duck specially designed to change colors if the water was too hot or too cold. A complete set of bath sheets that felt like they belonged in a luxury resort in Beverly Hills.

After the tub was filled, she went to the nursery to pick out clothes. Instead of letting the closet overwhelm her with too many choices, she closed her eyes and randomly grabbed a hanger. It was a cream dress with light blue polka dots. The skirt was pleated, and the collar tied into a large bow; it would look adorable on Vera. She noticed there was still a tag on it, so she checked the price. It was $108.

She also grabbed a diaper. The compostable packaging said it was made from biodegradable bamboo and that each diaper was dye- and fragrance-free. Every diaper was fragrance-free for only so long, she reasoned.

Now that she was fully prepared for bath time, she got Vera from her high chair in the kitchen. On top of smelling like a wet diaper, the girl had acquired a face and hands full of yogurt. The toddler protested having to leave the room her dad was in, but Leona sped them out of sight, tickling Vera's sides as a distraction.

Vera loved being in the tub, and she also seemed to love finding ways to get water out of it. She splashed with two outstretched hands, sprinkling the entirety of Leona's pajama top. Then she laid on her belly, kicking the water as high as she could.

"Keep the water in the tub," Leona said for the fifth time.

Vera took a cup and held it high in the air, then poured it over the side.

"Vera," she scolded, peeling off her wet socks one at a time and throwing them into the hamper. "You're like a breaching whale in there."

The little girl giggled.

"It's time we soap you up and clean the rest of the stink off you," she said.

She looked at Vera again and noticed her posture had changed. The little girl was still sitting up in the tub, but she was completely motionless.

"What's wrong?" Leona asked.

Vera leaned forward and looked at Leona. Her face was concentrating like she was bearing down.

"Vera?"

The toddler's face turned a deep shade of red. It looked like she wasn't breathing.

Every single alarm in Leona's head went off. She had no idea what was going on—why Vera was suddenly acting so strange. Maybe she was allergic to soap or maybe she was choking on something. She leaned down and rubbed Vera's back, but nothing changed. The little girl was clenching more and breathing less.

Leona needed a medical expert. She needed her husband.

"David!" she screamed as loud as she could. "David, help!"

She heard him run through the kitchen and down the hallway until he reached them in their bathroom.

"What's wrong?" He leaned next to the tub.

"I don't know! She's not breathing, and her face is turning red!"

Both David and Leona hovered in close. Each put a hand on her back. This couldn't be happening. Not again, she prayed. Suddenly, Vera breathed, smiling wide at the two panicked adults staring down at her.

A large turd popped out from behind Vera. It bobbed to the surface and then sank to the bottom of the tub again. That was when Leona finally understood.

David sprang into action. "Code Brown! I repeat, we have a Code Brown!"

He grabbed Vera and ran her slippery body over to the toilet in case she had more that needed to come out. Then, he laid Vera on a towel and cleaned her bottom. Overwhelmed by the odor, he dry heaved. "It smells so bad! Why does wet poop smell so bad?"

Vera giggled.

Leona started giggling too, first in disbelief and then at the entire scene. At herself for blowing everything out of proportion. At how gross parenthood could be. At David's gagging. She laughed until she was leaning over the tub, and then she laughed even more.

He was right. Wet poop smelled so bad.

She laughed until all the fear that had just paralyzed her was gone, and she sat back on the sopping wet floor. She walked over to the little girl wearing a biodegradable bamboo diaper and hugged her—probably too tightly. Watching Vera struggle to breathe triggered memories she didn't want to think about.

David was still smiling too. He grabbed a fresh towel and wrapped it around Leona and Vera. Again, there was so little space between them, but it felt a lot different than their close proximity twenty minutes ago. She and David were so close they could kiss.

She looked away. "I'm sorry. I . . . thought something was really wrong with her, and it scared me."

She felt something around her shoulders. When she looked up, she was surprised to see it was David's arm.

"When something's wrong with Vera, it scares me too," he said softly, hugging her closer.

It seemed like the tides were shifting for David. He wasn't melting all over her, but he was definitely more relaxed. He was being kind and friendly, a glimmer of the husband she knew. If she were home, she would eliminate the space between them and pull his head down until his lips were against hers. A kiss that could express the intricacies of love and parenting better than a mile-long essay.

This is what she wanted. To be with David *and* Vera.

Leona felt the warmth of his hand against the small of her

back. But when she felt it, she pictured another woman's hand touching him. Krissy's hand.

She recoiled. Thinking of it made her too sick to appreciate his help with Vera's bath. Even if he was warming up to her, her heart was icing against him. Everything he did couldn't be erased by one tender moment.

David cleared his throat. "It's supposed to be hot out today."

"Oh?" Leona looked away and fought the urge to roll her eyes. The weather was what people talked about when they had nothing else in common. Or when their relationship was burned down by an irreparable mistake.

"Maybe we could do something just the three of us," he suggested. "Like go to my parents' beach? It might be fun trying to keep Vera from eating sand for a few hours."

"I'm visiting my dad today," Leona replied in a way that said her decision was final. She'd made her plan a split second ago, but it was as good a plan as any.

David flinched. "Would you like me to tag along?" he offered. "I could be your chauff—"

"No," she cut him off. "I'll take Vera and give you some space."

When she knew he wasn't looking, she stole a glance at him. She couldn't believe he had the nerve to act hurt.

He patted his stomach. "I guess I'll go work out my dad bod in the basement for a while then. Maybe we could try the beach tomorrow?"

His eyes pleaded with hers.

Leona could tell he wanted her to say something, to let him in. For a second, she almost gave in. She held his gaze and remembered all they'd been through, the hard choices they had made to build their life together, and the choices they hadn't made at all—the tragedies that by only a miracle brought them closer.

But this wasn't the same David. And this David made the worst choice of all.

"I'll clean this up and disinfect everything," he said, his voice gruff, yearning. "You can get ready to go to your dad's house."

A HALF HOUR later, Leona was buckling Vera into her car seat. Before she even opened the garage door, she turned on Vera's favorite nursery-rhyme songs. She would not make the same mistake twice.

They drove across the city to her dad's house, to what used to be her and Rose and Evelyn's house too. It looked different than what she remembered but in a good way. There was brand-new blue siding. The porch was updated to a modern mix of wood and iron. There weren't old shingles littering the small strip of grass next to the house like they used to find after a big storm or mild gust of wind. Her dad even planted real flowers. It reminded Leona of when their neighbor Ms. Kathy put a pot of silk flowers—patterned red, white, and blue—on her front steps in anticipation of the Fourth of July.

Things like flowers and celebration were hard-fought luxuries in her neighborhood.

She unbuckled Vera and set her on the sidewalk. The uneven cement squares were a tripping hazard if you weren't paying close enough attention. Vera knew which steps to climb to her grandpa's porch, which made Leona hopeful for what this interaction with her dad might be like.

Looking around, she noticed a lot of adults sitting on their porches, enjoying their July Saturday by trying to escape the heat of their homes with fresh air and shade. A group of kids chased one another up and down the sidewalk, while another small crowd gathered around two kids playing Cans, a game native to the heart of Milwaukee.

One player tossed their basketball at the other player's smashed soda can and yelled, "I got twenty points!"

Leona smiled, remembering all the times she and Rose played Cans with neighbors. It was easy to find a smashed soda can on their street. The hard part was finding a fully inflated basketball.

"Let's knock on Grandpa's door." Leona demonstrated three knocks, which Vera copied with her little hand.

While they waited, Leona became self-conscious that she hadn't called her dad first. She couldn't believe this is what people did before phones: show up unannounced and unsure if anyone would be home.

Frank opened the door with a smile on his face. He looked the same, his red hair fading with age but not at all graying. Each time Leona saw him, he seemed more at peace, healthier.

"My babies! What a wonderful surprise." He came outside to give each of them a hug. "Come in. And please forgive the mess. The kitchen is still in the middle of updates, so keep your shoes on."

She gladly accepted his hug. "The house looks amazing, Dad."

He eyed her strangely. "You've been here plenty of times to see it, but I'm glad you still like it. It's all thanks to you and David."

She tried to recover. "Yes, but I don't think I've asked you enough what the updating process has been like."

That seemed to satisfy his suspicions.

"Well, after you gave me that completely unnecessary but incredibly generous Christmas gift last year, I was able to hire a contractor to finally start fixing up the place. One of our neighbors is a contractor, actually. Do you remember Mike Harris?"

Leona nodded. Mike was the one who kept Ms. Kathy's sidewalks shoveled and salted in the winter.

"I hired Mike, but he noticed I kept watching him while he worked and badgering him with questions. Eventually, he gave me a hammer and started bossing me around until I learned a few things. My expertise is engines, but between the money you gave me and a few free oil changes on his car, we've made the exterior brand-new and are making headway on the inside too. As you can see, the kitchen is next. I'm taking a whack at the cabinets, trim, and flooring, and Mike and his guys will handle the plumbing and electrical."

The kitchen was completely gutted and there was dust everywhere. Vera's dress didn't stand a chance.

"Now that I'm old and boring, I don't have much to do," he joked, "so Mike and I fixed Ms. Kathy's porch and redid Mr. Marshall's roof too. I know you offered to buy me a new place somewhere else, but look at how your gift just keeps on giving. On the same street you grew up on, no less."

It was touching to see their money being used for good. It reminded her of a conversation she had with Patrice Perry at the Medical Miracle Charity gala a lifetime ago.

"And don't worry about Vera's feet. I go through every night and pick up the sharp stuff so I don't surprise myself in the mornings. A nail in the foot doesn't go very well with a cup of coffee." He chuckled. "But I'm sorry if she gets that pretty dress of hers dusty. There's not much I can do about that."

"Oh, Dad, we both know kids get clothes dirty," she reassured him. "A little dust won't hurt her."

"I'm glad we can agree on that," he said. "Come sit in the living room. That's where I moved the dining table so I don't have to eat sawdust on my sandwiches."

There was a fan whirring in the corner, keeping the humid air circulating. Either Frank never added central air to the house or he was conscious of how often he turned it on. After they went so many years with so little, neither would surprise her. Frank had always tried saving pennies by walking the entire house to turn off lights and close doors. He'd remind her and Rose, "If you're not using a room, the room shouldn't be using the lights."

Leona quoted that line to David all the time now.

"Can I see the rest of the house again before I sit down?" she asked.

"Of course. Take a look around while I show this munchkin a few of the new toys I got her." He waved at Vera to follow him.

"You didn't have to get her anything, Dad."

"Now, now. I'm no Warlon, but that doesn't mean I can't get a few things for my granddaughter. I have to keep some fun stuff here so my sweet little girl wants to keep coming around." He winked.

"She just likes seeing you. I just like seeing you too. No strings attached . . ."

"Except my heartstrings," he finished for her.

It was another saying from the soundtrack of Leona's childhood. Frank often came home with the random stuff he found inside totaled cars at the shop that went unclaimed—an unopened air freshener, a coffee mug with Milwaukee's flag on it, a string of LED lights. Whenever he gave them to Leona and Rose, he wanted them to know he expected nothing in return because that's what made it a true gift.

He'd say, "No strings attached except my heartstrings. I can't seem to cut those away from my little girls no matter how old they get."

Leona looked in the bathroom and two bedrooms and was shocked by the freshly painted walls and new outlets and shiny hardware. It didn't feel like walking through the tired house she grew up in, home to nothing more than deprivation. The biggest surprise was her old bedroom where there was a handcrafted bunk bed and a large set of shelves filled with books, toys, and stuffed animals.

After her self-guided tour, she returned to the living room. "Dad, it's beautiful. I especially like my and Rose's room."

"I only wish it could have been this nice when you both still lived here." His smile was twinged with embarrassment. "But when Vera and Charlie get a little older, I want to have them over for some cousin sleepovers. I know you have plenty of help at home, but you have to let this old grandpa have fun with his grandkids every once in a while too. Rose has been teaching me how to take care of Charlie, with her condition and all."

The mention of Leona's niece took the breath out of her. She turned away so she could take a few deep breaths through the emotions trying to surface.

"Leona, what's wrong? You don't seem like yourself today." He patted the seat next to him at the table.

She obeyed, grateful that Vera was occupied with the box of toys Frank had pulled out for her.

"Is there something you want to talk about?" he asked.

Leona knew she could not take ownership of a life she'd been living for only a few days, but it tore her to pieces even imagining some of her most precious relationships falling apart.

"Dad, I'm grateful for my life, I really am. I love Vera so much." Her thoughts tumbled out. "But sometimes it feels like my life is falling apart. Stuff has been hard with David—" She broke off.

She wasn't ready to get into the details, to actually say it out loud. Frank and David got along well; he loved David like a son.

"I've messed things up with Eden. Me and Rose—" She stopped again. She still didn't know where she and Rose #2 stood here. "Things are just hard. It feels like I have more than I ever dreamed of, and at the same time I'm always missing something. It's not that I want more. I want . . . different."

She crossed her arms and rested them on the kitchen table—the same small table where she grew up eating bowls of cereal—and laid her head down. She wished there were such a thing as having the best of both worlds. She wanted David *and* Vera, her closest friend *and* her sister.

Why did each outcome leave her with one or the other?

Was there any place she could inhale and exhale without a heavy ache?

Frank leaned forward, put his elbows on the table, and folded his hands. "Leona, I appreciate your willingness to try and focus on the good in your life. That's a trait I wish more people had. But if there's one thing I've had to learn myself, it's that trying to force every cloud to have a silver lining won't protect you from the rain. The only way to get out of the rain is to walk through the storm to the other side."

She kept her head down in her arms. "Water metaphors about life are overdone," she groaned. "I need three easy steps to fix it. I need answers."

Frank patted her back. "Well, Ms. English Major, listen to this. Sometimes there aren't magic words or easy steps to fix the past. Sometimes you don't get the kind of answers that allow you to predict the future. Sometimes you have to face your life and have the hard conversations and ask for help. Surround yourself with good people."

"Thank you, Reverend Frank," she teased, sitting up again. Completely serious, she added, "Is that what got you through when Evelyn left?"

Frank frowned.

She knew he didn't like when she called her mother by her first name. She attributed it to generational differences. Frank believed that even if your elder ruined your life, they were still your elder and, therefore, deserving of their title.

"Yes," Frank answered. "It wasn't like walking down Sesame Street, but that is what got me through. Eventually." He stood up and went to the kitchen, grabbing the orange juice from inside the fridge and two plastic cups that were sitting upside down on top of it. "I wish I had the perfect advice to give you, but I don't. I have too many unanswered questions myself. But I will say this: Frank and Evelyn are not David and Leona. The two of you have something special your mother and I never had."

He laughed to himself. "Most marriages do, I guess. If there's one thing I would say after getting to know my daughter over the past three decades or so, it's that I know you like to keep the peace, but sometimes you have to fight for the ones you love before peace can live there. You can't fight for every person, but I think you have an eye for finding some of the good ones. Talk to David. Talk to Eden. Dreaming of some alternate version of your life won't make this one any better."

Leona sat up straighter in her chair, wondering how he knew.

Frank sat back down and opened the carton of orange juice. "Now, when it comes to your mother, there's something I want you to know. Even though I will never accept the way she's treated you girls, I don't blame her for our divorce. I made my share of mistakes."

She shook her head. "She's tried to tell me that before, but I'm not sure I believe it," she said, feeling defensive of him. "I'll never understand how the two of you crossed paths, let alone ended up married."

Her dad inhaled. "Our paths crossed on—"

"Homecoming night," she finished for him. "I remember the basics. You didn't love football, but you loved fancy cars, so you went to the game against her high school that night to meander the parking lot. I know that much, but you've never shared more than that."

Frank nodded. "Her high school always scheduled their homecoming game against my school. We didn't always have qualified coaches or jerseys where the numbers weren't peeling off. But a few of my friends were on the team, and that was the first year in a long time we had a chance of giving them a run for their money. No pun intended," he joked. "But yeah, it took everything in me not to pop the hood of that Porsche Turbo."

"But where did you run into Evel—er, Mom—that night?" she asked, correcting herself.

"Right away in the parking lot." He took a sip of his orange juice. "A limo pulled up right next to me, and out came their entire homecoming court. I asked her what her name was, but she wouldn't tell me. She wouldn't agree to go out with me on a date after the game either."

Leona felt like there were at least three plot holes to this story so far. "I want more details," she demanded.

Her dad hesitated. "It's not that this isn't an interesting story, Leona. It's just that we both know the story doesn't exactly have a happily ever after."

"I know," she said, "but we haven't really talked about this before. And for some reason, today it feels important to know."

"Well," Frank began again, "before she walked away from me, I told her we should bet on it. If my school won the game, I would get to take her out."

"And she agreed?" Leona asked.

"She said if my school won the game *and* she wasn't crowned homecoming queen, I could take her out."

Leona thought about it. "Basically, you were her consolation prize if she had a terrible night."

"Basically."

"So, then how did you end up going out that night if neither of those things happened? If you lost the bet?"

"I waited for her outside the dance."

"I can't decide if you're a dedicated romantic or a complete stalker," she joked.

"I like to think of it as being a foolish young man." He made a face. "Eventually, she came outside from the gym, trying to escape her mom. Mrs. Abbot signed up to be a chaperone for the dance that night, but she was the worrying type and that always made Evelyn claustrophobic. When I saw Evelyn, I told her I was there to take her out on that date."

"And she agreed? Even though her school won and she was crowned homecoming queen?"

He nodded. "I told her I made another bet that if I waited long enough, she'd let me take her out."

"Smooth, Frank Meyer." She tried to smile but felt sad. "And the rest is history?"

"Yes, sweetheart."

She sensed he didn't want to go on, but he took a deep breath and said, "That night, after . . . everything . . ."

"Please, Dad!" She cringed. "We don't have to talk about that part."

He laughed. "The point is, I was her escape and your mother was my siren, and it got the best of us. When I dropped her off, she refused to give me her number, and I thought I'd never see her again. I was shocked when she showed up at the garage three months later. She looked like a shiny pearl in a bucket of greasy bolts. She told me she was pregnant and that her parents were kicking her out. We got married the very next Wednesday. Grandma Vera and Grandpa Lawrence were the only witnesses."

Leona took it in. She'd always felt close to her dad, but this was the most he'd ever shared with her. Between the past two days, assuming her parents had the same backstory in World #1, she'd learned a lot about their past. About her beginnings.

"Six months later, you were born, and five years after that, Rose. I tried to keep the faith that one day we could make it work as a family." Frank cleared his throat. "But I didn't make it easier for her to stay. One night, my co-worker Bill invited me out to the bar after work. I was so stressed out about everything—money, your mom—that I joined him. One happy hour turned to two, which turned into a daily ritual. Eventually, my body told me I needed liquor at five o'clock like I needed oxygen."

She looked down and took a sip of her orange juice. Another complicated layer was being added to her own backstory.

"I tried to hide my drinking from you and Rose," he admitted, "but I couldn't hide that we couldn't afford mouse traps or new glasses or, during the worst month I remember that was my wake-up call, electricity. Your mom spent most of our money trying to make herself more comfortable than she had to be, but I spent the rest of our money at the bar. I am so ashamed about that. Like that day you drew me that picture of us in front of the house. What were you, ten years old? Seeing that picture made me recognize my failures as a father." He shook his head. "I should have done better by you girls."

"But Mom could have tried," Leona insisted. "She left us."

Frank sighed. "Your mother went through a lot when she was put out by her parents. She was grieving; she needed time to ease into our marriage. But I suffocated her. And then, when the pain of her pushing me away got too hard, I made it worse by drinking. No matter how much pain your mother caused me, she has a lot to forgive me for too. My AA sponsor reminds me of that."

His confession added another layer to Evelyn's backstory too.

"But Leona, you need to understand something. Even though I wish I did a lot of things differently and that a lot of things turned out differently, I have zero regrets. Zero. And I've been so blessed."

He placed his hand on top of hers, tears brimming in his eyes.

"Because the most amazing thing I'll never be able to fully understand is, through all my foolishness and pain and mistakes and unanswered questions, I was given you."

CHAPTER 15

Four Years Ago

IF ONLY IT COULD HAVE BEEN AS EASY FOR THEM AS sperm plus egg equals baby. But they couldn't get pregnant. Some assured them God had a very good plan for their lives, and *of course* that plan included the happiness of having a child of their own. Others encouraged them to work on boosting good vibes.

"The unsolicited advice is infuriating," Leona vented to David. "Have I tried hanging upside down from a chandelier after sex while eating an antioxidant salad and swallowing a bee pollen supplement?"

"The 'sex on a chandelier' thing sounds fun," David offered.

"That's not what I said. Also, I should stay active by taking long walks when it's partly sunny outside with a southeast wind blowing at ten miles per hour, but not so active I get too stressed because stress is bad for fertility."

"That's oddly specific."

"Even more than hating the unsolicited advice, I hate myself for trying all of it. Minus the 'sex on a chandelier' thing." She gave David a look. "And then there's the people who ask, 'Have you ever considered adopting because there are so many children out there who are already born and need parents?' "

David shifted in his seat. "I could set up a meeting with my parents to ask—"

"No," she shut him down.

"But—"

"No, David. Please don't ask again," she begged. A second later she added, "I'm surprised you're even offering to talk to them."

"I know." He looked down. "Me too."

His relationship with his parents was a sore subject, yet he'd brought up asking them for help multiple times. It cost twelve thousand dollars to do a single round of in vitro fertilization, something they wouldn't be able to afford until decades down the road when David's schooling was paid off and Leona's ovaries were already dried up.

But she couldn't do it. She would not subject herself to the humiliation of asking her in-laws for a loan—or subject David to it either.

So, they waited and they tried every natural, cheap method possible to boost fertility. They spent seventy dollars to get a paternal analysis on David, which came back normal. Leona took her temperature every morning when she woke up and charted her menstrual cycles. She took brisk walks to get her heart rate up before her school day began and did long sessions of stretching to soothing music under the aroma of a clary sage candle to get her heart rate back down again before bed. She kicked caffeine and her daily afternoon doughnut. She thought the doughnuts were the hardest loss, especially when she was staring at a plate of them in the teacher's lounge in all their glazed glory.

It was all so emotionally draining—every lifestyle change, every internet search, and the weeks of waiting to take a pregnancy test only to be let down again.

All the fighting too.

She fought guilt because her body was supposed to be able to do what she thought was a completely natural thing. She fought anger, like when her seventeenth test came back negative and she wanted to take a sledgehammer to a room full of glass. She fought envy, and she finally gave up social media because pregnancy announcements and photos of snuggly newborns haunted every scroll.

She fought tears when her students started getting nosy. "When are *you* going to have a baby, Mrs. Warlon?"

And, as she climbed onto the bus to go from work to her doctor's appointment, she fought doubt, mostly related to her issues with her own mother. Deep down, she worried that maybe she didn't even know how to be a mom.

Leona took her seat on the bus and checked her phone. There was still no call, text, or voicemail from Rose. Rose was a year and a half into art school and didn't answer her phone like Leona asked her to. At first, Leona didn't take it personally. Rose always did things at her own pace. But now it had been six months since she called her back.

Every once in a while, Leona texted: *Please tell me you're alive.*

To which Rose responded: *You're alive.*

She took the sarcasm as a good sign but hoped through the otherwise long stretches of silence that none of the ghosts Rose was trying to outrun had caught up to her.

Leona got off the bus and walked two blocks to the health center, sending one last text to David to let him know she'd arrived. He was going to pick her up after the appointment but wasn't able to leave work any earlier to join her.

Their insurance covered one wellness checkup with a gynecologist each year, so after eighteen maddening months of trying to get pregnant, she was finally going to an appointment. She had actually scheduled it sooner; she was considered infertile after twelve months. But this center—one of the few places with evening hours located on the bus line—had already canceled her appointment twice.

Even though the January temperature outside the health center was frigid, the air inside it was thick with illness and impatience. Patients sat shoulder to shoulder in lines of chairs, the hard plastic kind found in dank church basements across America. A couple of restless kids ran around, and a baby fussed as her mom bounced her on her bosom.

Leona made her way through a tangled sea of legs, each crossed or outstretched pair retracting one at a time to offer her a clear path. When she reached the front desk, she informed the receptionist she had an appointment at four o'clock. The receptionist handed her a clipboard of paperwork. A pen dangled from the clipboard by a frayed piece of purple yarn.

"Fill out these forms," the receptionist said. "You're eighth in line."

She didn't understand. "But I made an appointment?"

The receptionist looked at her. "Yes."

"Scheduled at four o'clock?" she pushed.

"That guarantees you see the doctor this evening," the woman explained. "It's first come, first served around here."

Leona switched from questions to a statement. "That could take hours."

The receptionist looked up like she was on her last nerve. "Are you experiencing a medical emergency?"

"Well, no," she stuttered, "but it's important."

The woman blinked, then said evenly, "Do you think everyone else here is in line for a ride at Disney World?"

Leona blushed and shook her head.

There would be no budging. This was the system. She turned to find a place to sit and begin waiting. She'd been waiting for over a year. She was tired of all the waiting.

An elderly gentleman wearing oversized dress pants and a weathered fedora waved at her and then pointed to the chair he was sitting in.

She waved back in polite protest. "I couldn't, but thank you."

He insisted. "I might be old, but I still like to treat a young lady like yourself with a little chivalry."

She gave in, grateful for his kindness.

He got out of his chair, his body crackling the whole way up. His chivalry would need a double knee replacement soon, she thought.

She filled out the forms she'd been given and then pulled out the pile of papers she needed to grade. At 6:14 P.M., the receptionist called a name similar to hers.

"Leon?"

Leona looked around the room. Nobody else got out of their chair, so she stood and started packing her bag.

The receptionist gave her a funny look and then double-checked her list. "Oh. It's Leahna. I'm sorry. Second room on the right."

As Leona undressed for the examination, she realized she'd shaved only one of her legs in the shower that morning. Just one. The epitome of "sorry, not sorry." The hairy leg was sorry, and the smooth one, not sorry. Now that she thought about it, her anxiety about the appointment had affected her entire morning. She'd dropped pretty much everything she tried to pick up and couldn't process any of what David said to her at breakfast.

She pulled off her red uniform polo and set it on top of her carefully folded pants, followed by her underwear and shabby bra. She forgot if the paper gown was supposed to go on with the split in the front or the back. After a quick debate, she tied it around herself like a robe, split front.

She was studying the blank walls when the doctor blew into the room. His medical coat was disheveled, and his glasses were crooked. He moved so quickly, with so much pep, that his New Balance 624s looked blurry. Leona could not match his energy after her full workday, slow bus ride, and hours in the waiting room.

"Good evening, there, Ms. Leahna. I'm Dr. Badgers," he said.

She was too tired to let it slide. "It's Le-*oh*-na," she corrected him.

"Ope! Sorry about that!" he apologized, flipping open her file. "Okey doke, what do we got here?"

Leona found herself overthinking the entire appointment. Dr. Badgers asked her to take deep breaths for her blood pressure reading, but all she could think about was that she'd eaten only a handful of cheese garlic croutons and a banana during her short lunch break without so much as a mint afterward. She tried hard to redirect her stale breath away from his face. Then, when he examined her for tumors, she tried to break the ice by joking she was exempt from getting breast cancer because she had the chest of a nine-year-old boy.

Dr. Badgers looked up from his kneading hands and said sternly, "Breast cancer doesn't discriminate," before he went back to work.

She did her time in the stirrups too. Everything made her feel exposed, invaded, vulnerable. She told Dr. Badgers about the last eighteen months.

No, she hadn't had any miscarriages.

Yes, her periods were regular.

Yes, David got checked.

No, they couldn't afford treatments or additional testing; they could afford nothing insurance didn't cover, which meant anything related to infertility.

No, she didn't partake in any recreational drug use.

Dr. Badgers popped up from below the paper gown. "Everything looks like it's in tippy-top shape as far as I can see! Yes, ma'am, that's one healthy looking birth canal. I'll send this sample into the lab, but unless we call you, no news is good news, and I'm thinking this looks like pretty good news."

Leona's eyes lost focus. She shook her head. She didn't know what was worse, receiving a diagnosis or not getting any answers.

Dr. Badgers was about to blaze out of the room. Before he grabbed the door handle, she said, "Wait. So nothing is wrong?"

He turned around. "Nope. Just relax and stay positive."

He gave her two thumbs up and left the room.

She *was* positive. Positive she could scream. Positive she wanted to grab those cold metal tongs and use them to swat the smile off the doctor's face. She'd tried to relax, tried to distract herself with the good parts of her life she loved, like her job and her husband.

Was it so wrong to want a baby too?

CHAPTER 16

Present Day

"LEONA." SOMEONE WAS GENTLY RUBBING HER shoulder, pulling her out of a dream. The voice was gruff, just above a whisper, and in her half-conscious state it sparked a sense of gladness.

Out of nowhere, two little hands smacked her face, which was as good as any morning alarm.

"Vera, don't hit Mommy," David said.

Leona opened her eyes. David was standing over her with a phone in his hand. Vera was on his hip, smiling down at her with a finger in her mouth.

"Hi, Vera," she answered the little girl's smile.

Leona pushed herself off a crumpled pillow, first onto her elbows and then into a sitting position. She rubbed the crusts out of her eyes so she could look around. She was sitting on the couch in the office, her legs tangled in the sheet that transformed the stiff black leather into a makeshift bed.

There was a laptop on the floor at her feet, which reminded her how she ended up there in the first place. She spent all of yesterday at her dad's house. Then she spent the rest of the night ignoring Frank's advice to talk face-to-face with David. Instead, she searched social media high and low for the name Krissy.

"Here she is, Eden," David said into the phone.

She heard muttering through the speaker: "'Bout time."

He held out the phone and whispered, "I'm not sure why she's calling you on my phone."

She shrugged as if she had no idea, unsure if he was legitimately confused or if he was testing her. He eyed her for two long seconds, then turned around and left the office.

She put the phone up to her ear, but her mouth was dry and her throat thick. She tried coughing to clear her morning phlegm, longing for a glass of water and a toothbrush. "Hey, Eden."

"Why are you still in bed? The day's half over."

Leona didn't particularly enjoy other people in the morning, but it was fun being on the receiving end of her friend's motivational critiques again.

"Eden, I know you don't know this version of me very well, but you should know my love for sleep is exactly the same as it was in college."

"All right, all right. But you need to get your butt out of bed because Carl is meeting us at BioThrive in an hour."

Leona perked up, fully conscious now.

At BioThrive two days ago, she had told Eden everything. She hadn't meant to tell her the entire story, but once she started talking about meeting David at the restaurant, how different David seemed, how she actually lived in Sherman Park instead of near the lakeshore, Vera's death—she couldn't stop.

She'd grabbed Eden's forearms. "I know this all sounds wild—that I'm from a completely different version of my life . . . or . . . something. I don't even know how to explain it. But I need you to believe me. I don't know what to do."

Eden had needed a minute. She'd paced her office to process, eyeballing Leona the entire time. Then she stopped moving and crossed her arms. "Honestly, I'm not sure what to believe. But I know a guy who's studying this exact thing. If there's any place to start trying to figure this out, it's with him. I'll call you on David's cell after I get a chance to connect with him."

A sound in her ear brought Leona back to where she was currently sitting in the office on Courtney Boulevard. "Girl, pay attention!"

"Sorry. I'm here," she apologized. "I'm just in awe you were able to connect me with Carl so fast."

"I'm a rare commodity. Now, as a thank you, please bring me a doughnut from the artisan shop on that street your neighborhood calls 'downtown.' I just shake my head because if there aren't people on the corner with cardboard signs in their hands, it ain't *downtown*."

Leona laughed.

"Anyway, they're delicious, and that's how you'll pay penance for making me miss church this morning."

"I promise I'll pray over your doughnut," Leona pledged.

"No need. They've already been touched by the angels," Eden said, then screamed, "Ah, this is unbelievable!" before hanging up.

Leona ran to the bathroom and gave herself a quick washcloth wipe down, then brushed her teeth.

She scoured the closet, and as she dug deep, she was surprised to find her old tie-dye robe tucked in the middle of the hanging clothes. Seeing it there made her stop for a moment to ponder the past couple of days. When she first came here to World #2, she mostly noticed the differences—the fancy, expensive luxuries that made this life feel so opposite from hers. But this beloved relic she'd had since she was sixteen was proof that pieces of herself existed here too. She took the soft material between her hands, comforted by its mere presence in the closet.

Turning to the shelves to look some more, she found and put

on a pair of buttery soft joggers, as well as an athletic tank top with so many cutouts in strange places she couldn't tell if it was supposed to be exercised in or worn to the beach. She threw her hair into a messy bun, put on her glasses, and looked in the mirror.

She thought she looked adequate for the day she might get answers to how she got here and why. She didn't know how to feel about that prospect, so she felt everything at once: Relief at the possibility of her circumstances making more sense. And, when she thought of Vera, she felt afraid too. Sometimes ignorance made things easier.

She walked to the kitchen where David and Vera were hanging out and was surprised it was already 8:30. By Eden's standards and a parent's standards, she'd slept in for hours. She would need to hurry if she wanted to get to BioThrive on time and pick up doughnuts on the way.

She set David's phone on the counter and then bent down to Vera. "Good morning again, cutie."

Vera walked straight to her and completely surprised her by putting her little arms around her middle. Leona thought she maybe even felt a tiny squeeze. Then Vera talked. It was all incoherent babble, but judging by her big facial expressions and hand gestures, the one-year-old knew exactly what she was trying to say.

Leona answered every one of her coded sentences:

"Are you serious?"

"That's amazing!"

"Same, friend. Same."

It was the cutest conversation she'd ever had. She wished it didn't make her want to cry.

David cut in. "Why did Eden call you on my phone?"

Leona froze. So far, he hadn't asked the same question twice, so she hadn't had to come up with excuses. She said the first thing that came to mind. "After we finally reconnected, she thought it would be fun to get together outside of work."

That was kind of the same thing as Eden telling her to invite her out for coffee instead of interrupting her workday, Leona told herself.

"And she chose a Sunday morning to get together?" He raised an eyebrow.

"Yeah." Leona started gathering what she needed for her meeting, including Vera's diaper bag. Busying herself with motherhood was the easiest way to distract herself from marriage. She grabbed her purse and rifled through it, thankful to find cash in her wallet. She didn't know what would happen if she tried to use her credit card.

"That doesn't seem like the Eden I remember, choosing a time that would conflict with church," he pressed.

"That's why I have to pick up doughnuts on the way. As penance."

He tilted his head. "And why my phone?"

It was the third time he'd asked.

"I'm not sure." She didn't look at him. "Maybe after all this time she only has your number saved?"

"You didn't give her your new number when you met up a few days ago?"

She stopped packing and threw up her hands. "I can't find my phone, David. Remember? That's why Eden called me on your phone."

She wished she hadn't exploded, but she was even more annoyed when she saw David grinning. He had an actual smile on his face.

"Are you saying *the* Leona Warlon lost something that belongs to her?"

She glared, knowing how much he enjoyed teasing her about this topic. Usually, she'd play along. Right now, she didn't want to give him that satisfaction.

David seemed to notice and backed off. "But I thought your phone . . ." he trailed off.

Leona looked at him, waiting for the rest of his sentence. For the first time, she noticed the lines in his brow and dark circles under his eyes. She wondered if he was tired from the way they kept tiptoeing around their problems or from her icy responses. She hoped he was tired of his own lies most of all.

He studied her again, his lips tightening into a frown. "Leona, we really need to talk."

She looked down at her purse and tinkered with the keys to their SUV. "I have to meet Eden right now, and I'm already running late. You know how she is about being on time."

"It's been days since we were supposed to sit down together," he pressed. "I've given you plenty of space after your . . . breakdown at dinner the other night."

He didn't even have the vocabulary for "panic attack," she thought. She was jealous of a few things in this version of her life—the obvious one being Vera—but her list also included the lack of crippling anxiety and panic attacks that snuck up on her in World #1. She rubbed the tender muscles in her neck.

David put his hands on the counter and leaned forward. "Please promise me you will prioritize this today. We can even wait until after Vera's in bed tonight if you'd prefer."

She was about to protest, but as angry as she was at him, the pleading in his eyes stopped her. "Okay," she agreed.

"Okay?" he asked again, his inflection full of hope.

"Okay," she emphasized. "After Vera's in bed, we'll talk."

David appeared relieved for a moment, until another question popped out of his mouth. "Does this mean you're not going to your workout class this morning? If you're meeting Eden, I mean?"

Leona didn't know what he was talking about, and she couldn't help but scoff internally at the thought of her working out in a room full of people. "No. I'm not sure how long this meeting will take."

David looked away, but a smile was tugging at the corner of his mouth.

Leona continued prepping Vera's diaper bag.

"Let me keep her while you're out," he offered. "That will give you a chance to focus on Eden without this adorable distraction." He picked up Vera, who was tugging on the ankles of his sweatpants.

Alarm bells went off in her head. She knew it wasn't realistic to spend every waking moment with Vera, but this was how grief messed with her. It made her want to smother those she loved while she could, before she was sitting next to their graves.

David was right, of course. It didn't make sense to drag a fifteen-month-old who needed naps to a place not designed for children. But keeping Vera with her was also the easiest way to satisfy her inner anger against him.

She let go of the diaper bag. "I'll leave her here. And when I'm done visiting with Eden, I'll come straight home." She bit her tongue to keep from adding "to Vera." She'd come straight home to Vera.

Vera squirmed to be let down and then ran out of the room after whatever suddenly struck her fancy. Leona felt an ache to follow her but remained in place.

David, on the other hand, crossed the kitchen until he was standing right in front of Leona. He placed his hands on her shoulders.

She sucked in a breath, thrown off by his sudden closeness.

He pushed a loose lock of hair away from her collarbone and leaned in. "I'm so glad we finally get to talk later."

The skin where his fingertips grazed her neck tingled.

Through the strangeness of the past few days, she'd forgotten about the power of physical attraction. She looked at her husband or, rather, Husband #2. Though his hair was cut shorter than her David's, his curls were still long enough to get matted into morning hair. Which, on him, looked good. His eyes—strikingly dark—drew her in. He smelled like an intoxicating mixture of cedarwood, sage, and lime. Compared to one short minute ago, she was confused about her feelings for him. She felt a familiar flicker of warmth.

If she had her journal, she'd write, *Are you genuine? Or a genuinely good actor?*

Suddenly, she remembered she had only thirty-two minutes to buy doughnuts and get across the city. She pushed through her peaked senses and took a slow step back. The next two hours of her life were too important.

"I . . . I have to go," she fumbled.

David nodded.

She could feel him watching her leave.

THE "DOWNTOWN" EDEN was referring to was actually in a neighborhood ten minutes north of Leona's House #2. There was an acupuncture wellness center, a boutique med spa, a fine jeweler, two Persian rug galleries, and many other luxury storefronts, including an artisan bakery. The term *artisan* could mean a lot of things—whole ingredients, ethically made, environmentally friendly—but Leona had always associated it with "expensive." Charging five dollars for one circular piece of baked dough was offensive when fifteen dollars could buy an entire custom birthday cake from Walmart.

Leona thought she was getting close to the bakery, but when she looked at the line of storefronts she was driving by, she noticed something that made her heart leap into her throat. She slammed on her brakes and swerved into one of the few remaining diagonal parking spots on the right side of the road.

The convertible behind her, already driving on her tail, laid on his horn as he sped around her. She jumped out of the car and stared at the sign. She couldn't believe it: Krissy's Gym. A wave of panic washed over her body.

Last night, she learned that at least thirty-one parents in the city of Milwaukee had named their daughter Krissy. She wasn't proud of the social media stalking she'd committed on the laptop, but she was also disappointed that in the process she hadn't discovered a business this close to home with the name Krissy on it.

She knew she would be late if she detoured into Krissy's Gym, but she had to go inside. The text she had discovered mentioned sweating together, and this was a gym named after a Krissy. Any nimrod detective on this case would put those two clues together. She had to go in and see the woman who was texting suggestive messages to her husband.

Besides, she was perfectly dressed for the occasion, she thought, remembering her joggers and trendy tank top.

Leona didn't know what she would do when she went inside, but she knew she already hated Krissy. She pictured a tiny, toned woman wearing a sports bra and short shorts, like some sort of fitness Barbie.

She took a deep breath and pulled open the front door. Inside, she found herself standing in an open room of adults who were stretching in front of a wall that was filled with—in Leona's opinion—too many mirrors. Techno music was blasting.

Leona felt like she was coming down with a sudden case of asthma.

"Hey, girly! You're just in time!" the peppy instructor said into her microphone, singling Leona out and sending everyone's looks her way. "Jump on in!"

The instructor was wearing a sports bra and even shorter shorts than Leona had first imagined. Leona still had no plan, so she decided the best course of action was to join in and observe. She went to the back row where nobody could see her, even though it felt like everyone was still watching her in the mirror.

An assistant trainer dropped a set of dumbbells at her feet.

Leona considered asking the woman on her left if it was okay to skip the parts that required heavy lifting. But when she glanced her way, the woman gave her a sharp look.

Leona began stretching, and much to her pleasant surprise, she was handling the pace well, able to keep up with the brisk "five-six-seven-eight and other side!"

"Way to go, Denise!" the instructor yelled at the woman next to Leona.

The music sped up and the instructor shouted even louder words into the microphone. It was sensory overload, and Leona didn't know how this could relieve anyone's stress. She looked to her right to see how others in the room were handling the workout so far. The guy next to her was wearing a cut-off T-shirt and had large sweat rings around his chest, armpits, and stomach.

The instructor pointed at him next. "You know when you step in my gym, I'm going to make you sweat! Isn't that right, Brock?"

Brock wiped his brow with his arm and then gave her two thumbs up.

"That's right," the instructor yelled. "Krissy isn't going to let you off the hook!"

Krissy, Leona fumed. There she was in the flesh. In so much skinny flesh, barely covered by bits of polyester. Speaking in third person.

Krissy yelled out the names of different stretches. Leona felt herself losing focus on her own movements; instead she thought about the derogatory names she wanted to yell back at the woman leading them at the front of the room.

The stretches became more dynamic, and Leona's heart rate

skyrocketed. They were only stepping side to side while crossing their arms, but it required more coordination than she was capable of.

"I don't care if it's Sunday! You! Are! Going! To! Work!"

Leona glared at Krissy.

Krissy pointed at her. "I love your intensity today!"

It was getting harder to multitask between hating Krissy and performing the "power skip plus reach!" She looked at herself in the mirror, which confirmed she was no longer keeping up with the rest of the class. Three rows up, a man stared at her reflection, smiling. He reminded her of someone, but she couldn't put a name to his face.

"That was the easy part! Now, let's see what you got!" Krissy yelled.

The music picked up the pace one more time, and Krissy led the class through a mix of aerobic exercises and strength challenges.

"Squat jumps!"

"Planks!"

"Mountain climbers!"

"Dumbbell presses!"

When she yelled "Burpees!" Leona thought she might burp her morning coffee all over the floor. She looked in the mirror again. The same guy was looking at her, but he wasn't smiling anymore. Her lack of coordination must have had a negative effect on him too.

Krissy's movements started covering more ground. She yelled, "Side shuffle to the right!" but Leona's brain didn't compute fast enough. She sent her body left, bumping into Denise's sharp elbows, and received another scowl.

She struggled, but she was able to regain her balance right as Krissy yelled, "Side shuffle to the left!"

Again, she wasn't ready, and Brock barreled into her.

It all happened so quickly, but in slow motion it looked like this: Leona face-planted into Brock's hairy upper arm. The sweat dripping from his body smeared all over her face. Two of his body hairs detached from his arm and adhered themselves with the glue of his perspiration to her cheek. And finally, the combination of his large mass multiplied by the high speed at which he side shuffled hurled her entire body to the ground.

In fast motion: She ricocheted off him like a pinball.

Leona stayed on the ground, disoriented and out of breath. She hated to admit it, but she was far more comfortable down there than she was exercising upright.

A crowd began to gather around her. Brock was the closest, and he bent down over her to apologize for what wasn't even his fault. "Sorry! I'm so sorry!" he repeated a few times. "I thought Krissy said go left, so I was just trying to shuffle like she said. But maybe I did it wrong?"

As he loomed over her, a large bead of his sweat fell onto her forehead.

"Oh no! I'm so sorry," he apologized again.

Next to him, Denise rolled her eyes.

"I'm just . . . going to . . . clean myself up in the bathroom," Brock excused himself, clearly mortified.

Krissy budged into the circle next. "Are you okay, girly?"

Leona felt her embarrassment being overcome by a fresh wave of fury. She was going to do it. She was going to let Krissy have it. "Please, don't call me—"

"Leona," someone interrupted. The crowd seemed to part for him as he came in close and bent down next to her. "How's the view from down there?"

It was the guy she'd caught watching her in the mirror earlier. Leona knew there might be plenty of people in World #2 who knew her even though she did not know them. But it was still weird to hear a stranger call her by name.

He held out his hand, which she took. Between him pulling and her pushing, she got up off the floor. Now that her body was forced to change positions, her injuries throbbed.

The man brought his hand up toward her face, then plucked something off her cheek—one of Brock's stray hairs. Then he patted her on the butt. With a hand that communicated a little more than "Go team."

"Do I know you?" she asked, wiping away the invisible imprint he'd left.

Krissy laughed, but Leona thought there was an edge to it.

The trainer crossed her arms and stuck out her hip. "Know him? The way the two of you act around each other, I thought you were dating." The words traveled through Krissy's microphone and amplified tenfold over the loudspeaker.

Leona blushed and looked at the man to see his reaction.

He stood smug, and he didn't deny Krissy's accusations.

"I'm married," Leona said.

Krissy arched a pretty eyebrow. "Mm-hmm."

Leona blinked, not sure what to say. What to do. She needed a second to think.

Krissy uncrossed her arms. Covering her microphone, she whispered to Leona, "Why don't you go outside for some fresh air? I have a class to run." She turned on her heels and jogged back to her platform at the front of the room, shouting the whole way, "Okay, people! That show is over, so let's get back to the gun show! PUSH-UPS!"

The music turned back onto blasting.

Leona agreed, push-up time was the perfect time to exit. She walked outside and stood facing the street, frozen in place. The last twenty minutes flipped everything she thought she knew upside down.

Krissy said she thought Leona and that guy were dating. And Leona still didn't know why he looked so familiar.

"I think you made Brock cry back there," came his voice from behind her.

Leona didn't want to turn around. She was terrified to face the truth. She wanted to climb into her car without looking back.

"Such a nice guy too," he teased her. "He'll probably feel awful about it until next week's class."

She nodded, feeling stuck in this man's expectation that she would be friendly toward him. "I can be a bit of a bully sometimes," she joked, but her words came out flat.

Leona sighed, taking a moment of silence for Brock. For Denise too, and whatever might be causing her midlife rage.

"You've been avoiding me," the guy said.

She continued staring straight ahead.

"You haven't texted me back or come to class."

She could sense him walking closer. Her insides deflated.

"Why aren't you talking to me, Leona? Did you fall on your head back there or something?" He put his hand on her shoulder, the same shoulder David had held that morning.

She flinched and took a step away. But she also made herself turn to look at him. He might not be her mistake, but she was the one currently facing the consequences.

The guy certainly wasn't horrible to look at. She studied him, more and more convinced she knew him from somewhere. Her eyes widened in horror when she finally remembered.

"Derek." It came out almost as a growl. "Derek Carter."

"Um . . . yes? That's me." Derek laughed.

The sound grated her ears.

Derek was the one boyfriend she'd had in high school. Neither Eden nor Rose cared for him, but she went overboard, pouring herself into him anyway. He broke up with her, and less than a week later he was in the halls holding hands with their classmate Janet. Eden was gracious enough to let Leona cry on her shoulder and say only one time, "I warned you he's fake."

Leona couldn't believe this entanglement—emotional affair, she corrected, not wanting to downplay it now that she was the one involved—was with Derek.

"You look so different than I remember," she said, then covered her mouth with her hand. She wasn't supposed to say things like that out loud.

Derek frowned. "From when, the last time you saw me?"

He smiled. He had a beautiful, wicked smile. "Or are you reminiscing about that hot emo look I used to rock in high school?"

Leona blushed, which seemed to satisfy his confusion.

She remembered the look he was referring to—his painted nails, the white-and-black checkered book bag, the skull-and-crossbones stickers on everything he owned. For a while, he even dyed his hair blue and had a lip ring. He was so independent and mysterious, completely uninterested in the throwback jerseys and matching Jordans their classmates were into at the time. Yes, a long time ago she dug that look.

Now his hair was cut short with a high fade and hard part—all business. And he was here, at Krissy's Gym, working out in tiny pieces of polyester like their instructor.

Krissy.

Everything was hitting Leona at once. One of the reasons she hired a Bella Luna Nanny was so she could "engage in self-care," and workout classes might fall under that category for some people. If she was the one with connections to Krissy's Gym, then the phone in the office was actually hers. "Hers" in this version of her life.

How did she miss that?

The phone David handed her this morning also had a black case, so it would have been easy for her to mistake one for the other. Derek must have been programmed as "Krissy" to keep David off her trail.

She wondered what came first: Derek or the gym? Within the bigger picture of whatever this was, it didn't really matter.

She needed answers, and she needed them now. She turned to Derek, who was eyeing her as she mentally gathered the pieces of this life. "Derek, I need your help. I need you to pretend we haven't seen each other since . . . let's say . . . fifteen years ago. So, there's a lot I don't know about us."

Derek leaned back and frowned.

It was just like they were back in high school, she thought. He abruptly broke up with her back then, and it was possible he still backed away from anything more complicated than pleasure. If she burdened him too quickly, he might run the other way.

Derek surprised her by leaning in again. "Wait. Are you asking me to do a little bit of role-play?" He wormed his eyebrows up and down.

Leona pinched the bridge of her nose. She couldn't believe this guy, but this was probably the only way to reach him for the answers she needed.

"Sure, Derek. Let's role-play. I'm an . . . adult female with Alzheimer's."

Derek turned up his nose.

"And you're . . . you're a punk rocker named . . . Eric." She had no sexy ideas, so she went with the first rhyme that came to her head. She just hoped he'd take the bait.

He thought about it for a second. "Okay. I'll play your little game." He gave her a smoldering gaze and deepened his voice. "Hello, I'm Eric. What's your name?"

"Hi, I'm Leona," she said with no steam. "Did you recently text me that you 'missed sweating with my bod'?" She almost gagged on the words as she said them.

Derek seemed unimpressed by her role-playing skills, but he simpered at her question. "Guilty."

She clenched her jaw. This interrogation was not starting out well.

"Since high school, where did we first cross paths again?"

"Krissy's Gym."

"How long have you and I been"—she tripped over how to ask the question—"flirting with each other?"

Derek puffed out his chest. "Seems like you've been into me ever since the first class you came to."

"And how long ago was that?" she asked.

"I don't know, eight months? When Krissy made everyone say why they joined, you said you had a baby and your mother-in-law wanted you to take care of the extra pounds. You didn't seem thrilled to be there."

Delaney, Leona seethed. Forever the thorn in her side.

"Although"—Derek scanned her—"it looks like some of those pounds you shed might have come back."

Leona was instantly enraged. She reverted to Mrs. Warlon, high school English teacher, and pointed her finger at him. "You are not invited to comment on my body. Ever."

Derek's eyes widened. "Did you just change roles?"

Eight months. Eight months she'd spent messing around with this guy. She wondered what would ever push her toward him.

She looked down at her feet, unready to ask the next question. Derek wasn't wearing any shoes.

"Have we ever," she hesitated, "spent time together outside of class?"

"I've had to beg," Derek said, "but yeah. Sometimes we've gone out for a coffee, talked for a while."

She couldn't imagine what they'd talk about.

Derek cooled his charm and got serious. "It's been nice being with someone who grew up . . . not around here, you know?"

That hit her; his reasoning made sense. They knew where each other came from. Derek was an escape for her; someone she could commiserate with about this place that was lovely on the outside but so different from what they knew as normal. She wondered what brought him here, if he was truly one of the rare Cinderella stories Hollywood loved to make movies about.

She was about to ask him.

Then Derek said, "Even with the baby weight, I think you've gotten hotter since high school."

She shook her head. It didn't matter if they had a shared history. As far as she knew, Derek had cheated on every girl he had ever dated. Janet didn't last more than three weeks before he moved on to the next one. And now, he was into women who were also being unfaithful.

She didn't want to ask, but she couldn't leave without knowing. "Have we ever done . . . anything else?"

Derek stood taller. "Well, if we're finally going to stop beating around the bush, then no." He stepped toward her, too close, and reached for her hips. "But I wouldn't be sad if one thing led to another."

She swatted his hands away, grateful to be a stranger to this version of her life. It made her next words easy to say.

"This"—she pointed between the two of them—"whatever this is, is over. I am happily married. Well, not super happily obviously, but that's not the point," she stuttered, balling her hands into fists. "I'm sorry if I led you to believe this could turn into anything."

Derek scowled. Whatever allure she may have held over him a few minutes ago seemed to vanish.

She turned toward her SUV. She had a few artisan doughnuts to buy and a lot of explaining to do. "Maybe you and Krissy would be a better fit," she offered.

"Krissy?" Derek yelled after her. "Been there, done that!"

Leona didn't give him the satisfaction of turning back around. However, as she was climbing into her vehicle, she did yell back, "The contraction *it's* has an apostrophe!"

And she slammed the door.

CHAPTER 17

Three Years Ago

MONTHS AFTER HER DOCTOR'S APPOINTMENT, LEONA stood in her kitchen on a rare weekday off from school, blending together a concoction that was supposed to naturally boost her fertility.

It felt like she was trying to create a magical potion. An ineffective, worthless potion with avocado, raw honey, flaxseed, frozen fruit, and a protein powder containing vitamins A, B6, B9, B12, D, and E as well as omega-3, selenium, and zinc. At first, she thought she would get used to the chalky texture of this daily practice, but in reality, she learned it was better gulped down than slowly sipped.

With all the conscious eating, walking, and stretching, she was in the healthiest shape she'd ever been in. Too bad she was only a shell of herself on the inside.

The blender stopped whirring, and Leona heard a knock on the front door. She wasn't expecting anyone, and David was long gone to the lab. Grabbing her smoothie, she made her way from the kitchen at the back of the house to the front door to see who it was.

Standing on her front porch, alive and in person, was her sister.

Rose didn't look as rough around the edges as Leona was used to seeing her. She was more stylishly edgy, wearing a loose button-up shirt and skinny jeans. Her plum brown hair was cut into a sleek shoulder-length bob, and her eyes were no longer outlined with an angry pencil. Her natural features—which were all Evelyn's—spoke for themselves, though she did still have on her favorite shade of lipstick, a mauvy maroon.

It had been almost a year since she'd seen her last and nearly eight months since they'd talked beyond a few "are you alive" texts. Leona was so excited to see her, she forgot to scold her for never calling her back.

"Rose!" she squealed, quickly moving to set the smoothie on the coffee table so she wouldn't spill it all over her sister.

"Hey, Leona." Rose looked down and shuffled her shoe.

"This is the best surprise ever! I can't believe you're here!" Leona took her hand and pulled her inside. She wanted to hear all about Rose's classes, talk about how Dad was doing, and brag about David and Eden's research. She wanted to dish about her students and vent about how infertility was killing her. And then, she wanted to talk about nothing important at all—just like when they were little girls, giggling about a funny movie they'd watched before falling asleep in the bed they shared.

She turned to Rose. "I can't wait to catch up with you, but before I heat some water for tea, let me hug you—"

Leona pulled Rose close, and that was when she felt it—something between them. A firm, round bump. Hidden by the optical illusion of Rose's flowy shirt.

The thrill of seeing her long-lost sister was overcome by turbulent shock. She crossed her arms and looked Rose up and down. Rose was standing on their entryway rug, which was designed to look like the periodic table of elements and had words printed on it that said *Ah! The element of surprise.*

She stared at Rose's pregnant belly, speechless.

"I didn't want to say anything," Rose began. "I know how much you and David want . . ." She trailed off, like she realized that whatever she said wouldn't actually help.

Leona needed space; she needed air. When her head stopped spinning enough to take in the news, she moved from shock into the next stage of grief: asking a million questions.

"What happened? Are you okay? What—how?" Each one came out in breathy disbelief. She couldn't even look at Rose when she asked them.

Rose chuckled. "I think you know how this happens."

She was not amused. "I'm not asking how babies are made, Rose. I'm asking you how your baby was made."

Before Rose could answer, Leona added, "How is Dad going to react when he finds out?"

She assumed Rose wouldn't make an effort to inform Evelyn she was going to be a grandmother. Even the thought of Rose making Evelyn a grandmother felt like a kick to Leona's womb. They could both agree Evelyn would make a second-rate grandma, but Leona was the one trying to give her the first grandchild.

Rose raised her eyebrows. "Well . . ."

Leona watched her for a second, then narrowed her eyes. "Wait, Dad already knows?"

Her sister nodded.

Leona knew she was supposed to show compassion for everything Rose had been through, whatever it was she'd been through until now. But all she felt was a lot of sorriness for herself.

"Leona, I'm sorry," Rose made a second effort to explain. "There's been so much going on and—"

"How would you even know what's been going on?" Leona interrupted.

Rose took a step toward her. "I know I haven't called you recently, but—"

"Do you even know who the father is?" The question slipped out of Leona's mouth before she could bite it back. She took a step farther away from Rose and collapsed onto the couch.

Rose seemed hurt by the question, but she didn't fight back. Whatever riled her up so easily in years past seemed absent.

That *fighter* lower back tattoo must have worn off, Leona thought.

Past her shock and out of questions, she moved on to another stage of grief: blistering rage. She didn't know what she should be the angriest about—Rose dropping off the face of the earth over the past two years or Rose not telling her she was pregnant. Or Rose, her little, uncommitted sister conceiving a baby when she couldn't.

"Leona, if you would just let me talk—"

"Let you talk?" Leona yelled. "I've been begging you to talk to me for eight months. I wanted to talk to you, but you weren't here and you didn't answer your phone."

She looked at Rose. Her sister's hand was cradling the bottom of her belly, gently holding—and protecting—whoever was inside.

"It's like watching an oxymoron. My angry mess of a sister, who partied away years of her life and couldn't hold down a basic job, being motherly." Leona couldn't believe the words coming out of her own mouth.

Rose gasped.

There was something about her sister's softened edges, the way motherhood looked natural on her, that outraged Leona. She knew she was getting worked up, which was bad for her stress levels, which was bad for fertility. She turned away so she would have the bravery to keep being mean.

"I've been trying for almost two years to have a baby with my husband. I've needed you. Not that you couldn't go to art school or chase your dreams—not that. But you're my sister, Rose, and I needed you. A simple text. A phone call every once in a while. And you're off . . . doing this."

She expected Rose to start yelling back, to unleash her pain, to let her short fuse finally blow, but she didn't. It was like the two of them had reversed roles. Now Rose was the sad one. Leona, the angry one.

Leona got off the couch, her fury still flaring hot. She stomped over to where her smoothie sat on the coffee table and grabbed it. "I've been drinking these disgusting drinks and taking stupid walks and staying away from coffee. Do you know how hard it is to teach a room full of teenagers without a lick of caffeine in your veins? I've been doing all the right things—everything I'm supposed to do. And yet, here we are. I'm not supposed to be an aunt. I'm supposed to be a *mom.*"

She looked down at her smoothie one more time, and then, screaming as loud as she could, hurled the plastic cup across the room. It smashed into the wall and broke into pieces, leaving a brown splatter. The thick sludge began to run down the wall.

Leona crumpled to the floor. She wasn't judging Rose for how she ended up pregnant, even though she knew that was exactly how she sounded. She was broken at the unfairness of it all. She'd been trying to have a baby for what felt like forever, and here her sister was, making one by accident.

Leona hoped this would be the part when they finally talked through everything, when they apologized to each other. But she also knew they'd never been taught how. Growing up, she and Rose got over being mad at each other by getting mad at Evelyn together.

As it turned out, anger wasn't a strong enough tie to bind.

She wanted Rose to fight again, to weather the storm of her

rage and push herself back into Leona's life. But Leona didn't ask. Her sorrow had made her tired, and she decided humility was too exhausting of a sacrifice to pile on.

So, Rose left through the same door she came in. And Leona didn't go after her.

After the baby was born, their dad was the one who told Leona.

CHAPTER 18

Present Day

LEONA HANDED THE BOX OF DOUGHNUTS TO EDEN. "I bought a half dozen extra because I'm so late. I'm really sorry. I got caught up with . . . something."

She didn't want to think about what just unfolded at Krissy's Gym. She wanted to compartmentalize it into a part of her brain where it would remain under lock and key until she got through this important meeting in Eden's office at BioThrive. The knot in her chest reminded her brain that would be easier said than done.

Leona turned to Carl, planning to thank him profusely for his time.

He was already right next to her, grabbing her hand and shaking it. "Thank you so much for your time, Mrs. Warlon. It is thrilling to be able to share my ample knowledge regarding the many-worlds interpretation of quantum mechanics and—"

"Please slow down, Elmer Imes," Eden interrupted. "I think we need a little artisan magic before we're ready for your TED Talk."

"I'm letting my excitement get the best of me." Carl released

Leona's hand and took a step back. "It is truly an honor to meet you. Carl welcomes you to this universe."

Carl had frizzy light brown hair that was warped into the shape of an hourglass by the strap of his safety goggles. The goggles rested on his pearly forehead while a pair of orange-rimmed prescription glasses sat on the bridge of his nose.

Leona would take all the excitement and enthusiasm and knowledge he had to offer. "Thank you so much, Dr. . . . ?"

He clasped his hands together and slowly nodded. "You may call me Carl."

Eden turned from the files she was moving on her desk. "You went to school for a decade, and you don't want the title you outright earned?"

He adjusted the goggles on his brow. "My last name is Flatus."

Eden's eyes widened. She put a hand over her chest like she was having a heart attack.

"Imagine the fun my AP Chemistry class had with that," he said to Eden. "They called me ChemiCarl Flatus."

Leona looked around, waiting for understanding to drop out of the sky because she didn't get the punch line. She leaned over to Eden and started to ask, "What does that mean"

But Eden grabbed her elbow and whispered, "*Flatus* is Latin for 'fart.'"

Leona turned to Carl and said, "'Carl' it is."

Eden fetched a dry-erase marker from her desk and brought it to Carl, then nodded at the whiteboard wall of her office. "Please, Carl. Make it make sense for us."

Leona felt nervous again. How could anyone, even the two highly educated people with her in this office, explain her unbelievable circumstances? Where would Carl even begin?

For over twenty minutes, he gave an animated lecture about the existence of many universes. Specifically, the many-worlds interpretation of quantum *blah, blah, blah.* Even after all that,

Leona still didn't understand any of the graphs or Greek symbols sprawling across the whiteboard. She still had no idea how she got here. The only thing she learned was a grammatical term. The plural form of universe was *multiverse*.

Even Eden was lost. She shoved another bite of doughnut into her mouth and muttered under her breath, "This is why I research medicine. A plus B eventually equals C for 'cure.' This is just nonsense."

Leona whispered back, "I studied English, but I'm pretty sure that's not the language he's speaking."

She was overwhelmed. Storming around in her brain was everything that went down with Derek, how uncomfortable she was away from Vera, and now, the burden of whatever Carl was trying to teach her about how in the world she got from her life into the life she was visiting now. Her problems were suppressed but piling on without any resolutions. And her insides were threatening to detonate.

She missed her safe place. David.

Carl held his elbow in one hand and used the other to tap his chin. "I'm not sure this is the best way to explain such sophisticated subject matter, but have you seen any of Hollywood's recent superhero movies?"

Eden and Leona answered at the same time:

"Yes."

"Not really."

Leona looked at Eden in disbelief. "Yes? I thought a long time ago you said you didn't have time for any superhero nonsense. Or any nonsense in general."

Eden rolled her eyes. "Ugh, I know. But my fiancé Tamaree is really into them, so now I've seen all of them. In chronological order. I admit, I think they're pretty entertaining too."

"David loves all those movies too." Saying his name sent a pang through her heart. "The problem is that he always starts them way too late at night. I have such good intentions to watch them with him but end up falling asleep on the couch fifteen minutes in."

"Spoken like someone who's no longer in her twenties." Eden laughed.

"But, speaking of Tamaree," Leona said, "I have a lot of questions I'm dying to ask you."

Eden's smile radiated. "And I can't wait to answer all of them. He's the best—"

"Ladies?" Carl interjected.

Leona and Eden glanced at him.

Eden folded her hands into her lap and reverted her attention. "We're sorry, Carl. Please continue."

Carl nodded. "My point is, the idea of existing universes with different versions of your life is not new. Many science fiction movies play off this idea, and relevant scientists have written theories about it." He paced in front of the whiteboard. "The problem is that there's little evidence for or against these theories because it's so hard to observe and experiment. A theory isn't necessarily true only because it can't be disproven."

Leona finally understood a sentence that came out of his mouth.

"However, according to what Dr. Williams told me when we spoke on the phone, you claim to have a very different life from this one. You live and work on the north side instead of in one of Milwaukee's lakeshore neighborhoods. Your husband works at BioThrive with Eden. And your daughter . . ." he faltered. "It's just that . . . there's a lot of evidence that you are not the same woman she knows as Leona."

"*Knew,*" Eden corrected. "Leona hasn't been a part of my life for a long time." She leaned her shoulder into Leona and said, "It's not your fault."

She shrugged. "It's okay. I'm mad at me about a few things right now."

They turned back to Carl.

His excitement was turning jittery. "What I'm saying is, these theories are not extraordinary, Mrs. Warlon. *You* are. You are the evidence."

She wished she could reciprocate his excitement, but too many thoughts were swirling around in her head to get excited about her monumental presence.

"But how? And why?" was all she could think to ask.

"That's where scientists often disagree," Carl said. "In fact, one physicist wrote nine different ways a new universe might be formed."

Leona sucked in a breath. Over the past few days, she hadn't let herself dwell on the idea that she might not be able to get home. She also hadn't let herself dwell on the fact that she might have to say goodbye to Vera again. She'd made a habit of not dwelling on much of anything except for that sweet little girl. But hearing Carl say that out loud—that it might be impossible to understand how she got here and how to get home—was like taking a sucker punch.

Eden squeezed Leona's shoulder, then spoke up. "You are all we have, Carl. What do you think?"

"As I was saying earlier," he continued, "I've come to adhere to what's called the 'quantum multiverse' theory. Every time a life-changing event occurs or decision is made, a new universe is created with another version of yourself that reflects the outcome of that decision."

Eden crossed her arms and squinted. "So, let me get this straight. Your theory is that every time something big happens, bang! A whole new world? A whole new you?"

Carl nodded. "Precisely. A new world reflecting the new trajectory of that person's life. With a new person living out that trajectory."

Eden rocketed past instruction into personal application. "You're saying there's a different world out there where a different Dr. Eden Williams married Ryan?"

Carl looked at Leona for help.

Leona whispered to Eden, "I don't think he knows who Ryan is. Also, what happened between you two? As far as I remember, you were pretty hot for each other. Most of the time."

Eden rolled her eyes. "It's a long story, but the short version is that if Ryan was in your shoes, one of the moments his life split into another world was when he let his ego take over again. My aspirations were too much for him. He was always trying to make me small so I could fit into his comfortable little box. Tamaree couldn't be more different than Ryan in that regard." She held up the sparkly band on her left hand. "He's a real one, and he even gave me this shiny friend to keep me company. Till death do us part."

Leona let out the scream a supportive best friend makes during moments like this, taking Eden's hand so she could closely examine the ring. "It's gorgeous, Eden! I'm so happy for you."

She kept it to herself that in World #1, Ryan let his ego go.

Eden circled back to the multiverse. "I know the science on this is still developing, but my brain can hardly handle the philosophical implications. Like, isn't this saying our choices literally alter the universe?"

Leona countered based on her own experiences. "But there are still some key similarities between my life and this one. I married David. I have a daughter named Vera. Eden was one of my closest friends growing up. If these fundamental pieces remain the same, do we actually have that much control over where we end up?"

"True." Eden nodded.

Carl seemed to be taking that in too.

"I also wonder how people would react if this became common knowledge," Eden added. "Would they be paralyzed from making any decisions, knowing they could choose themselves into a worse world?"

Leona sighed. "Or would they have a sense of meaninglessness? Because they try to make the right choices but still can't control the bad things they've done or the bad things happening to them?"

Eden glanced at her.

Leona took a deep breath. She could tell she was dragging down the room, raining on the parade of this philosophical conversation. She tried to push her thoughts into a more positive place. "Maybe there are some pros to this." She folded her hands in her lap. "It might be kind of nice to know there are worlds out there where it's easier to do the right thing."

Eden agreed, "Yes, that would be fantastic. Maybe in another life, Vel Phillips got to spend less time fighting housing discrimination and more time . . . I don't know . . . watching baseball?"

"Which brings up the debate over how many choices a person actually has based on their neighborhood or any other number of demographics," Leona added.

"Dang, Carl," Eden exclaimed. "You're opening up quite the can of worms with all of this."

Carl beamed. "That's why physics is so remarkable. I get to study tiny molecules while unearthing the universe's biggest philosophical questions."

"Well, I'll be taking these questions with me back to Bible study," Eden declared. "You're welcome to join, Carl. Wednesdays at seven."

Carl placed a hand on his heart and nodded.

"I have a less philosophical question," Leona spoke up. "Why did my purse come with me but my phone didn't? It's possible my keys and ID were left behind too."

"That's fascinating, isn't it?" Carl re-intensified. "These are the rules nobody knows. It's possible your purse wouldn't upset the dynamics of this universe as much as some of the contents in it, such as your phone. Especially today when our phones hold so much of our personal lives in them."

"But I still need to know *how*," Leona said. "Everything you've told me explains what happened, but I need to know how I got here."

Carl's glee faded. He cleared his throat. "We are unsure how the multiverse forms or interacts within itself. Some scientists believe these worlds are like bubbles, expanding and bouncing off each other. Others envision a line graph constantly splitting off from itself. Still others picture the multiverse forming separate waves of time collapsing onto one another to form a single reality."

Suddenly, Leona lost focus of her surroundings. She felt like the room was starting to spin.

He continued, "What you've been through suggests your world and this world intersected. Even though your life previously broke away from this one, the two overlapped again because of circumstances that created a door between worlds. You, Leona—and *this* world's version of you—didn't know you were walking through that door."

Leona willed herself to focus in on Carl, hoping she was starting to get it. "So, you're saying that at some point in my life, a choice *I* made set the course of my life on a different trajectory from this one. A completely new life and a completely different Leona was made."

Carl nodded.

"And you're saying it's possible these two different trajectories overlapped again because of some random set of similar circumstances."

He nodded again.

"Is it possible the place we overlapped and 'opened a door' could be somewhere as simple as a restaurant?"

"Yes."

Leona whispered out loud to herself, "Bartolotta's."

Eden looked at her, impressed. "Bartolotta's? Fancy."

The questions were rolling off her tongue, and each of Carl's answers were building a foundation of understanding. But Leona didn't want to hear the answer to the next one. "And what you're also saying is that there is another version of me out there. Another Leona who belongs to *this* world. This world I'm visiting right now."

Carl nodded.

"So, I'm not just jumping from one timeline to the next all by myself, but switching places with myself from another timeline. With . . . let's call her . . . Leona #2."

"Yes," Carl answered. "That is what I'm saying."

"Which means, the version of me from *this* world is probably in the life I left behind."

"Precisely."

The tension in her neck started to flare up again.

Eden jumped in. "But how are you supposed to communicate with the other version of yourself to switch back?"

"The same physicists who support these theories also believe it's impossible to cross over into a different existence," Carl explained. "They theorize these worlds split and go their own ways and that you'd have to travel even faster than the speed of light to cross over into a different reality." He hesitated. "Which . . . isn't something humans are capable of."

Leona gasped. "But then how . . ."

She couldn't finish her sentence.

A heavy silence fell across the office, like everyone sensed the weight of her circumstances.

"I do have one hunch," Carl said, "but it doesn't involve communicating with the version of yourself that you switched places with."

Eden grabbed Leona's shoulders and shook her. "You hear that, Leona? Where there's a Carl, there's a way!"

Carl took to the whiteboard again.

Leona knew she should be completely tuned in to his teaching. The trajectory of her life depended on it. But her mind was elsewhere, everywhere.

It was with David, the one with whom she'd weathered sorrow. And it was here, with Vera. Depending on Carl's hunch, she could go back to a life with her husband, or she could have a life here with her daughter.

Her mind spun anxious poetry:

I'm stuck
between
you
and us.
You, my baby.
Us, my love.

One part of Carl's theory made sense to her. He'd said, "You can try creating a door at the place where you made a life changing decision. A decision that split your life off from this one."

Leona closed her eyes and inhaled. She knew exactly where that door was.

"But it's up to you, Leona," Carl said. "You're the one who has to choose if you're going to even try to go home. Or simply stay here."

CHAPTER 19

Two Years Ago

LEONA'S THIRTY-SEVENTH PREGNANCY TEST WAS POSItive. She didn't believe it, so she took another test. Number thirty-eight was positive too. She stared at the two tests sitting next to the sink, heart pounding.

"David!" she screamed.

He came running to the bathroom. He looked terrified. "What's wrong?"

She pointed to the tests and then sank to the floor. She was already crying too hard to say anything else.

David stared at the tests for a long time. He blinked his eyes and looked at them again.

"Does this mean?" he asked.

She nodded, smiling through her tears.

"Are you serious? You're pregnant?"

She nodded again.

"You're pregnant. We're going to have a baby."

This time he didn't wait for an answer. He put his hands on his head and yelled. He then proceeded to dance in the doorframe of the bathroom.

She laughed. "I'm not quite sure what you'd call those moves, but it looks like the perfect dad dance to me."

David joined her on the floor and cried too.

BUT THREE YEARS of infertility had changed Leona, put some cracks in her heart. Which was why, when there was finally a baby growing inside of her womb, she couldn't let go of all the unsolicited advice and Google research she'd followed when she was trying to get pregnant. Now she followed it all to a point that was obsessive. She attributed it to motherhood—she was about to be responsible for another human being, and she wanted to start doing a lot more things in her life intentionally, on purpose. However, a medical professional might have labeled it anxiety manifesting itself as control.

Morning sickness wrecked her. There was no hiding from her colleagues or students that she was pregnant, especially when one of her ninth graders brought an egg salad sandwich into her classroom and she had to run to the trash can in the corner to throw up. She was also so tired she fell asleep during a staff meeting.

But Leona wouldn't let herself complain because she needed to be grateful and stay the course and follow all the rules for making this the healthiest pregnancy ever. She never took showers that were too hot. She avoided deli meat like it was an actual plague, and she yelled at David when he brought home his leftovers from Subway.

"Are you trying to poison me? I can practically smell the listeria in the air!"

David looked at her, not saying anything.

It wasn't until Leona heard her own huffing and puffing that she realized she was being illogical. Her shoulders drooped, and she covered her face with her hands.

"Let's go for a drive," he said gently.

He took her to the lakeshore—the place they first talked about wanting to become parents. The sun was setting west behind Milwaukee's cityscape, and the sky over the water blazed from pink to somber violet. Leona's thin jacket wasn't a match for Wisconsin's cool autumn breeze, so she huddled her back against David for warmth.

They were quiet for a long time, listening to the waves lap onto the sand.

"You can tell me I'm being ridiculous," she said, bracing herself for the confrontation she knew she needed.

"That's not why I wanted to come here," he said, chuckling into her ear and tightening his arms around her.

She patted one of his hands. "Really, it's fine. I can handle it."

"Okay, then. I wanted to come here so that . . ." He took a deep breath, then paused.

"Spit it out, David," she coaxed.

"I wanted to come here to ask if we could go to Jimmy John's for supper. Wow, I'm so glad I got that off my chest."

Leona shoved his arms off her while he laughed.

She whipped her head around to give him her most pointed teacher glare. When she saw his smile, she broke character. "You and your diseased deli meat can go to detention, Mr. Warlon."

He drew her close and kissed her softly. "Okay, Mrs. Warlon."

After a few more minutes of quiet, David said, "Leona, I wanted to come here so we could acknowledge how hard the past three years have been."

Her insides tightened.

"We've been so busy working and trying to have a baby and trying to 'stay positive,' that we haven't even taken the time to sit down and talk about how devastated we were for thirty-six months in a row. It wasn't only infertility but also what happened between you and Rose."

Rose. The ache reached deep inside Leona. She missed her sister.

"And now there's actually a baby, but you're miserable," David continued. "We wanted this good thing, and we have it, but it feels like morning sickness and bad gas."

"You can't blame your smelly digestion on my pregnancy."

"Shh." David put a finger over her mouth. "I just want you to know that I think it's okay if it feels hard to let go of all that disappointment and get excited. I get why you're trying to do everything perfectly and why you're acting a little . . ."

"Irrational?" She glanced back at him.

"Grieved," he corrected.

She'd never thought of it that way.

David tucked a loose strand of hair behind her ear. "I do hope, however, that after all the barfing and the gas, this gets a little more fun. The past three years have been pretty awful, but who knows, the next three could be pretty grand. Besides"—he held out his hand, gesturing toward the great expanse of water in front of them—"look at all we've been through so far. If we can get through this, we can get through anything."

A wave of inexplicable calm washed over Leona. For every time she'd cried out in anger over the past thirty-six months, she'd also had a moment of gratitude for her husband. This was what it felt like to be known, for better or worse.

"You know, Leona"—his tone turned upbeat—"I recently read something really inspiring that feels appropriate to share considering our current circumstances. It's a poem entitled, 'Footprints in the Sand.'"

She groaned. "Just when I thought you might actually be a perfect human being, you bring up that tired—"

"One night, I dreamed I was walking along the beach with our Lord," David recited dramatically.

"Spare me."

"Many scenes from my life flashed across the sky—"

"Nope."

"During the parts of my life that sucked, there was only one set of footprints—"

"Stop it," Leona said. "That's not how it goes."

"But you didn't even let me get to the good part," David complained.

"I don't care."

He threw out the last line quickly, like it was a hot potato he needed to get rid of. "The Lord replied, 'It was then that I carried you!' "

She laughed, and he tightened his arms around her.

"You're stuck with me and my brilliant prose forever, babe."

She absorbed his warmth. "And you're stuck without Jimmy John's tonight. Or Subway. Any restaurant that sells deli meat between bread."

The sun disappeared behind them. The water, once calm and serene in the daylight, was now a churning expanse, sinister and chaotic in the dark. Tragically prophetic.

Her teeth chattered in the cold. She made one more statement before getting up to signal she was ready to leave. "I want to name her Vera. After my grandmother."

"And how do you know the baby is a girl?" David asked, indignant.

She sighed, the most at peace she'd been for a long time, and the most at peace she would be for a long time after.

"I just know."

CHAPTER 20

Present Day

A NOTE WAS LEFT OUT ON THE KITCHEN COUNTER:

> *Vera refused nap. Out for a stroller ride. Pray her tantrum doesn't escalate from a 5K to a marathon.*
>
> *—D*

Even in writing he was charming, Leona mused.

She placed her purse and car keys on the counter, still trying to process everything she'd learned that morning. Between Krissy's Gym and BioThrive, she'd collected several pieces of information that explained this version of her life. But she still had to piece together the bigger picture. And decide what to do with the bigger picture after it was assembled.

She hoped her conversation with David would offer the direction she needed.

"David," she said. She was so sorry, so torn up. Not only about what Leona #2 had done, but over the way she, Leona #1, had assumed the worst of him.

Standing alone in the large kitchen, she decided she needed to do something to occupy her mind. She didn't want to get stuck dwelling too long on all the things she couldn't change. Or on Carl's words, "It's up to you, Leona."

Try to go home.

Stay here.

Choose.

She went to the office, this time walking past the desk and laptop to the end table next to the couch. The phone, charger, journal, and prescription glasses were still sitting on top of it. She picked up the phone, ready to test a few combinations of numbers for the password. However, she couldn't turn the phone on to get to the lock screen. The battery was dead.

It made sense. The phone hadn't been charged in four days. Anyway, she didn't need to creep through texts and email to confirm it didn't belong to David. The fact that it was left untouched in the office for so long—on top of the text from "Krissy" (aka Derek)—was proof enough.

She plugged the charger into the wall and the phone into the charger. It would be a good five minutes before she could turn it on, but she didn't wait idly. Something in her gut told her there was more information waiting at her fingertips from a different source. She went back to the side table and grabbed the journal. She opened it and immediately recognized the handwriting. It was the same as hers.

She tossed a chef's kiss into the air. Phones and laptops couldn't give her the answers she wanted, but pen and paper were about to say everything.

She believed there was nothing more thrilling than reading another person's journal, but also nothing more invasive—even if the leatherbound notebook technically belonged to another version of herself. She paged through its contents, her heart breaking a little more with each entry. The thoughts flooding out in poetry confirmed everything she suspected.

Leona #2 was angry and in pain.

Sophistication.
Art collections.
Vacations.
Shiny distractions.

Education.
Competition.
Social connections.
"Self-made" delusion.

Fixation
on nominations
bought by donations.
Fraudulation.

Entry fee:
self-reinvention,
social exclusion;
isolation.

For every effort Leona #2 had put toward being someone who belonged at Delaney's brunch and gala tables, she'd lost pieces of herself. Fitting in cost her the community she'd always known.

The next pages of the journal told a tale as old as humankind.

Honestly?
It's easier to hide
than to confront.

Honestly?
The light invites me,
but darkness embraces me.
Honestly?
I'm adrift.

She knew that fear intimately. Growing up in a home riddled with conflict, it was hard to believe any kind of relational clash could end in a peaceful resolution. It had taken every ounce of courage to bare her heart to David right after he proposed to her.

She just wished David #2 was given the same chance in the ten years since he'd proposed. That he was trusted to listen.

She turned a few more pages. The journal never mentioned Derek by name. Maybe Leona #2 didn't want to admit anything to herself by writing it out loud or maybe she didn't want to leave such an obvious trail for David to discover. Nevertheless, there were plenty of coded entries referencing her emotional entanglement.

It isn't love.
It's the culmination
of my unhappiness,
my self-doubt.
It's reminders
of who I am,
of who I was—
the parts I must now cover under Neiman Marcus.
It isn't love.
It's glimpses
of where I came from.

A few feet away, the phone dinged.

Leona looked and saw the screen light up with the charging icon. She got up from the couch and sat next to the outlet where the phone was plugged in. After powering it on, she tried the digits of Vera's birthday for the password. It remained locked. She tried her anniversary. That didn't work either.

Suddenly, there was a commotion at the back of the house. It sounded like metal keys, a diaper bag, and a plastic sippy cup were being unloaded onto the counter. David was making his way inside. Vera let out a happy squeal to announce her arrival too. Hopefully that meant she took the nap she needed.

"Leona?" David called from the kitchen.

"I'm in the office," she called back.

He changed his voice to address Vera. "See if you can find Mommy's room while I go tinkle," he said like he was sending her on an adventure.

The sound of little feet padding across wood floors came closer and closer until Vera arrived outside the office. She knew Mommy's room wasn't the same place as Daddy's room, Leona noted.

Vera peered in and looked around.

"Hello, Vera," she said. She held out her arms, bracing herself for the possibility of another rejection.

The little girl hesitated, then walked over to Leona and accepted her hug. Vera was warm, and there were blankie lines printed on her left cheek.

"You're the best," Leona whispered into her sweaty hair.

Vera sat up and started babbling a bunch of words that only made sense to herself.

Leona pretended she knew exactly what she was saying. "Wow, that sounds like an exciting stroller ride. Please, tell me what happened next."

"An evil squirrel attacked us," David interjected from the doorway, "but Super Daddy saved the day with his own brute strength." For show, he flexed his arms.

Vera let out a trill of giggles, and Leona smiled at the two of them. They were adorable together.

"After being attacked by squirrels and humidity, I'm feeling a little sticky." David wafted air into his shirt. "I'm going to take a quick shower and let you two have some girl time. Maybe catch up on the city's latest scandals."

He stepped toward the hall.

"David?" Leona called him back.

He turned to face her.

"Actually, I was hoping we could talk right now," she said. "If that's okay with you."

His eyes bounced back and forth, like he was getting his thoughts in order. "Yeah, definitely," he agreed. "I'll set Vera up with some fruit snacks and PBS Kids. That should buy us a solid fifteen minutes of uninterrupted chat time."

Leona nodded. "Desperate times call for desperate measures."

A few minutes later, she could hear an episode playing on David's tablet in the nursery. When he came back into the office, he sat down on the couch two cushions over from her.

"I apologize if you can smell me from over there," he said half-seriously. "Hopefully I'm giving off more of a manly musk than the stench of a boys' locker room."

She laughed, enjoying what this moment felt like.

The two of them glanced at each other and then looked away. It seemed like they were both unsure where to start.

"I see you found your phone." David nodded toward the wall where it was charging.

"I did," she replied. "This probably sounds strange, but I thought it was your phone."

"That does sound strange," he agreed, "but they both have slender black cases, so I guess I won't hold it against you."

She took a deep breath, praying the oxygen would be full of bravery. "I know you've wanted to talk, and I understand why you would want that. But I think it's important for me to say that I might not have all the answers you want."

She rubbed her temples. She knew she probably wasn't making any sense. She was about to try again, but David jumped in.

"Leona, there's something else I want to ask you." He looked down at his hands. "And it has nothing to do with what I wanted to talk about the other night at dinner."

"Okay?" Her stomach started to tie up in a nervous clump.

David seemed stuck now. "It's just that, there's something . . . different . . . about you."

Her mouth fell open, and she quickly shut it again.

"I've noticed a lot of . . . changes?" he continued, looking her up and down like he was taking inventory. "And I've been trying to run through all the possibilities of how those changes could have happened, but nothing makes sense. Not when you're so different so suddenly. I'm not sure science could even fully explain what it is I think I'm seeing. Which makes me wonder if I'm losing touch with reality—"

"David," she interrupted, needing to reassure him, though she was surprised at how much he'd already figured out on his own.

He looked up, straight into her.

She held his gaze. "You're not losing touch with reality."

He tucked his chin and frowned. "I'm not? You're not going to refute anything I just said?"

She shook her head.

"You're not even going to give me any weird looks? Let me know with your face that I'm clearly saying some strange stuff?"

"No." She smiled. "And when you hear what I'm about to tell you, I need you to believe me too."

He nodded.

"I'm Leona, but I am not your wife." She gave him a second to take that in. "I mean, I *am* your wife, but not here. With you. I'm from a completely different outcome of our lives that looks . . ." She didn't want to say "both tragically and wonderfully different," so she said, "a little different."

David put both his hands on his head and blew out a loud breath of air. It looked like everything was hitting him at once. Relief, then more confusion.

"But how?" He didn't finish the question.

"That's what I went to BioThrive to talk to Eden about today," she admitted. "Unfortunately, I'm still not sure I fully understand. All this science stuff goes way over my head. In a way, you're not losing touch with reality. You're in touch with a different reality."

"Which means the whole phone thing this morning—"

"I didn't know until this morning that the phone in the office was mine. Because, again, it's not *mine* mine. I don't have my own phone or house keys or driver's license either."

"So, when did you . . . arrive?" He shrunk back, as if he wasn't sure if he was using the correct terminology.

"Three days ago. At Bartolotta's."

He nodded. "That makes sense. That's when I started noticing the changes."

She nodded back.

"So, what did Eden say?" He leaned in. "Last I heard, BioThrive was a research start-up, not a time machine."

"It was Eden's friend of a friend named Carl who tried to explain everything," she clarified. "He claimed that I came here through some sort of portal? A door created by circumstances that overlapped your timeline with mine."

David clapped. "As in the many-worlds interpretation of quantum mechanics?"

"Yes, dork." She laughed.

"Wow."

"That's exactly what I said when I got here. *Wow.*" She raised an eyebrow.

"I don't care what science can explain. This is wild."

"Literally unbelievable," she agreed.

They sat together in silence, letting it all sink in.

Leona still couldn't believe she was here. And she couldn't believe how much easier it was to be here when she didn't have to hide her identity from David #2 anymore. She was still lost, technically, but she wasn't living under the pressure of being some sort of spy or fugitive. They could finally talk about stuff. Like husband and wife. Sort of.

"I want to know what tipped you off that I'm different from your wife," she said.

"Oh, Leona." His laugh was teasing but not cruel. "The first night you were here, you climbed into our bed. You haven't done that in a very long time."

She flinched at the pain hanging from that statement.

He kept going. "You've been fumbling around the kitchen, struggling to find a simple coffee mug, even though everything in this house has been meticulously organized by you."

She chuckled. "I could have had a forgetful case of mom brain or early onset dementia."

"Possible. But not likely."

"More likely than a different version of your wife traveling from another dimension to visit you?"

He smiled. "Touché."

She reciprocated with a smile of her own.

"Usually, when my wife gets home," he added, "she follows the same three steps: Wash hands, get a drink of water, and put on house shoes. It's almost a religious ceremony."

"That sounds obsessive, even for me."

"And your wedding ring is different," he said, motioning toward it. "I spent two months picking one out, agonizing over the right one for you, so I'm not sure what this thing is."

She looked down at her hand. After her David proposed to her the second time, she was so high on courage she asked if she could pick out a simple rose gold band instead. It was what she really wanted.

"You're wearing glasses I've never seen before," David #2 explained. "My wife wears contacts most of the time, except at night when she's reading."

She remembered the pair on the end table. It reminded her of another detail she had noticed on the oil portrait hanging in the sitting room: Leona #2 wasn't wearing glasses.

"But the very first giveaway was your tattoo," he said. "I know I can be oblivious at times, but I think I would have noticed it before you arrived at the restaurant."

She looked down at her forearm. *Vera* was written into her skin, scripted in a light font that flowed into an artistic daisy, the flower for Vera's birth month, on each side.

"I caught you staring at it multiple times," she said.

"What made you get the tattoo?" he asked. "I thought you were terrified of needles."

Leona didn't know the ramifications of sharing details in a situation like this. How much information about her life was too much information to share with David? The line between oversharing and remaining too closed off felt like a delicate balance to maintain. She didn't think she should pile on the idea of Vera's death when David #2 had enough troubles of his own.

She shrugged off his question and asked another one of her own. "What I want to know is *why*? If I'm the one who's been sleeping in the office, why were your clothes next to the couch a few days ago?"

He chuckled. "I was working late in here one day and took my clothes off before going to the bedroom to get my pajamas. I wasn't leaving you a clue; I'm just a slob. Don't you know me at all?"

"That is a true statement," she agreed. "You're a slob in every world I've met you."

Leona covered her face with her hands and groaned. "I just want to let the record show that I'm both a terrible actress and an unexceptional detective. I thought I was being sneaky, but your long list of evidence says otherwise."

Her amusement dwindled. Sure, she wasn't cut out for acting or investigating, but the moment she saw Vera, her goals drastically shifted. She didn't even want to look for clues anymore. She just wanted to be with that little girl.

"This is going to sound terrible, but"—David lowered his voice—"there's another thing I noticed. . . . My wife attends workout classes regularly. So, you look . . . a little different?"

She crossed her arms and raised an eyebrow. "What are you implying, David Warlon? And why would you even say that?"

"Nothing! I'm not implying anything. My wife is just a little more . . . toned?"

"Is that a question?" she challenged.

"It's not a bad thing, not at all! It's just another thing I noticed that changed."

"Oh, please. Spare me your—"

"And that's why I put the gym in the basement," he cut in. "I wanted to give you—or, the other you—a reason to work out at home. You were so adamant about starting an exercise regimen, but I wanted you here with me. Whatever size you are, I'd rather be together than know you're at the gym with . . ."

She looked down, so heartbroken for him. "You saw the texts?"

He raked a hand through his hair, his short curls clearly defined by the sweat and humidity. "I know you're not to blame. I just wanted to say all of that because even though my wife and I have been drifting apart for a long time, I still know her enough to know you are not my wife. Or the woman I asked to marry me? I don't know. This is all really weird and fascinating and freaky. My mind is still blown, and I'm going to need a bit to recover."

There were times Leona was annoyed by how aloof David could be, when his social detachment kept him from noticing the blaring details she thought he should see. But even in this trajectory, he must have learned a few things over the past ten years. Or, maybe, watching his marriage slip away was a wake-up call to look harder.

"Leona #2," she said.

He furrowed his brow. "What?"

"Your wife," she explained, "is Leona #2. That's the labeling system I came up with to keep everything straight. You're David #2, and your wife is Leona #2."

"That's a very sophisticated system," he said dryly.

She lifted her chin in the air. "I agree."

"But why do you get to be Leona #1? And why can't I be David #1?"

"Because I created the system. I get first dibs."

He tilted his head and scrunched his shoulders. "That's fair."

"I didn't ask if you thought it was fair." She put a little snoot in her tone.

"Can I fill out a petition to become David #1?" he queried.

"Is that seriously our biggest problem right now, David #2?"

He laughed, as did she. This was the connection Leona knew and loved.

David's shoulders stiffened. "So, are you here . . . to stay?" he asked.

Leona looked at him. The lightheartedness that warmed the space between them began to cool down again from her own uncertainty. She couldn't tell what he wanted the answer to be.

Try to go home.

Stay here.

Choose.

"That's certainly the million-dollar question," she said, the weight of the choice suffocating her. "Honestly, I don't know how to answer that."

CHAPTER 21

Fifteen Months Ago

LEONA PULLED HER CELLPHONE OUT OF HER POCKET and called David. It didn't complete its first ring before he answered, and she didn't complete her first sentence before he blurted out a nervous string of questions.

"Is it happening? Are you okay? What should I do? I should come get you. I am coming to get you. Do you want me to come get you?" As a medical research scientist, David was calm and collected under pressure. As a father, he already had zero chill.

Leona had been sitting in a chair at the front of her classroom teaching creative writing to a class of uninterested high school juniors. Sitting because standing up this late in pregnancy made her out of breath in mere minutes. She was in the middle of talking about different plot types—ironically, rags to riches—when she felt the gentlest pop below.

She yelled at her students, "Don't do anything dumb!"

Then she radioed the front office for backup while she waddled to the bathroom. She sat on the toilet so more of her water could break into the bowl.

"Yes," she said into the phone from the bathroom stall. "My water broke, so it's really happening. Please come get me. And bring a towel."

It was two days past her due date. Far past the point of glowing, now she was just swollen and sweaty. She'd had many light contractions over the past two weeks, enough that she'd gone to the hospital twice for false alarms. Now it was really time. She would finally get to meet the baby who'd been kicking and hiccupping inside her.

Her hospital bag was already in the car, so all she had to do was get to the parking lot. Outside, she shivered in the spring chill as she waited on the curb. There was a strange fluttering in her chest, which moved down and turned into a strong contraction that clenched her body.

David pulled the car up next to her, so she rested a hand on the side of it to brace herself through the pain.

He jumped out of the car and ran to her.

"Are you okay? What do you need?" He put his hand on the small of her back.

The contraction ended, and she inhaled a deep breath. "It's like they turned on the lights, started dancing the polka on my uterus, and yelled 'Surprise!'"

David looked around. "Who's they?"

"The contractions," she said through gritted teeth. "That was a really strong one, and they're starting to speed up. I thought you invented medicine and knew some of these things."

David patted her back. "Let's save your energy for giving birth instead of ridiculing your doting husband," he joked.

Another contraction ripped through her, and she no longer felt like his affectionate bride. Ten seconds later the contraction lessened, and she caught her breath.

"Just get me to the hospital," she demanded.

He opened the door, and she bent over her cramping middle to get into the car.

"Are you too hot or too cold?" he asked, pulling the car onto the road toward the hospital.

Another contraction began, morphing her into a hellcat. "Why would you ask me such a stupid question?"

His eyes widened. He turned back toward the road.

She tried to explain herself. "David . . . I think you should . . . know . . . that until this baby is . . . out . . . you will not be able to do or say anything right."

He leaned over and placed his hand on her leg. "Got it."

She started to wonder if this baby would come out of her in the car. The speed limit was only thirty-five miles per hour, and—as usual—her husband was driving one mile under it.

"Drive faster," she said through gritted teeth.

Fifteen minutes and three contractions later, they practically skidded onto the parking ramp of the hospital and swerved into the first open space they could find. When labor and delivery were only theoretical to her, Leona firmly declared she would have an all-natural birth. But by the time she was taken to triage to undress and register, she realized just how naïve she'd been to labor pains. All she wanted was cold hard drugs.

"Can I get an epidural?" she pleaded with the nurse, who was calm and looked like she'd been delivering babies for at least a couple of decades.

The nurse checked to see how dilated she was. "Honey, you're at nine and a half centimeters out of 10."

Leona looked at David, who leaned in and tucked a piece of her sweaty hair behind her ear.

He whispered, "I think that is fancy hospital code for *no.*"

"I'm at nine and a half?" she asked David in a frenzy. "How did this happen so fast?"

The nurse explained, "For some, it goes zero to sixty once your water breaks." She turned to another nurse who Leona thought looked like she'd graduated college two seconds ago. "I've wanted you to get to see a case like this."

Leona looked at David. "A case like what? What kind of case are we?"

David squeezed her hand. "A case where we arrive at the hospital and our baby gets here relatively soon after."

The nurse wheeled her to a delivery room, then began asking questions that felt like rocket science during late labor, like "When was your last period?" and "Do you have any religious preferences?"

Another contraction hit her, and she reeled over in pain.

David took her hand and rubbed her back. "In through the nose, out through the mouth," he repeated, quoting the breathing technique they'd picked up from movies. "Or something like that."

When the contraction ended, she said, "How did Mr. Lamaze make millions of dollars by coining a method of breathing?"

He laughed. "I don't know the history, but why do you assume Lamaze is a man?"

"Because 'breathing like this takes my labor pains away,' said no woman ever," she groaned.

Something changed within her. Not only was the next contraction the most intense one yet with almost no time to recover from the last one, but now she wanted to push. Her body was screaming at her to push.

"I need . . . to push," she told the nurse.

"I can't let you push until I check the position of the baby," the nurse warned her. "If the baby is the wrong way, it will tear your cervix. The doctor will be here—"

"I'm here!" A doctor rushed into the room pulling gloves onto her hands and a mask over her face.

Leona was glad that the doctor seemed in as much of a hurry as she was.

The woman examined Leona, then she said, "All right, it's time to go. On your next contraction, I want you to push."

When the next contraction hit, Leona did as she was told. She pushed, and she didn't recognize the sounds coming from deep within her body. When the contraction subsided and she caught her breath, she apologized.

The doctor smiled from behind her mask. "That's okay, Leona. It's kind of like Vegas in here. What happens in Labor and Delivery stays in Labor and Delivery. Use that energy to push instead, okay?"

She squeezed David's hand so hard she wondered if it would liquify. "It hurts so bad," she said.

He squeezed hers back. "I would trade places with you, but it looks pretty awful."

She pushed and sweat and tried to breathe, and after three more contractions, the room was filled with the cries of a newborn baby.

David raised his free fist in the air, then he kissed Leona on the cheek. "She's here, Leona! You did it! Our little girl is here!"

The doctor invited David to cut the umbilical cord, and then she gently placed their baby against Leona's chest.

"Vera," she whispered over her pink newborn. She felt like she was falling into a new kind of love.

After a few minutes, Vera settled from her cries into a warm, swaddled sleep.

Now that the delivery room was quiet of nurses and doctors and pain-filled screams, Leona looked at David, so content. "Thank you for being such a good, doting husband. Even if I didn't appreciate it for a second there."

He brushed her hair back and kissed her. "Leona, the day I married you, I promised I would not hold you accountable for the things you say while giving birth."

"Hmm." She smiled. "I don't remember that being part of our vows."

After two nights in the hospital, both of David's girls were given a clean bill of health and cleared to go home. Leona was ready—so ready—to start this new beginning. Between maternity leave and summer break, she would have four full months to spend at home with Vera.

The only months she would get to spend with Vera.

CHAPTER 22

Present Day

"THERE'S ONE LAST FUN FACT I'M EXCITED TO share." David #2 leaned back into the couch. "The other night at Bartolotta's? That wasn't our anniversary. We were trying to do something with just the two of us, meeting to talk about everything that's been going on. I was hoping it would be our chance to learn how to live again."

Those words sounded scarily familiar, Leona thought. She couldn't believe it. Last Thursday, she met her husband at Bartolotta's for their anniversary. Last Thursday, David #2 met his wife at Bartolotta's to talk about their marriage.

All four of us were hoping to learn how to live again.

These were the overlapping circumstances that opened the door from her life to this one.

She sat up straighter as she connected the dots. "That's why your Leona and I switched places. We went to the same restaurant at the same time to—in a way—try and restart our lives." Another lightbulb went off in her head. She retrieved the phone from the charger and sat back on the couch. David seemed to enjoy watching her rebounding thoughts and movements.

"What is your anniversary?" she asked him.

"September 17," he answered. "You wanted a July wedding at the beach, but my mother insisted the temperatures of an 'autumnal nuptial celebration' would be far more comfortable for a large crowd of guests wearing black-tie."

Leona put her palm to her face. "Let me guess, Delaney insisted on paying and then took over all the preparations. Instead of a simple ceremony we got married with a guest list as large as the Grain Exchange would allow."

David blinked. "Yeah. You're good."

She entered the five digits of his anniversary into the phone. It unlocked.

David watched her. "I'm surprised she kept our anniversary as her passcode," he muttered.

Leona winced; a fire lit in her heart. She looked straight at him, then reached over and tipped his chin up to make sure he was looking back at her.

"I'm not surprised at all," she said. "She loves you. She chose you. But life here has been a huge struggle for her. I'm not saying that's a good excuse for what she's done, but it's a factor."

The journal was still on the floor next to the couch. She grabbed it and handed it to him. "I'm not speaking for her. She spoke for herself."

David grabbed the journal and flipped through the pages. His face changed with each entry. Anger. Helplessness. Pain.

Finally, he said, "My marriage didn't fade overnight, you know. It's been slowly unraveling for a long time. It's almost like it got tired. Like a cliché." He said it like he knew she would appreciate the word choice.

He'd always argued that words and phrases became cliché

for a reason, while she countered that clichés lacked original thought.

"I can't believe I'm about to say this, but just because something is cliché, that doesn't mean it's wrong. Your marriage may have become less novel, but that doesn't mean the original definition is lost."

"That's a strong statement coming from you, English Major."

"Yes, it is." She paused, choosing her next words carefully. "I don't think it would be wise for me to say a lot about my life, but one of the biggest differences is that David #1 and I chose to live on the other side of town so I could have more overlap with the neighborhood I grew up in. Well, that, *and* it's one of the few neighborhoods we can afford to live in. But just look at how our . . . your . . . friendship with Eden has all but dissolved here, for example."

"So, the answer is to move?" He sounded desperate for tangible solutions.

Leona's mind immediately jumped to Vera, and her entire body flooded with anxiety. Moving would not be a guaranteed so lution to their marital problems because living on the other side of town was also the source of her deepest grief. Besides, a long time ago she'd resigned herself to believing there weren't always three easy steps to fixing something as complicated as life. Maybe that was a long time ago. Or maybe that was yesterday when she visited her dad and he shared those exact words.

She shifted the conversation with a different question. "Have you ever considered more separation from Warlon Tech? Maybe what she needs is better protection from your mother. I mean, you've seen the way Delaney tries to control her, starting with your wedding day. Did you even know Leona started working out only because Delaney told her she looked a little soft after Vera was born? I think we both know that those kinds of words coming out of her mouth aren't meant to be a compliment."

David's jaw clenched. "No, I didn't."

"Partnering with her might start by giving your wife space from comments like that."

"As in, four feet of space?" David chuckled, but his eyes still looked sad. It looked like he was still working through everything he just heard.

"While I do believe four feet is the perfect personal space bubble, I'd start with at least ten thousand feet," she clarified.

David leaned forward until his elbows were resting on his knees. "You wouldn't know this, but I've done a lot of good work at Warlon Tech. I've led great reform within the company, righting past wrongs and making change."

Leona thought the words sounded like he was reading them off of a brochure. "I'm glad for you," she said.

A silence fell between them. She was starting to hate the silence. It made her ponder her impossible situation.

Try to go home.

Stay here.

Choose.

David broke the stillness. "I forgot to ask you, but how was brunch Friday morning?"

She shifted in her seat. "You know how much I love spending time with our mothers."

He raised his eyebrows. "Evelyn was there too?"

"Yes. Delaney invited a few other prestigious ladies to brunch." She mimicked the way Evelyn emphasized the last word in her sentences and said, "It was her midyear check-in between her annual *galas.*"

David placed a hand on his collarbone and joined in the mimicry. "Is it true they're expecting to break the record for the most money raised in one *night*?"

"That's what I've been *told.*" Leona laughed at his impression.

Something shifted in the room between the two of them.

David #2 was staring at her. "Do you remember when you said your glasses protected you from other people being able to read your thoughts?"

She smiled at the memory. She still felt that way sometimes, like her lenses were a comfortable barrier protecting her soul.

"Well, even though you're wearing some now, I'm pretty sure I can still see what you're thinking." His lips curved.

The slightly suggestive comment sent heat charging through Leona's body. She could only make eye contact for a split second before it was too hot to handle. She felt like a girl with a crush again.

"Oh, really? And what exactly do you think you see?" she flirted back.

David moved himself a cushion and a half closer, opening his body to her like they were close companions sharing intimate conversation. In the most perplexing way possible, that was accurate, she thought.

He was close enough she could smell him—a little bit of sweat like he'd worried earlier but plenty of pleasing hints of whatever scents his deodorant was made of too.

She half expected him to put his arm around her or take her hand like David #1 did all the time. Instead, he put his hand around the back of her head, gently, and leaned in.

He whispered against her neck, "I've been angry for so long."

Her skin absorbed the intensity of his words.

"But then," he continued, "the last few days showed me things could be different. We could be us again."

Try to go home.

Stay here.

Choose.

Leona put her hand on his cheek, leading him away from the tingling skin on her neck and resting her forehead against his. It felt like neither of them knew what they were doing, but both of them knew what they wanted to do.

David's eyes were closed and he was breathing heavily. "I know my science-y brain should be geeking out about how you got here, but honestly, right now you have me thinking with a different body part."

Leona blushed. She wasn't new to this kind of talk from him, but in the moment, it still felt new.

David's palms traced the sides of her figure all the way down to her waist. A few of his fingers made it under her shirt. Leona shivered. She could tell he wanted to let his hands wander a lot more, but he kept them in place, kneading her sides to restrain himself.

He whispered, hoarse, "I want you. You are the woman I asked to marry me."

She looked down. He didn't know just how different she was from the woman he asked to marry him ten years ago.

CHAPTER 23

Eleven Months Ago

"HER TEMPERATURE IS STILL 102 DEGREES," LEONA said the second the front door of their rental house on Thirty-Fourth Street groaned open.

David appeared in the frame, ragged. "Another long day of trial and error at BioThrive," he said half-heartedly.

He closed the door and turned toward her.

"Did you hear what I said?" She watched him as he took a second to accept his surroundings.

Swaddling blankets covered the floor, tiny clothes draped the couch, and wadded tissues peppered every surface. She'd used just as many to wipe her own tears as she had for Vera's runny nose. Even the most patient mothers tired from rocking a feverish baby all day.

Leona paced the only trail of clear floor left, holding four-month-old Vera in her arms. "I've tried everything—a cold compress, a lukewarm sponge bath, taking off her clothes. She hasn't nursed in forever, and I haven't been able to set her down so I can pump. I think I'm going to burst."

David set down his backpack, adding more debris to the disaster zone, and took Vera from Leona's arms.

Her shoulders drooped as she ran for her breast pump.

Vera wasn't magically better, but she was already fussing less for David. He smiled down at her.

Leona untangled breast pump hoses while David looked under a set of pajamas and three dirty tissues for the thermometer.

"You're sure you were able to get an accurate temperature?" he asked.

"Of course I'm sure," she barked from the couch. Her breasts were tucked into plastic flanges, and the machine next to her revved and hissed. This was not her finest hour.

"How long has it been since she last ate?" He kept his voice low, laying Vera on the couch to get another temperature reading.

She closed her tired eyes to do the math. "I don't know. Almost four hours now, I think? Much longer than her usual three hours between feedings."

"You're right. Her temp is 102."

"I'm not an idiot."

He ignored the comment. "Has she seemed lethargic?"

"No? Yes? I don't know," she groaned. "She's been fussy most of the day so she hasn't slept, but she hasn't been super awake either."

"And you said in your texts she's been coughing too? Any wet diapers?"

"Don't trip over them." She nodded at the floor where they lay scattered.

David stopped his examination and picked up Vera, cuddling her close. "I know I'm not a pediatrician, but my advanced degree in medicine says this isn't anything severe enough to take her in for yet when the threshold for four-month-olds is 103. Let's see how she's doing in the morning."

Leona did not like that answer. "But everything online said she might have something terrible, maybe even RSV, which is respiratory syndrome virus . . . or something."

"Respiratory syncytial virus," David corrected, then bit his lip.

"Whatever." She glared at him. "Have you seen all the news stories about babies who die of RSV? You're not supposed to kiss babies anymore because they might get RSV. She's irritable; she's not eating. She's had this runny nose for a couple days now. Her cough seemed a little wheezy earlier . . ." she trailed off.

"It's August, Leona, not exactly RSV season. And you know you're not supposed to research symptoms online. It gives you cancer."

"What else was I supposed to do all day while I was taking care of her and nothing seems to be making her feel better?" she argued.

"Leona—"

"I want to take her in. I know you're a smart . . . medicine guy . . . but I'm a mother, and sometimes mothers know something is off. I've been with her all day, and something is off."

"Yes, she's obviously sick, babe, but I don't think something is off enough to take her in. Especially with the price of the insurance co-pay. Can we wait one more night and call Vera's pediatrician for her opinion in the morning?"

Leona glowered loud and clear.

"I'll get the car seat," he said.

Leona put on a bra and brushed her teeth for the first time that day. Then she grabbed the diaper bag, locked the front door, and met David and Vera at their only car, a red Buick LeSabre. David had nicknamed it Trusty Rusty, after the color of the car and the name of the salesman who sold it to them years ago. David would have driven his black BMW M6 convertible forever, but shortly before they got married, he received a formal letter from the Warlon estate demanding he return it. Leona suggested they park it at the front gate, filled to the brim with whipped cream.

She also reminded her devastated husband, "The BMW isn't a super practical car for Midwest driving anyway. We have snowy winters and future children to think about."

Days before their wedding, they went to Car Dealz Dealership and laid eyes on Trusty Rusty for the first time. It didn't have any license plates on it, and when David asked to bring it to a mechanic for an inspection, Rusty the salesman scoffed, "What, you don't trust me? Man, get out of here. I'll save this deal of a lifetime for someone else."

Not wanting to be the guy who assumed the worst, David signed his name on the dotted line next to Leona's. This car was the best they could afford anyway.

When the salesman handed him the title, David noticed it didn't have Car Dealz Dealership listed on it. A felony in the state of Wisconsin called "title jumping."

Leona shrugged. "Welcome to Car Dealz, where the deals are shady but the prices are unbeatable."

Unlike the house they rented, they'd had no issues with the car since they bought it. They decided they'd drive Trusty Rusty until it broke down on the side of the road.

DAVID AND LEONA checked in at the urgent care center and found seats in the waiting room. Vera slept in her car seat at their feet.

Leona couldn't remember the last time she was this exhausted. She rested her head against David's arm. "Is it killing you to not be in a lab coat and referring to yourself as 'Dr. Warlon'?"

"A little bit," he joked, brushing her cheek with his hand. "How will people even know I'm not like a regular dad, I'm a cool biomedical researching dad?"

"If I had more energy, I would laugh," she said. "But I promise you're the coolest dad I know."

She looked down at Vera, her fear rising up again. "Why does the world seem all wrong when something is wrong with her?"

David took Leona's hand in his. "Because you care. And because you're a really cool mom. The coolest I know."

"I've been worrying about her all day and at the same time feeling sensory overload from holding her for so long. For a bit there I was so overwhelmed I wanted to run out of the house and down the street. I didn't think I could give another ounce of myself. And now look at her." She squeezed his hand. "She's sleeping peacefully, and I feel like the luckiest person in the world to get to be her mom."

A medical technician called Vera's name. Their family of three was escorted from the waiting room to a patient room to wait another twenty minutes for the doctor to come in.

"Hello, I'm Dr. Zhao. And who do we have here?" the doctor asked as she flipped through the papers on her clipboard. "Vera Warlon?"

"Yes, this is Vera," Leona said. She carefully took her baby out of the car seat and handed her to the doctor. Vera protested with more cries.

"Tell me more about what's going on," Dr. Zhao said.

Leona shared everything she could, and the doctor followed up with a series of questions as she took Vera's temperature, listened for her heart rate, and examined her ears.

David tapped Leona on her shoulder and whispered, "Did you hear that? I asked those questions too. And don't you dare roll your eyes at me because we're in public."

She rolled her eyes at him anyway.

Dr. Zhao carefully tucked Vera's arms and legs back into her pajamas. "It was good you brought her in," she said.

Leona tapped David's shoulder violently.

He rolled his eyes.

Dr. Zhao tucked Vera's hands into her jammies and placed her in Leona's arms. "It's not anything serious like RSV, but she does have a cold and an ear infection."

The couple looked at each other and shrugged. They both won that round. Not that anyone wins when their baby is sick.

"The infection explains her lack of sleep and unwillingness to eat—the pressure Vera feels in her ear makes it difficult to sleep or swallow," the doctor said.

Leona liked having a diagnosis.

The doctor continued, "In babies this young, sometimes bacteria in the eardrum can spread to other parts of the body and cause serious infection, so I'll send a prescription to the pharmacy you can pick up shortly."

Dr. Zhao described a few home remedies to make the duration of Vera's illness more comfortable, then dismissed herself from the room. Leona kissed Vera's soft baby cheek and fastened her into her car seat, shushing her remaining cries.

It was only a short drive from the urgent care center to the pharmacy, but Vera had already fallen asleep again.

"She had a long day too," Leona said to David once they were all settled in the car.

"So then, shall we take Trusty Rusty along the scenic route? Let silence revive us a little?" he asked.

"Why, yes. Yes we should," Leona replied, leaning back with a contented smile.

For a while, David drove north on Lake Drive parallel to the lakeshore as the August sun began to set. Then he turned left onto Capitol Drive and drove west for home.

The traffic light at Capitol Drive and Sherman Boulevard turned green, so David pressed his foot on the gas pedal. With the sunset glaring off the windshield, he didn't see the car on Sherman Boulevard sprinting toward them at seventy miles per hour, about to run their red light.

"WE'RE PUTTING TOGETHER a strong improvement plan," Alderman Straights explained to Leona over the phone. "Beyond handing out steering wheel locks to car owners, the police will tow unregistered vehicles involved in reckless driving incidents. We'll also be offering free driver's education courses. Even roads will be re-engineered."

The statistics he quoted to her were shocking. Over seven thousand vehicles had been stolen so far that year in Milwaukee, averaging out to one every hour. Most of these vehicles were boosted by teens without a license, so the issue on top of the issue was drivers joyriding their "stolie" until they ran out of gas or crashed.

Leona had seen plenty of news articles and broadcasts about it before. She'd witnessed plenty of reckless driving too: cars going eighty miles per hour in thirty-five-miles-per-hour zones; drivers weaving through traffic with passengers hanging out of the windows; cars passing in the bike lane on the right—a move nicknamed the "Milwaukee slide."

Drivers also ran red lights.

Which was why Alderman Straights was on the phone, asking her to speak out and join their Auto Theft Task Force to address reckless driving once and for all.

"And if that sounds like too much, we'd still love it if you would simply speak at the upcoming town hall. As a grieving mother affected by this issue, your testimony has the power to make change," Alderman Straights said.

She came up with a polite response but declined his invitation, hanging up and running straight to the bathroom to vomit. She wiped her mouth and flushed the toilet, dragging herself to the kitchen to get a glass of water.

Later, she'd journal:

Why
is the pressure
to make change
always placed on
grieving
mothers?

Leona understood why Alderman was calling her. City officials were at a loss for how to address the issue. Because they were unable to pinpoint one reason for the uptick in these specific crimes, everyone chose something different to blame. The police chief accused social media, where anyone could learn to steal a car in as little as thirty seconds. Common Council complained about the two car companies whose models were easiest to hot-wire. A cable news network criticized the government and "today's parents." One minor charged in multiple car thefts admitted that the consequences were too insignificant to fear—a mere three weeks of jail time.

The effects were too horrific to not try something, anything. Multiple pedestrians were injured; hard-earned cars were stolen and destroyed; insurance rates were skyrocketing. And now, a baby had been killed. A baby related to the Warlon family of Warlon Tech.

It was popular local news for an entire week. The details of the wreck, the injuries sustained by the baby's parents. Journalists pried for more information, but nobody was willing to comment on why a Warlon heir wasn't living in a more affluent neighborhood.

Leona set her glass of water down and rubbed her tender neck and shoulders. She had plenty of blame to place too, but the driver who struck their Buick was killed on impact. She wondered how long it was acceptable to hold a grudge against a dead teenager.

Had he paid for his sins? A life for a life?

He was seventeen, still in high school. His mother was grieving too.

Leona blamed herself most of all.

Millions of thoughts beginning with: *Why?*

CHAPTER 24

Present Day

"YOU ARE THE WOMAN I ASKED TO MARRY ME," DAVID #2 had said. Leona pushed herself away from him. An entire couch cushion away. He was wrong for so many reasons.

She stood up, suddenly claustrophobic inside of the office. Her breathing was getting shallower, and her heart rate was quickening—the beginnings of another panic attack. "I . . . need . . . some air . . ." she gasped.

This time, David didn't ignore the attack on her body. He stood up next to her and rubbed her back. "You're okay, Leona. I'm here. You're safe."

She took the hand he was holding out to her, and they walked through the house until they reached the front door. Outside, she pulled fresh air into her lungs. It was muggy, but she found it easier to breathe than when they were sitting close to each other on the couch.

David left the door open. "In case Vera needs us," he explained.

She couldn't hear him. She was trying to breathe slowly, in

through her nose, out through her mouth, counting *one, two, three, four.*

"Leona, look at me." David put his hands on her shoulders and turned her toward him.

The pain in her chest was still there, but she listened.

"Tell me three things you see."

She couldn't believe it. How did he know what to do?

Apparently, he could read the question in her eyes. "I looked it up while you were gone this morning. I wanted to be able to help you if it happened again."

She nodded, grateful. Using another intentional breath, she said, "I see . . . the door."

"Yes, that's right. The maroon door Delaney keeps insisting we paint to match the neighbors' doors."

She glared at him.

David nodded. "Okay, I see it now. Delaney is running our lives."

Running and ruining, Leona thought, exhaling hard. Taking in another lungful of air, she noticed the landscape was in full bloom. There were fluffy white hydrangeas, not a single branch sagging out of place. It was stunning, serene.

"I see . . . flowers."

"That's correct, Leona. Those are the bushes Delaney gave you for Mother's Day."

She straightened, ready to throw a pebble, a punch—something.

"I'm kidding!" He laughed. "Now, let's get back to your breathing exercises. You're making me look like a terrible helper."

She shook her head and smiled. And then her smile turned into a laugh. And then her laugh took over her entire body until she was shaking and had to sit down on the front steps. She was having trouble breathing, but it was no longer because of anxiety. It was because she was enjoying his company.

She didn't need to say the third thing she saw. *I see you, David.*

He sat down next to her. "Was it something I said?"

She grabbed his arm. "You're a jerk."

"I know." He smiled. His eyes were full of light, playfulness, and desire.

They sat in the quiet for a moment. She noticed that the silence was becoming more comfortable to sit in with David #2.

He took her hand, intertwining his fingers with hers, then rested their hands on her leg.

She didn't pull back or push him away—it was a gesture too familiar for her to resist. She might not be the woman he asked to marry him, but according to Carl, it was likely they had bits and pieces of a shared history. That had to count for something.

"When did you start having panic attacks?" David asked, no longer kidding around.

She hesitated. "In the past year."

"Do you know why?" he pried.

"I don't know if I should tell you." She looked away.

"Well, that seems unfair," he argued with a twinge of sarcasm. "You got to see my version of our life. You've been all up in *my* business."

"You're right." She nudged her shoulder into his. "This has basically been a vacation for me."

"Exactly. Which means I need more details. Give me some details, Leona," he pleaded.

She looked at him, wondering what she could even say. At home, her husband was her safe place. And now, in this trajectory, David #2 was becoming safe too.

She let go of his hand and pulled hers away, resting her elbows on her knees. Then she covered her face with her hands. A sudden wave of emotion was threatening to knock her over, but she didn't want to cry. She was tired—so tired. Tired of navigating this version of her life on the east side; tired of struggling to survive on the north side. She was tired of missing Vera at home; tired of missing her David here.

Try to go home.

Stay here.

Choose.

Her heart couldn't take being pulled between two places at once much longer. But her heart couldn't bear choosing between the man she loved a world away and the chance to be with the child she lost.

David took her hand again, but this time he tilted her forearm so he could see her tattoo. "If I ask you about the tattoo again, will you tell me why you got it?"

He traced the letters of Vera's name with his finger, which sent a wide realm of thoughts running through her head.

She used her free hand to rub the tension in her neck, thinking about telling him more. Giving him the details he was asking for. Sharing the pain that had become her life.

Because what if telling David #2 gave her the chance to stay?

CHAPTER 25

Eleven Months Ago

THE CASKET WAS SO SMALL. DAVID AND LEONA STOOD near it as a line of people formed to offer their condolences.

Each time the church doors opened, streams of hot August sun flashed through the opening. Leona couldn't decide if the sunshine and blue skies outside were uplifting or ironic, like the weather didn't know how to read the room.

Frank was the first to arrive. Leona looked to see if Rose was following behind him. She wasn't.

Leona let her shoulders drop. It was just the beginning of visitation, which would lead into the funeral, luncheon, and burial, but she could already feel a headache building behind her eyes. She didn't know how she would get through the day. All the hugs, all the words. It was meant to be a show of support, but she didn't have the strength to receive it. She was empty, her insides wrung out like a gray sponge.

The mammary glands in her breasts, however, were not yet empty. She'd nursed Vera from birth and too abruptly didn't nurse anymore. She was engorged with milk and had no baby to feed.

Multiple clogged ducts had formed, which made each hug she received painfully tender. Soon, she might have to excuse herself so she could express some of her milk into the church's bathroom sink for relief.

Nature was amazingly designed, and yet sometimes, nature could be cruel.

Delaney arrived at the front of the line, wearing a mourning veil over a sizable black hat and dark glasses. Leona had heard her weeping loudly in line a few minutes ago and couldn't help but wonder if the display was for the cameras waiting outside the church.

David leaned in to give Delaney a polite embrace, only to hit his forehead on the brim of her hat.

"I'm surprised to see you here, Mom," he said. "I haven't heard from you in months."

"Vera's death is all over the news," Delaney replied, as if that was a perfectly rational explanation for why she was suddenly in the same room as them again. "It didn't take long for reporters to connect her back to the Warlon name."

David clenched his jaw. "Are you here for your granddaughter's funeral or for public relations damage control?"

"What are you accusing me of, son?" She dabbed her eye with a handkerchief.

David looked around his mother and scanned the small crowd. "Where's Dad?" he asked.

Leona had spotted Charles across the narthex earlier. He was leaving the bathroom, checking his wristwatch.

"Your father stepped outside," Delaney said. "He had an important phone call."

David's face twisted into anger as tears gathered at the corners of his eyes.

Usually, Delaney's mere presence made Leona's own anger flare, but right now all she felt was numb. It took everything she had in her, but somehow she was able to lift her hand and place it on her husband's forearm. She wished Delaney was anywhere but standing in front of her, but she also didn't want there to be a scene at her baby's funeral.

Delaney leaned in to David. "If only you'd listened to me and stayed on the side of town where you belong," she hissed, "that little girl wouldn't have—"

"Enough," David said, loud enough that both Leona and Delaney jumped.

Everyone's eyes were already on them, but now Leona sensed that their whispers were too.

David put his hand on Delaney's arm. "Excuse us," he said to the people waiting next in line. He guided his mother away to a far corner.

Leona could no longer hear what either David or Delaney were saying, but as she went through the motions of hugging two co-workers from the English department at school, she watched them anyway. Delaney was performing a monologue while David stood with his arms crossed, shaking his head.

Leona couldn't believe how Delaney was acting, mostly because seeing her torn up like this felt like a rare glimpse into her humanity. She wished she could peel back her mother-in-law's diplomatic layers to understand her better. It made sense to her that Delaney was shrouded with genuine sadness, that her maternal reflexes left her grieving. What didn't make sense to Leona was Delaney's mission to crucify, as if enough pain hadn't already been inflicted.

But Leona also couldn't believe how unfeeling she was toward Delaney at the moment. This display of hers was something that on any other day would push Leona over the edge, make her rage. Instead of breaking down, she felt dead inside. A zombie.

Evelyn stepped up to Leona, right in front of the co-workers she had been half listening to.

"You're young, Leona," she said. "You can always have more children."

It was Evelyn's second platitude since Vera died. Earlier in the week, she dropped via text message: *Vera's in a better place.*

Leona shook her head. Barely, because the movement required too much effort, but she wanted to communicate to her mother that she had zero interest in anything else she had to say.

Thankfully, David returned to her side. He was breathing heavily, which she guessed was due more to emotion than the walk across the room. He took her hand and clasped it tightly. She couldn't squeeze back.

"Thank you for coming, Evelyn." He nodded and then looked around her to the next person in line. It was the clear dismissal Leona needed, though her body still wasn't capable of reacting.

Evelyn lifted her chin and walked away.

The next person in line was Eden. Seeing her friend cracked something open in Leona. She'd remained numb through awkward conversations with acquaintances, targeted words from family, as well as miserable, trite explanations for why it shouldn't hurt so bad that her daughter was lying dead in the casket next to her.

She let Eden pull her in for a hug and then broke down into deep, ugly sobs.

"I can't do this," she said into Eden's shoulder.

"You shouldn't have to do this," her friend said through her own tears. "Mothers shouldn't have to bury their babies."

Eden stroked her hair and held her tight. After a few minutes, Leona pulled back and wiped at her mascara-less eyes.

Eden was holding a book in her hand, which she gave to Leona. "I didn't wrap it because I didn't want you to have to use any of the strength you needed to get through the day."

Leona looked down and realized it was a children's book called *We're Going on a Bear Hunt.*

"You probably remember this book. It's about a family going

outside on a hunt to look for bears," her friend explained. "They have to go through all these obstacles—tall grass, squishy mud, and a dark forest—before they get to see the bear."

Leona knew the story, but she wondered where Eden was going with this.

"Each time they reach an obstacle, they remind each other, 'We can't go over it, we can't go under it, we have to go through it.'" Eden put her arm around her. "This is grief too, Leona. You're facing every day without Vera while trying to move, trying to breathe."

Leona's shoulders started to shake.

"Each time sorrow comes back to the surface, you can't just get over it. You can't hide from it. For any healing to take place, you simply have to go through it."

Leona grabbed the tissue David was holding out to her so she could wipe her eyes and nose. She wondered if there would ever come another day she didn't cry. She nodded and let Eden hug her again.

"I'm going to be right here with you the whole way," Eden promised.

VERA WAS BURIED seven days before the first day of school. Wisconsin state law didn't require employers to provide bereavement leave, but the city of Milwaukee permitted up to five paid workdays off for the death and funeral of an employee's immediate family member, to be used within ten calendar days of their passing. In order to be approved for funeral leave, city employees—including Milwaukee's public school teachers—had to fill out an application and have it signed by their supervisor, attaching a copy of the obituary, or submitted with a statement from the mortician. When Leona tried to staple Vera's obituary to the back of her application, the stapler jammed.

Funeral leave covered four days of staff meetings, as well as the first day of classes after summer break. She tried to put on a brave face for her students and perform the duties expected of her to earn a paycheck, but everything else felt foggy. She could barely manage a few bites of her lunch. So many things triggered sadness, like going to the grocery store and seeing a little baby, walking past Vera's nursery, or the smell of lavender. Even though she lived in Sherman Park, it wasn't guns popping a few blocks away that set off her heart rate. It was the sound of screeching tires.

There were moments she was distracted enough to think maybe she would be okay. But at the end of every day came the night, the darkness, and—worst of all—the quiet. She thought it might swallow her whole. Whenever David got home from work, she was usually lying awake on their bed staring at the wall, her journal lying open next to her, completely blank.

She couldn't bring herself to write about the funeral—the extra pain some of their family members had caused or the end of the day, when she and David collapsed onto the grass near the deep hole that housed Vera's casket, no tears left to cry.

She remembered only one thing the minister said from the pulpit. "On the days we wonder if God cares about our suffering," he'd preached, "we can remember these two words: 'Jesus wept.' His compassion for David, Leona, and all who loved Vera will always abide."

Sitting in the pew, her mind had spun another round of bitter poetry:

"Loved"?
Did I stop
loving her
when
she stopped
breathing?

She wrote that in her journal, followed by another entry consisting of only two words.

My baby.

IN THE WEEKS since then, her mind had gone blank. All the thoughts that used to flow so easily from her pen were blocked. She didn't know how to articulate what it was like to carry a child inside of her body and then at her breast and then have to put her in the ground.

When they were struggling to get pregnant, her grief showed as anxiety, an effort to control every environmental condition until she became a person who yelled at her pregnant sister and threw her smoothie at the wall. She'd been angry, but present and participating.

Since losing Vera, her grief showed as losing herself. She didn't know who she was anymore. For three years of infertility, nine months of pregnancy, and four months of infanthood, she'd done her best to do everything right. And it all ended this way.

Why should she even try?

After work, she had nothing left to give, including to David. When he joked, she didn't laugh. When he climbed into bed and laid himself parallel to the curve of her back, she felt neither comfort nor connection. She used to see elderly couples holding hands and assume that would be them someday. Now she started to wonder how couples made it so far. How did friendship in marriage survive one spouse losing the brightness in their eyes?

She knew David was worried about her. Four months had passed, and she was a shell of the woman she used to be. She was barely able to take care of herself, going days without showering and rarely eating much of her dinner. She didn't want to go for walks, didn't want to write. She was sluggish, tired.

When David asked her a question, it was like she snapped out of a daze, surprised to see he was in the same room as she was. There was a gaping void between them, which she knew was unfair. A reminder that grief left no survivors. Everything was vulnerable to wreckage, including their vibrant companionship.

Mid-December, David came home from work early and announced he was going to take Leona to her favorite place in the world.

"We'll feel the crisp winter air off the lakeshore as the blazing orange sun sets behind us over glassy buildings and trees," he said, marketing the outing with his usual can-do attitude. "Together, we'll inhale new oxygen and exhale the stale air of our somber house."

Leona stayed curled up on the bed, unmoving.

"We don't have long," he tried again with simpler words. "I checked, and the sun is scheduled to set by 4:18 P.M."

She didn't want to go.

David pursed his lips. Instead of asking, he helped her sit up and dressed her. He found her thickest sweater and gently draped it around her shoulders. She didn't resist as he pushed each arm through a sleeve. He hoisted her off the bed and walked her to her parka and winter boots. He tied a scarf around her neck and put on her hat and gloves.

She felt his hands on her face, a kiss on her cheek. All she could think was that he was supposed to be doing this for Vera, not his grief-stricken wife. She couldn't bring herself to look at him.

David took her by the hand and led her outside to the curb in front of their house where their car was parked. They'd only had it for four months. It was new to them, but it was a very old Toyota Corolla. Taupe.

The numbness that turned her into a ghost was replaced by loud fear. She wanted to escape, to flee the reminder.

David's hand was pulling her forward, but she started pulling back against it.

He opened the passenger door for her.

She took a strong step back.

"David, I can't." She was fully awake to her surroundings again, terrified.

"I'll drive slowly," he promised. "*Please,* just get in the car."

Her brain was on fire. She was in distress but didn't know how to tell her husband.

He noticed, then pulled her in and hugged her. "Hey, I know you're scared."

"D-d-d—" She couldn't even say his name. Her body was acting in a way she'd never experienced before. She was sweating. Her heart was racing.

Why am I breathing so heavily?

"Leona?" David was looking down at her. "What's wrong? Leona?"

She couldn't answer. She could hear David's voice, but his words no longer registered; they just echoed around meaninglessly in her head. She was dizzy. Breathing, but unable to push the air out of her lungs. Her hands tingled; her feet were cemented in place.

"Leona, breathe. Please!" David put his hand on her cheek.

She still couldn't answer. She heard him say, "I'm taking you to the hospital."

From the car all the way to the emergency room, Leona was frantic for relief, for oxygen. She worried there would be no end to her suffocating fear. She wanted to die, and at the same time she was afraid she might die. She might leave David a grieving dad and widower. Could life be that punishing?

David carried her into the emergency room and yelled for help. "My wife can't breathe!"

Two nurses flocked to them while David tried to explain what happened. "I was just trying to get her out of the house to take her for a drive, and now my wife can't breathe." He choked up on the last word.

Leona wanted to curl up into a ball on the floor. She was seeing spots and there was a sharp stabbing in her chest. Somehow, she ended up in a wheelchair, and a nurse rolled her away until they were behind a privacy curtain. An oxygen mask was placed over her face, and she was hooked up to a heart monitor.

The nurses broadcast her vitals to each other.

A third nurse arrived and turned to David. "The doctor would like to give her some medicine to help calm her body, but I need to know: Has she recently experienced any symptoms of depression?"

He stuttered. "Our baby . . . died . . . four months ago. Besides going to work, she rarely gets out of bed."

A knowing look passed between the group of nurses. The head nurse nodded. "I see. For now, we're going to avoid using this medication."

The head nurse settled in front of Leona next. "Honey, I'm going to walk you through this, but the first thing you need to know is that you are safe." She told Leona to breathe slowly, inhaling the oxygen under the mask through her nose and exhaling slowly through her mouth. She said it over and over, "You are safe."

After a few minutes of guided breathing, one of the other nurses announced that her heart rate had decreased.

"Very good, hon. Next, I want you to think of three things you can see. What are three things you see around you?"

Her mind was slowly returning to her body, but it was still hard to concentrate. She looked straight ahead and found her feet.

"Boots," she said, muffled by her mask.

She looked to her left and saw the two women and one man who were caring for her.

"Nurse," she said next.

And then she looked to the right and really saw him for the first time in four months. He was wiping his eyes.

She lifted her mask to say, "David."

Tears were falling down his cheeks, but his mouth turned up.

"That's right, David is here with you." The nurse patted her shoulder. "Now, sweetheart, I want you to tell me three things you can hear."

It was working. She was reconnecting with the world in front of her. Most of the noises she heard were coming from the bustling emergency room.

"Beeping . . . wheels . . . your voice."

The nurse nodded again. "You're doing great. If we weren't at the hospital, I would also ask you to tell me three things you can smell, but I don't want you to think about the guy across the curtain who soiled his pants earlier," she joked.

One of the other nurses handed her a cold glass of water. "This will help too. Lift your mask, take a sip, and think about what it tastes like. Using your senses helps bring you out of your head and back into reality."

Her body was finally calm enough she could form a complete sentence, but she was stuck on the exercise they skipped over—the things she could smell. She recognized the strong antiseptic odor most people referred to as "hospital smell." She remembered the warm scent of Vera being laid in her arms for the first time. Neither was the smell she fixated on now.

She smelled death.

THE DOCTOR SAID they would do a blood draw to rule out any concerns with Leona's heart, but he was confident what Leona experienced was a panic attack.

"Based on your symptoms and the stress you've been under

since losing your baby, you could even call this a 'grief attack.' Something triggered a painful memory, causing extreme panic and anxiety."

She knew exactly what that something was. Their new car.

He handed her three pamphlets. The first one defined panic attacks and described various methods for coping with them. "The important thing to remember is, once a panic attack begins, you can't magically make it disappear. You have to learn how to cope through it. These coping mechanisms begin with reminding yourself you are safe. Even a severe panic attack that makes you feel like you are going to die very likely won't kill you."

She skimmed the first pamphlet and recognized the breathing technique and senses exercises the nurse used with her earlier. She gave it to David who also scanned its contents.

"The second pamphlet is about antidepressants. Some of what you and David have described going on for the past couple of months are signs of clinical depression, which can be caused by a traumatic life event. Antidepressants aren't painkillers. They help you better function. I want you to consider talking to either a psychiatrist or your primary care doctor about going on a small dose for six months or until some of the brain fog goes away."

The doctor closed his file. "The last pamphlet is a list of support groups in the greater Milwaukee area. I know appointments with a therapist can be expensive, but these groups are free and can be very helpful. A couple of them are specifically for parents who lost an infant." He looked back and forth between David and Leona. "I recommend going once a week for a few months and then deciding together how often you'd like to go after that. It really helped me and my wife after our baby was stillborn."

Before disappearing behind the curtain, he addressed Leona one last time. "It's not your fault, you know."

But that was exactly what Leona didn't believe. Like Delaney, she blamed herself that Vera was gone.

"I WANT YOU to set one small goal for the future," Chaplain Davis said. "If you are here with a spouse or a partner, I want the two of you to work together on setting a goal. It can be more serious, like creating a budget or painting a room in your home. Or it can be something playful, like taking a dance class. There are no rules except to set a goal."

After her panic attack, Leona still couldn't find the energy to open up to David. But their time in the emergency room stirred something in her. It reminded her how much she loved him, and that love made it worth getting help so someday she could move toward him again. If she wanted her marriage to last, if *she* wanted to last, she needed help.

Help began with a prescription for antidepressants, and after a week of taking her little blue pill, she was amazed at how much easier it was to get up and perform everyday tasks like taking a shower. They also began attending one of the support groups listed in the pamphlet the doctor gave her. After their first meeting, in which neither of them volunteered to talk but both of them quietly cried, they collapsed into their car.

There was a moment of silence, then David said, "Everyone in there seemed really sad. Do you think it's because they haven't gotten their Bereaved Parents Club T-shirts yet either?"

Leona swatted his arm.

Their fellow club members lost babies at all different times—pregnancy, birth, and shortly after. One parent lost their baby decades ago and was just now learning how to process the pain. The main idea of their group was to "resolve through sharing," to say their ugly thoughts out loud with others who understood.

Chaplain Davis spent a lot of time addressing the couples in the room too, reminding them the most important thing was to learn how to communicate.

"Two people might be grieving the same child, but the language one person speaks while they're grieving might be completely different than their spouse's language," she said. "Consider how you can respect their needs while not stifling your own. And remember that it's normal to feel disappointed if your spouse doesn't react the same way you do."

How true for David and Leona Warlon, Leona thought. She needed to emotionally decompress while physically hiding under a rock. And David needed normalcy, to be around people who were willing to talk about Vera and something other than Vera.

One day at a time, one pill every morning, and one support group every Thursday night, she lived and grieved. Evenings with David were her favorite, when they streamed episodes of their favorite sitcoms and ate their feelings with ice cream and a glass of wine.

All of it loosened her pen:

The same methods
for celebrating
are also
fitting
for mourning.
Cheers.

Chaplain Davis reminded their group often that grief wasn't about trying to forget their babies.

"The same is true about your assignment," she explained. "The point of setting a goal is not to pretend everything is all better; it's about stepping forward. You will never forget the baby you lost. But you also have permission to do something new."

David wanted more than anything for their goal to be frivolous, extravagant. Something to symbolize them learning how to live again.

"Why not our tenth anniversary?" he suggested. "It's still months away. We could save up and go out to eat somewhere really fancy. You could wear that one dress, and I could take that one dress off you after dinner. You know, *that* dress?" He moved his eyebrows up and down dramatically.

"But just think of what we could do with all the cash we'll fly through in a single meal," she argued. "The funeral was a massive addition to our school debt, not to mention the bathroom sink needs to be repaired."

"I'm thinking Bartolotta's by the lake," David continued.

Leona smiled. "It's hard to say no to your boyish enthusiasm. I need some of that eager spirit to rub off on me."

He kissed her on the cheek. "Just think about it. Have your people call my people, mkay?"

She hoped that their date would help the places of her heart still languishing.

Even though she was functioning better, more present, she still hadn't told him about what she'd received in the mail shortly after the funeral—the card with the beautiful hand-painted flowers on it, embossed with the letters "EF" on the back.

She'd opened it and realized it was a note from Rose. Her sister didn't come to the visitation or service, but she wrote,

> *I didn't want to complicate the funeral with my presence, but I still wanted to write to say I am so sorry for what you're going through. I know you are an amazing mom to Vera. I wish I could have known her too. I miss you, sister. If you're ever ready, please call me.*
>
> *Rose*

Rose's phone number was listed at the bottom of the card. In the six months since Leona got it, she hadn't the strength to dial the ten digits.

CHAPTER 26

Present Day

SHE DIDN'T KNOW HOW TO BEGIN TO EXPLAIN TO David #2 all that had happened. How Vera died, how she became depressed. Her panic attack, which sent her to the hospital, which sent them to group therapy, which sent her to Bartolotta's clutching her purse with the note in it from Rose so she would finally have the guts to call her. Which somehow brought her here, sitting outside of the house she didn't choose next to another version of her husband, near Vera again.

These pieces of her story were too much, too heavy for her, as she sat on the front steps with David #2 on Courtney Boulevard. The details remained trapped inside the gaping wound in her heart, unable to make their way out of her mouth for him to hear.

She shook her head, hoping he would understand.

"It's okay." David put his arm around her, his look painted with concern. "I'm here if you ever need to talk about it with me."

She was grateful he didn't push her on this. She also wondered if they would be given that kind of time. If sharing her story would give her the chance to build a life here.

"David?" She turned to face him, but when she caught his gaze, the thoughts running through her head vanished.

Stay here.

Choose.

It was strange sitting so close to a man who looked just like her husband. Holding his hand, laughing at the types of jokes her husband loved to tell, receiving his kindness. The air between them was thick with chemistry, and she wondered if he noticed it too.

For a moment, she forgot about the choice weighing over her. She set aside east side estates and north side neighborhoods. Her husband a world away and her child here. Her messed up relationships with Rose and Eden. Instead, she welcomed the awakening of her senses right where she was.

David put his hand on her cheek and leaned in. This time, he wasn't looking her in the eyes, he was looking at her lips. He was going to do it, she thought. He was going to kiss her.

And she was going to let him.

She put her hands on his sides. She could feel the hours he'd spent in the gym downstairs. She wouldn't say it felt bad, but she'd always liked the round middle on her husband. The David who hadn't completed a crunch in the past ten years.

That startling thought reminded her of the choice she couldn't ignore forever. Her body was begging for something carnal, but her mind needed answers to impossible questions. She didn't know how she could choose between two drastically different versions of her life. Between her husband and her child. The one who made her heart skip a beat and the one her heart beat for.

There were still so many things left undone in her own life too, like with Rose. However, her friendship with Eden wasn't exactly thriving here.

Do I walk
through

the door?
Or
close
it?
Is there a greener side of the fence?

David laid the softest kiss on Leona's lips. It was achingly familiar—a kiss she'd been kissing for the past twelve years. She wanted to lose herself in him. Her inhibitions were gone, and decisions were being made.

She could make this marriage work. She could persuade David to leave Warlon Tech. They could rebuild each of their lives together, and she could still be with—

"Mama!"

Leona and David jumped a foot apart. They looked at each other like two teenagers caught by a parent. Except they weren't caught by a parent; they were the parents. Caught by a toddler whose fruit snacks ran out.

Vera was standing in the doorway.

The toddler turned around and climbed down the front step, then walked straight to Leona, holding out her hands to be picked up.

"Mama!" the little girl said again, clearly voicing each syllable.

Leona's heart welled. She was a mom—she would always be a mom. But she'd never been called that by her own child before.

"Of course you can come by me." She picked Vera up and held her tight.

David put his arms around both of them, and Leona soaked up the moment that felt like they were a family of three again.

She knew exactly what she wanted to do.

And what she needed to do.

CHAPTER 27

LEONA HELD VERA CLOSE, THINKING ABOUT HOW THE rest of her night could go. She could go back in the house. She could eat another grandiose meal assembled by Emily, carried from oven to table by David. The three of them—a family—could leave their dinner mess to spend the rest of the humid July evening playing outside. Emily was paid to wash the dishes anyway, a job that Leona learned was covering the costs of Emily's first semester at LMSU in the fall.

She could put Vera to bed, kissing her little belly before covering it with unicorn pajamas. She could rock her in the dark, inhaling baby shampoo and summer sweat. She could rock her for an hour if she wanted to, then carefully tuck her into her crib and close the door.

She could stay.

She wouldn't have to lament that the horizon wasn't strong enough to hold the sun up a few days longer, because more sunrises with Vera were possible here. She could live in anticipation of another day with her daughter.

Sitting on the front steps with Vera on her lap, she closed her eyes and kissed the little girl on the cheek. She ran her fingers through Vera's silky curls and hugged her, trying to memorize every detail.

"Can you go by Daddy for a minute, sweet girl?" she asked.

Vera pointed. "Dadda."

Leona leaned forward, and Vera crawled into David's open arms. Then Leona stood up on the steps leading to the front door of 2638 Courtney Boulevard.

She held out her hand to David.

He looked up at her and smiled. Shifting Vera to the side of his lap, he reached out his free hand to take hers.

The scene felt familiar to Leona. A lot like the one she remembered ten and a half years ago when he proposed.

To both of them, she said, "I love you."

Try to go home.

Stay here.

Choose.

CHAPTER 28

LEONA FELT A STRANGE SENSATION RUN THROUGH her body, like she was being pulled in at least five different directions. She was still standing on the front steps of the stunning Victorian dwelling on Courtney Boulevard, but she was *home* home. She knew because when she looked down at the man in front of her on bended knee, helping her re-create a door back to her own life, he was no longer wearing sharp activewear but a drabby T-shirt from his undergrad physics club. The print said, *Be nice to science geeks. We have potential (energy).*

His hair was longer, his gaze afflicted. She could see their Toyota Corolla parked toward the front of the driveway.

All of this evidence meant Carl's theory actually worked.

Carl had warned her it was a long shot. He went as far as recommending she start grieving the life she lost so she could begin making the most of where she ended up. Exhausted as she was, the thought of surrendering didn't sound so bad. If everything was out of her control, there was no reason to agonize over what choices to make or which theories to test. She could simply take a nap and get back to being with Vera.

But everything changed when that little girl called her "Mama."

Being on the receiving end of that sacred name jolted her to accept the thought in the back of her mind she'd ignored for days, the thought Dr. Carl Flatus brought to the forefront. While she was living someone else's life, someone else was living hers, and that someone was Vera's mom. Leona #2.

She would do almost anything to have more time with her baby, but she wouldn't do that. She couldn't keep Vera at the cost of causing someone else the same pain she carried with her every single day.

So, she'd stood up on the front steps of 2638 Courtney Boulevard and taken the hand of David #2, re-creating the moment that changed the course of her life forever. The decision that sent her life on a wildly different trajectory than the one she'd just visited.

Her door back home was located where David first proposed.

Even with the grief that tried to suffocate her, and chronic neck pain from the accident, she knew she was exactly where she needed to be. She needed to be here, with her David.

"David." She announced her arrival with only his name. She'd hoped she would be able to get back home, but she didn't know her husband would be here waiting for her.

He looked up from where he was kneeling on the brick pavers and stared at her like he was seeing a ghost.

"Get off that knee of yours, old man," she teased, taking his hands in hers and pulling him to his feet.

The anguish on his face said he wasn't ready for joking around.

"It's me." She turned over her forearm. "Look, the tattoo I got in memory of Vera."

He didn't say anything.

Leona gave him another moment to take her in and then kept going, trying to recite the list of clues David #2 gathered much faster than she did. "I'm wearing my glasses. And, apparently, I am also 'less toned' than whoever you've been hanging out with the past couple of days."

"I know it's you!" he snapped. He stepped away, raking his hands through his hair.

She flinched, holding her hands up to signal she wasn't a threat. This wasn't how she pictured their reunion. She was hoping for something happier, like all the predictable chick flicks she pretended to hate. She noticed then his hair was greasy and his face was unshaven.

"I'm sorry," he tempered his tone. "I just thought . . . I thought I was losing my mind. You walked into the restaurant looking so different. And, no, I don't mean your weight," he said, flustered.

She smirked. "Yes, I know. You positively love my body."

"The difference was, you were so cold, so distant," he went on, still processing. "You warmed up a little during dinner even though you didn't understand why we were celebrating our anniversary so early—"

"Wait, you actually got to eat the food? The pork tenderloin that, according to Google, costs four dollar signs?" she teased, wishing he was in more of a celebratory mood. More himself.

He ignored the interjection. "But when we left the restaurant, you asked why we were driving the Toyota and why we were going to your old neighborhood. And then you . . . you kept asking where Vera was." He forced out the words. "You screamed over and over, 'Where is my baby?' "

Leona gasped, covering her mouth with her hand. Her sparkle sobered.

"You had a panic attack, and even after you got through it, you couldn't recover. You wouldn't get out of bed. It reminded me so much of when . . . when we first lost her. All I could think was that I lost you again too."

While she was soaking up the unexpected gift of more time

with a version of the child they'd lost, the other version of herself was grieving like she had—unliving and unable to get out of bed.

As David processed his side of this story, a trace of that pain rose up in her again. "You—or, the other you—refused to go to a hospital, refused any sort of help. I didn't know what to do. You finally got out of bed today, but you demanded to come here, and . . ."

Leona lowered her head.

"It was the first time you . . . she . . . wanted to go anywhere in days, so of course I was willing to take her here. I didn't understand; we haven't been here since—"

"You proposed."

"I proposed."

They said it at the same time.

It made sense. Leona #2 wanted to get out of bed so she could see if Vera was here.

"It didn't matter if it didn't make sense to me," David cried. "I just needed to follow you, to make sure you were all right."

It was possible this all made Leona's door home that much stronger. She'd not only re-created a door at her big choice, but their overlapping circumstances once again helped pry it the rest of the way open.

Leona placed a hand on David's face, making herself his focal point. "I'm so sorry you had to go through all that again. I . . . I know I've been gone a lot longer than a few days. A part of me has been gone ever since Vera died." Her eyes filled with tears. "But I'm back; I'm here. And I want to start living again. I want to honor her life by living ours. I love y—"

His kiss stopped her short.

He tilted his head back but pulled her body closer. "I'm sorry, Leona. I was so scared. What I meant to say the moment I saw you again is I'm so glad you're home. I missed you. Profoundly."

"I missed me too," she agreed. "Profoundly."

Giving Vera back to Leona #2 wasn't the only reason she tried to come home. She drew her other reason in for a second kiss, pressing herself into him. Absence had flamed her fondness for David, and she wouldn't mind getting a room to see where her fondness could go. She dug her hands into his hair and savored the closeness of his arms around her.

Suddenly, the door of 2638 Courtney Boulevard blasted open, interrupting their reunion.

An elderly man neither of them recognized appeared in the doorway.

"Hey! Get your fornicating off my property or I'll call the police!" He glared with more bitterness than an amino acid supplement.

Leona gawked. She'd forgotten that—as of a few minutes ago—she was no longer married to the owner of this house. It now belonged to the gentleman throwing open his door to see who was making all the racket on his property.

David put his arm around her and addressed the homeowner. "Is it technically considered fornicating if we've been married to each other for ten years and three days? Because that's how long we've been married—ten years and three days."

The man snuffed, "You mean you're married to this riffraff?"

Leona's eyes were already wide at David's bit, but they bulged even more after the man insulted her. Then it hit her. The man wasn't looking at David when he'd said that; he was looking at her.

He turned to David. "Sounds like you have quite the Cinderella story, young man." He grumbled something about drabby T-shirts and hippie hair, then yelled, "It's against the rules of our neighborhood association to loiter!"

The door was slammed shut.

Leona looked down at herself. She was still wearing the luxury exercise apparel she borrowed from Leona #2's closet. She looked like a socialite ready for class with her personal trainer. Her husband, on the other hand, appeared a bit more downtrodden.

They looked at each other and burst out laughing. The troll had their backstory entirely wrong. They walked hand in hand to their car and then David drove them across the city to the little bungalow they rented on Thirty-Fourth Street.

They crossed their threshold together for the first time in days. David walked Leona to their bedroom. Their four walls had absorbed so much sorrow, but through the past couple of months, they were gently turning into more than a holding place for despair. She wanted that hope to keep rising.

David kissed her with an aching tenderness.

She grasped at his soft middle and traced the lines on the back of his body, the contours that always did something to her. Then she pulled his shirt off, inviting him to do more.

He laid her on the bed. Hovering over her, he dropped heavier kisses on her mouth and then nibbled at her neck. Leona loved the feel of his stubble against her skin. She let herself get lost in the moment without confusion or worry that she might regret it later.

"You're beautiful," he whispered reverently.

She thought of David #2, not in a way that stole from the moment she was in with her husband but in a way that affirmed it. He'd wanted Leona to stay, to have a do-over with her. What he didn't understand was that she was no longer the woman he'd asked to marry him. Vera's death made her a completely different person. She was more than her grief, but her grief now shaped the way she saw, touched, and tasted the world.

Her husband knew that part of her. He knew *her.*

When they finished, she drifted into a deep relaxation, nearly asleep, with only one thing on her mind. Every day, no matter which person she was on her timeline—the one who fought for a life with him or the one who lost her baby—David chose her.

CHAPTER 29

LEONA SAT UP IN THEIR QUEEN-SIZE BED AND LOOKED around the bedroom. The lone decoration was a hand-stitched quilt draped over a small chair. Its faded blues, greens, and yellows were "so nineties," and not in a way that would be posted to Instagram. Her Grandma Vera had spent countless hours making it for her, and it was as dear to her as her tie-dye robe.

Beyond that, the floors needed refinishing, the chipping paint on the window trim needed to be addressed, and the leaky roof was causing water damage that warped their ceiling. The house was more than one hundred years old, but it hadn't been stylishly modernized. It probably wasn't even up to code.

Leona threw on her glasses and climbed out of bed, nearly tripping over a pair of David's pants that had somehow ended up on her side of the room. She walked out of their bedroom and snaked through the closed floor plan to a door at the back of the house that she hadn't opened in at least six months. She turned the handle and stepped inside.

This nursery was far barer than the one on Courtney Boulevard. Nesting before Vera's arrival had consisted of pulling rusty nails out of the wall and repairing a hand-me-down crib with zip ties. There was no collection of toys and books, no chic rocking horse. There was one dresser. Leona couldn't bring herself to open any of the drawers, but she knew the clothes inside were no bigger than size six months. There was a picture frame sitting on top of the dresser that had a photo of her, David, and Vera at the hospital on the day Vera was born. It was the first photo of them—from a very small collection—as a family of three.

This time, Leona allowed herself to be completely swept away by sorrow. All her angry questions exploded to the surface.

What if Vera never got a fever?

What if I hadn't insisted on taking her to urgent care?

Mostly, *What if Vera were still alive?*

Her body shook with sobs, raged with pain, and, a long time later, slowly returned to calm.

She forced her body to move so she could pick herself up off the floor and turn toward the dresser. She grabbed the picture frame, holding it in her hands and staring at the faces in the photo. Then, using her pajama T-shirt, she dusted it off and placed it back on the dresser. She didn't like the placement, so she moved it again, carefully tilting it at the perfect angle like she was staging the room.

That was enough steps forward for today, she thought.

She walked to her small bathroom. Pushing back the plastic shower curtain, she turned on the shower as high as she could and got in. Two minutes later, the stream was so hot it was close to scalding, but she didn't care.

When the water hit her skin, she wanted it to bite.

CHAPTER 30

"I HAVE SOMETHING FOR YOU," LEONA SAID, SITTING down next to David at their kitchen table. The door to Vera's nursey was in her peripheral vision. It stung, but she could still breathe.

"Is it one million dollars?"

David was working on the finances for BioThrive, something he did before and after his many hours in the lab. He hid his stress well, but she knew he was losing sleep over getting BioThrive off the ground and FlourX into the market. They needed funding, and neither he nor Eden could take any more pay cuts than they already had.

Leona laid down the anniversary note she wrote for him in the taxi ride to Bartolotta's. "I was going to go out and get you more of a gift during the past three days I've been back, but then I decided my presence was present enough after the weekend we both had." She put her arms around him.

"But I wanted one million dollars," he said, "and a pony."

She patted his back. "Your million-dollar pony will have to wait until our eleventh anniversary."

He picked up her note and took in her written words. "How did I get so lucky to be on the receiving end of your sonnets?" He leaned in and kissed her. "I love you too, Leona Warlon. Then, now, and forever."

She stood up from her chair and grabbed her purse from the other side of the kitchen.

David said, "My anniversary gift to you is this: I promise to buy you a new bathroom sink handle and then watch YouTube videos about how to install it."

"Really? I'll take it." She smiled at the prospect of a fully functioning bathroom.

She dug through her purse and handed him the other note, the one she'd been holding on to all this time. "This one isn't for you, but I need to show it to you."

David looked at the hand-painted flowers on the small greeting card, then he opened it. His eyes widened as he read it to himself in a whisper. "I wanted to write to say I am so sorry. . . . I wish I could have known her too. . . . If you're ever ready, please call me . . ."

When he reached the end of Rose's note, he looked at Leona. "Wow," he reacted. "How long ago did Rose send this?"

She looked at her feet, ashamed to say the truth out loud. "Shortly after Vera's funeral."

He fanned himself with the card. "Oh."

"After everything that happened between her and me, I didn't know how to call her or even how to tell you about it. The other goal I set for therapy besides meeting you at Bartolotta's and getting that tattoo was to finally show you this. I messed things up with Rose, but I really want to try to fix it."

"What are you going to do?" he asked.

"What I should have done a long time ago."

"Call her?"

She pointed a finger in the air as her smile perked. "Actually, I have a different idea. Did you see what's embossed on the back of the note?"

David flipped it over. "EF?"

"Yes, EF. While I was gone last weekend—"

"Exploring the multiverse and other galaxies of the beyond? That kind of gone?"

She laughed. "Yes. While I was exploring a different universe at brunch last weekend—"

"Wait. We didn't even get to that story yet. You went to Friday morning brunch? With my mother? No!"

"Yes," Leona asserted.

"But it's written in our marriage vows that you would never have to go to Friday brunches with my mother."

"Correct."

"I'm sorry, babe." He gave her a side hug. "Thoughts and prayers; love and light."

"Anyway"—she playfully pushed him away—"Delaney and her henchwomen were talking about someone who sounded eerily similar to Rose."

"Oh, this sounds juicy." David leaned in.

"They were talking about an artist named Ember Finch, who does high-level decorating on the east side of town and even around the world. Everything they said about her sounded like Rose. I don't know if Rose would have taken the same path in each outcome of my life, but I think it's worth a shot to find out."

David raised an eyebrow. "But Rose hates everything associated with your mother even more than you. Like, she's outwardly angry most of the time."

"That is one of many holes in my theory," she agreed, "but they described her as having an 'alternative look.'"

"In Delaney's circle, that probably means she doesn't wear pantyhose under her skirts," he argued.

"Yes. Thank you for poking another hole in my argument, here.

But Cynthia Brand said she thinks she also has a child 'out of wedlock.' "

"Those clues certainly don't rule out Rose. So, does this mean you're going to go look for her at her secret identity's office? EF's office?"

"She doesn't have an office, not a publicly listed one anyway. She doesn't have a website either."

He frowned. "How are you going to find her? At this point, wouldn't it be far more efficient to simply call her?"

"Yes, David, but I want to hug her. So, can you spare an hour before going into work this fine Monday morning?"

He walked toward her with his arms open wide. "For hugging? Always."

"Get in the car, David."

LEONA DID MOST of the required sleuthing the day before they climbed into their taupe Toyota Corolla to reunite with Rose. Taking what she'd learned over the years about David Warlon's world, she decided to use the art of social networking to her advantage.

First, she made a call to Booker Perry at his financial firm during business hours. His administrative assistant was hesitant to put Leona through to Mr. Perry's office until Leona explained she was the daughter of Evelyn Porter, second wife of George Porter of Porter Law Offices LLC. According to Evelyn, Booker and George were members of the same golf club. They played eighteen holes every Saturday morning in the summer, and Mr. Perry's administrative assistant was the one who booked their tee times.

Hearing Leona's connection to Mr. Porter, the assistant transferred Leona's call to Mr. Perry's office right away.

After Leona's brief explanation of the reason she called—so as not to "waste Mr. Perry's valuable time, sir"—Mr. Perry was willing to share his wife's cellphone number. Patrice Perry was more than amicable on the phone, remembering the first time she met Leona at the Medical Miracle Charity gala.

"You were pretty unforgettable that night." Mrs. Perry chuckled. She said she still heard David Warlon's name pop up in her circles from time to time too.

Leona went out on a limb and asked if Mrs. Perry had completed a large renovation project in their home and hired a decorator. Specifically, world-renowned decorator Ember Finch. EF.

"Yes," Mrs. Perry confirmed. "Ember is working for us. I just so happened to hit it off with her. We even grab coffee from time to time to talk about things other than décor."

"Well, Mrs. Perry, the reason I wanted to call is that I really want to connect with Ember. I think I might know her—and have known her for a long time. Is it true that her name is actually Rose Meyer?"

Mrs. Perry hesitated, so Leona added, "Rose is my sister."

She explained to Mrs. Perry what she hoped to do and was given an address. Leona was thrilled . . . until she found herself in front of Rose's home on the south side of Milwaukee. Suddenly, her courage was gone.

Standing on the sidewalk, she turned around to look at David, who'd stayed in the car. He was close enough to run to but far enough to give the two sisters their privacy. Over the years, he'd been careful not to boss her into anything regarding her relationship with Rose.

He nodded and waved his hands forward, encouraging her to knock.

Leona turned back around to face the door and took a deep breath. Maybe she was too late. Maybe she'd beaten her sister with her own pain, and now she had to live with the consequences.

Maybe I—

"Leona!"

She didn't have time to entertain any more doubts. Rose's front door flung open and she was in her sister's embrace, nearly suffocated by the strength of the hug from the woman with a sleeve of tattoos and a pierced eyebrow. Apparently that was what Sandra meant by "alternative."

"Rose" was all she could get out at first.

"I saw you through the window coming up the sidewalk. I couldn't believe it, so I had to come outside and see for myself," her sister said, a smile lighting up her entire face.

Leona inhaled a deep breath so she could finally begin the apology she should have offered a long time ago. "Rose, I'm so sorry. I lashed out at you for reasons having nothing to do with you, and I pushed you away. And then I never came after you. I regret it so much. I should have been there for you and your little girl."

Rose hugged her again, even tighter. "We'll get to all that. I have plenty of things to apologize for too. Leaving you hanging while I was at school, not coming to you after Vera . . ." She trailed off.

They pulled back and looked at each other, feeling both the pain of lost time and the joy of being back together.

"I'm just so glad you're here," Rose said. "But first, I need to know—how did you find me?"

"One of your prestigious clients," Leona gushed. "What I would like to know is, how have you been Ember Finch all this time without anyone figuring out you're Evelyn Porter's daughter?"

"Oh, please." Rose waved a hand at her. "I don't think Evelyn is pulling out her phone to show people pictures of us like some proud mommy. A few people said I reminded them of someone, but I think my artsy vibe keeps them off the trail from connecting me to Evelyn." Rose patted her edgy, asymmetrical haircut.

"But how long have you been working with Evelyn's acquaintances? You used to hate anything associated with Evelyn. Even David said that."

Rose looked past Leona and shouted to her brother-in-law, "Hello, David!"

He waved at her and got out of the car.

"There have been a few people I didn't particularly like, but that's most neighborhoods." She shrugged. "Besides, I figure I might as well steal a little of their money using my 'world-renowned talents.'"

"It isn't stealing when you're worth every dime," someone called from the sidewalk.

Leona and Rose turned to see who it was.

"Mrs. Perry?" Rose was confused. "Did I forget about a coffee date we scheduled?"

"Actually, I'm not here to see you, Rose. I'm here to meet with a certain Dr. Warlon and Dr. Williams."

David heard his name and turned around.

At that moment, Eden pulled up to the curb too.

"Wow," exclaimed Rose, "looks like we have ourselves a whole family reunion." She dashed down the sidewalk to greet the small crowd gathering.

Eden got out of the car and hugged Rose. Then she turned to Leona. "What am I doing here, Leona?"

The group stared silently for a second, waiting for Eden to notice who was in their presence. When Eden finally turned and noticed Mrs. Perry, her mouth fell open.

"Are you?" She turned to Leona and whispered. "Is that?" She turned back to Mrs. Perry. "*The* Mrs. Patrice Perry? The woman I've seen included in Forbes Top 100 lists?"

Eden turned back to Leona and whispered, "Am I dreaming? I must be dreaming."

Leona guided her starstruck friend over to Patrice for an introduction. "Dr. Williams, I'd like you to meet Mrs. Perry. I called

Mrs. Perry to help me reconnect with Rose. Long story. However, during that conversation, we got to talking about your and David's work. I shared that the two of you were close to your breakthrough but that you needed more of a financial base and help connecting with labs overseas. Mrs. Perry is here because she would like to hear more about BioThrive and FlourX as a potential investor."

Patrice locked eyes with Eden and nodded.

Eden straightened, then nodded back.

Mrs. Perry said, "Dr. Warlon and Dr. Williams, there's a Colectivo around the corner. Would you be willing to take me out for a cup of coffee?"

They both snapped to attention, each choosing a different side of Mrs. Perry to walk next to. Before they disappeared around the corner, David whipped around and mouthed to Leona, "You got me my million-dollar pony?"

She smiled and blew him a kiss.

The front door of Rose's house opened again, and Leona turned to see who it was. There was a little girl standing there. Leona felt it all again—the pain, the regret, the sorrow. But alongside all of it, she also felt a sliver of joy.

"Mommy?" the little girl said. She wasn't looking at Rose, but to the side at the grass, clutching a blue plush bunny.

Rose turned to Leona and beamed. "There's someone special I would like you to meet."

Epilogue

ON THEIR ELEVENTH ANNIVERSARY, DAVID AND LEONA stayed as far away from Bartolotta's Lake Park Bistro as possible. However, since the meeting with Mrs. Perry, they'd started receiving paychecks that allowed them to treat themselves on special occasions. To celebrate their anniversary, they picked up a tin of Lush Popcorn from Sherman Phoenix and ate it at the beach.

Leona was pregnant again. With a boy.

"Let's name him FlourX for good luck," David insisted for the tenth time.

She laughed, rubbing her belly as she absorbed her son's kicks.

She already felt sad thinking about what to say when people asked how many kids she had. Eden said she recently read an article about moms around the world who answer that question, "Two, with one who is living." She might try it out.

Each day was a fight to be at peace. Mostly because she knew the tiny life inside her was out of her control. She had to take one day at a time.

She missed Vera.

And
she feels
so
happy.

WORLDS AWAY, LEONA #2 found a note in her journal, not only written in her own handwriting but in her own language. She didn't know it, but it was part of the same note Leona #1 wrote to David #1 on their tenth anniversary.

For David #2 and Leona #2:
Only in my season of
Unlovable
did I understand
the depth
of your
Compassion.
For better or
for worse;
in sickness and
in health.
We are trying.

READERS GUIDE

1. How does Leona react to conflict, both in ordinary circumstances and unbelievable situations? Do you think her reactions are realistic? Why or why not?
2. Describe the progression of David and Leona's relationship, including the various hardships they face. What would you consider the strengths and weaknesses of their relationship?
3. Leona talks about motherhood being exhausting, but she's offended by a nanny showing up at her doorstep to watch Vera. Why do you think she has these mixed feelings? How do the struggles of parenting look different in each outcome of Leona's life?
4. Talk about Leona's relationship with her sister, Rose. How do they grow up to react differently to their shared adversity? Which character do you relate to more?
5. How do Evelyn's experiences shape her perspective and motivate her behavior? Does learning Evelyn's backstory make you feel more compassion toward her? Why or why not?

6. How does grief drive Leona's decisions in both timelines? What do you think about Eden's assessment that a person can't get over grief; they can only go through it?
7. Leona suspects that David #2 is having an affair only to find out Leona #2 is the one who has been unfaithful with her high school ex-boyfriend, Derek. Explain why Leona #2's indiscretions with Derek might be considered understandable or unforgivable.
8. How does Leona's view of wealth compare to the views of Evelyn, Delaney, and Patrice? Whose views do you relate to? What do you think of David's decision to walk away from his family's money? In your experience, have you seen access to money build community or isolate people from community?
9. When Leona goes to BioThrive to ask Eden for help, Eden ends their conversation because Leona #2 hasn't invested in their friendship in a long time. What do you think about Eden's boundary? How does Eden show both strength and vulnerability as a character?
10. Leona visits an outcome of her life that answers some big what-if questions about how things might have turned out differently if she'd made different choices. Do you agree with her final decision between the two trajectories of her life? In what ways would visiting this different outcome affect the reality she came from?
11. Discuss the significance of the title, *Between You and Us.* How does this capture the tension Leona feels between motherhood and marriage? Where else do you see Leona and David living in tension? (Consider their neighborhoods, marriage, relationships, and roles.) Have you ever felt caught between the different roles you embody?

NOTES AND ACKNOWLEDGMENTS

After writing nonfiction for over a decade, this novel was the wild turn in my writing career I wasn't expecting. I was in a place of burnout and decided to create something for the pure enjoyment of writing, and this story was born. That being said, this story wouldn't be the published book you're holding in your hands without the many generous people who helped me along the way.

The first group I want to acknowledge are the ones who either read drafts, listened to me talk about drafts, or were subjected to an email chain of updates waiting to see if the latest draft would be offered a publishing contract. This group includes Dave and Renee Potgeter, Amber VanderVennen, Kyle and Becky Potgeter, Mackenzy Roosien, Madison Konyndyk, Savannah Noorman, Dan and Karen Broekhuis, Kayla Vande Kamp, Kristin Fraser, Kaylee Sleeman, Jennifer Cosgrove, Linda Schroedermeier, and Rachel Carlberg. Also, via Voxer, Aubrie Benting. To them, I say thank you for your literal thoughts and prayers and listening ears.

A special thank-you goes to Rachel Carlberg for also nerding out with me over everything book-related through the publishing process. Thank you for your thoughtful input on everything from covers to discussion questions to the story between them.

Writing can be lonely, which is why I'm grateful for the Redbud Writers Guild, American Christian Fiction Writers, and my local writing group with DesAnne Hippe and Ben Parman. For years, DesAnne and Ben, meeting with you has been a highlight of each month. Thank you for not only being willing to talk about craft for a few hours at a time but also about the complexities of neighboring in cities like Milwaukee. To Greta Sisu, a member of this same group for a season, I thank you for prophetically encouraging me to keep going. Your talent of saying profound things in few words inspired me to try adding poetry into Leona's thought life.

With a variety of sensitive content in this book, I'm grateful for helpful feedback from people whose lens of experience is very different from my own. So, thank you to Jasmine Jones and Hannah Hippe for your feedback on Eden as a character so that I could shape her in a more authentic way. And thank you to Lisa Crayton for doing the authenticity read and helping me think through difficult subject matter throughout.

To Nicole Baart, thank you for your amazing class on the basics of fiction in the summer of 2022. Your coaching, as well as that of Betsy St. Amant, gave me solid direction with my first chapters and book proposal, and furthermore, gave me the courage to try.

I also want to thank my literary agent, Tamela Hancock Murray at the Steve Laube Agency, for representing me, both now and through years of closed doors. Tamela, this fun twist in my publishing career is thanks to your kind advocacy and cheerleading.

And then there's Jamie Lapeyrolerie, my editor extraordinaire. Jamie, I'm incredibly grateful you saw potential in this story. Thank you for patiently applying your vision and expertise to this book so that it could become the best version of itself. I've thoroughly enjoyed working with you and learning from you.

Kristen Defevers and Laura K. Wright, thank you for smoothing out the tiny details of the manuscript in ways that made a big impact.

And thank you to the rest of the team at WaterBrook for acquiring this manuscript and getting it launched into the world. It has been an honor, and I'm so grateful you took a chance on this debut.

To Jocelyn, Levi, Cecily, and Marre—I love you more than life itself. Your constant coloring, cardboard taping, and Lego building inspires me to create for the fun of it more often. And to Aliza, thank you for all you've taught me about grief, though I'd give up all the lessons I've learned in a second to still have you here with our family.

To my husband, Collin, who would never ask me to acknowledge him—thank you. Thank you for supporting my desire to write by solo parenting so many nights and weekends. As strangers like to tell you when they see you out with four kids: You're *such* a great dad. I'll add to that—you're such a great husband and friend.

To you, dear reader, thank you for reading this book! Your support allows me to continue to do the work of writing, and that means so much to me. Related to the themes of Leona's story, I pray that through life's sorrows you'll find safe spaces to lament as well as glimmering reminders of hope.

Last, but most, I thank Jesus, whose deep love I've often experienced through other people, including the many listed above in this acknowledgments section. I'm giddy excited about this publishing opportunity, Lord, and so grateful for Your presence through it.

ABOUT THE AUTHOR

KENDRA BROEKHUIS lives in Milwaukee with her family. For her day job, Kendra stays home with four of her children and drives them from one place to another in her minivan. You can find her sarcastic ramblings and serious encouragement—including her grief over losing a baby at thirty-three weeks pregnant—on social media and at KendraBroekhuis.com. *Between You and Us* is her first novel.

ABOUT THE TEXT

This book was set in Caledonia, a typeface designed in 1939 by W. A. Dwiggins (1880–1956) for the Merganthaler Linotype Company. Its name is the ancient Roman term for Scotland, because the face was intended to have a Scottish-Roman flavor. Caledonia is considered to be a well-proportioned, businesslike face with little contrast between its thick and thin lines.